MAKING MEMORIES AT THE CORNISH COVE

KIM NASH

Boldwod

First published in Great Britain in 2024 by Boldwood Books Ltd.

Copyright © Kim Nash, 2024

Cover Design by Alexandra Allden

Cover illustration: Shutterstock

A CIP catalogue record for this book is available from the British Library.

Paperback ISBN 978-1-80549-481-2

Large Print ISBN 978-1-80549-482-9

Harback ISBN 978-1-80549-480-5

Ebook ISBN 978-1-80549-483-6

Kindle ISBN 978-1-80549-484-3

Audio CD ISBN 978-1-80549-475-1

MP3 CD ISBN 978-1-80549-476-8

Digital audio download ISBN 978-1-80549-479-9

Boldwood Books Ltd
23 Bowerdean Street
London SW6 3TN
www.boldwoodbooks.com

Beryl Ivy Robinson
21/9/1932 – 11/12/2023

At the grand age of 91, sadly our lovely Aunty Beryl was taken ill and passed away after a two-week stay in hospital. This all happened while I was editing this book, so it seemed only fitting to dedicate the book to her. She was a very special lady who became a surrogate Mom to my sister Lisa and me, and grandparent to our boys, after we lost our own lovely Mom. Aunty Beryl will always be remembered so very fondly.

To Aunty Beryl,

Thanks for all the chats we had about books on our nightly check-in calls, and the surprise in your voice when you told me you'd read one of my books and said 'actually I quite enjoyed it!'

Thanks for the inspiration for many of Vi's anecdotes too. You were funny without knowing it. And the fact that you flirted with the crew as they wheeled you into the back of the ambulance and the dishy doctor in A&E has inspired me to always be a flirt however old I am!

I hope there's a library in heaven, because I know how much reading and books meant to you and you always said you were never alone if you had a book to read. On the morning we lost you, I sat beside your hospital bed and read to you (missing out the rude bits obviously!). I hoped you could hear.

You'll be so very sadly missed by us all but know that there will have been a huge welcoming party up there.

So here's to you, Mrs Robinson...
Until we meet again.

xxx

1

In a world full of constant distractions, sometimes it's nice to just look at the sea and ponder life.

However, my peace and quiet was suddenly shattered by the sound of the doorbell. I groaned as I stood, a habit I had acquired over the last couple of years, more than for an actual reason, and walked through the kitchen, towards the door. As I glanced through the window, I saw a parcel delivery van on the drive and a courier on the doorstep.

'Coming!' I yelled as loud as I could. The delivery drivers around the area were quicker than Lewis Hamilton at the Monaco Grand Prix, dump and drop their normal delivery tactic. By the time you get to open the door, they're already back in their van and driving off down the lane. But this one greeted me with a smile and a very large box.

'Thanks so much for holding on for me. I was out the back.'

He grinned.

'No worries, madam.'

I wondered if he knew how old a simple word could make a

woman feel. I'm sure he didn't. He only looked about twelve. Was he even old enough to drive?

I frowned, trying to remember if I'd ordered anything.

'It's heavy to be honest. Do you want me to put it down somewhere for you?'

Years ago, I wouldn't have hesitated, especially if it was someone as good looking and cheeky faced as this young pup, but these days you shouldn't just be inviting anyone into your house. I had two choices: the first to let him in, and the second for him to leave it on the mat and me not be able to budge it. Besides, he had an honest face. When he grinned again, I made a split-second decision. He looked like a nice boy. And now, laughing to myself, even I realised how old I sounded.

'If you don't mind popping it just there on the kitchen table, that would be amazing.'

He did just that and headed back to the door.

'Thank you. That's so kind of you.'

'No problem,' he shouted over his shoulder as he headed back to his van. 'I'd have had to do that for my nan too. Bye!'

Cheeky sod!

Thankfully, I had just escaped the possibility that the man-boy I'd just invited into my house wasn't a serial killer. As I walked past the hall mirror, I noted that the face reflecting back at me could be mistaken for someone's nan, even though I still felt ridiculously young on the inside.

My pondering session resumed as I thought about my life; the past, the present and the future, although over the years, I'd learnt not to dwell on what looms ahead too much. The reason for that was that I'd just celebrated my seventy-first birthday. But I wasn't sure I could really be seventy-one. How could that be possible? There was still so much that I wanted to do with my life and I didn't really feel that different to when I was twenty-three. I still felt full of life and had so much more to give.

I made myself a cup of tea and grabbed my iPad, taking it back through to the conservatory where I googled where the nearest cosmetic surgery clinic to Driftwood Bay was. Maybe it was time to give in to Botox and fillers after all.

For the next couple of hours, I was distracted, somehow falling back into the world of internet surfing for the first time in ages. My quest for eternal youth started with me looking at Botox and fillers and ended up with me ordering an electric blanket that was on offer at Marks & Spencer and that I definitely didn't need until winter. It wasn't until I took my empty bone china mug back to the kitchen to swill it that I remembered the box on the kitchen table.

'Ah.' The familiar postal address told me that the person who had sent this on to me was my ex-husband, Peter. I thought I already had everything that had been cleared out from our house in the United States, my last home before I moved here, but the attached note told me differently.

My dearest Lydia,

I hope life in your new home is treating you well. I do think of you often with such great fondness even though we both know that we've done the right thing by parting ways. You have left a huge hole behind in both my home and my heart and while I am keeping myself busy, I miss you more than I ever thought I would.

I went up in the loft recently and found this box with your name on at the far end, tucked behind my fishing gear. Whilst the things that are inside are not in the greatest of condition, I thought I would forward them on to you anyway for you to do with them whatever you desire.

I wish you nothing but happiness in your life, my love. I hope you find the peace that you've always been searching for.

Take care and be kind to yourself.

Much love,

Peter x

Ah, my darling Peter. My fifth husband and the man who eventually taught me that I didn't need anyone else to make me happy. That I had to find it within myself. Such a kind, thoughtful, lovely man – but not right for me.

I took a sharp knife from the kitchen drawer and slit the packing tape to open the box. As I lifted the lid, I gasped as the memories came flooding into my head. A waft of strong, aged perfume hit me full on and took me back over fifty years to a time and place where nothing else mattered. My heart filled with joy as I saw the other things under the garment on the top.

I thought this box must have got lost over the years and I couldn't be happier that Peter had found it and sent it on. He would know how much these items meant to me. I picked up the dress on the top and held it to my nose, breathing deeply. As I closed my eyes and reminisced, trying to process the emotions that were overwhelming me, I heard the slam of a car door which jolted me back to the present. A familiar car came into my line of vision.

Bugger. I couldn't let her see me like this and I certainly didn't want her to see what I had here. Maybe one day but not right now. I needed to process it all myself first.

The back door opened, just as I was swiftly cramming the dress back into the box, and I closed the lid just in time – not only on the box but also on my memories and emotions.

'Hi, Mum, what you got there?'

My breath was still trying to return to normal.

'Oh, nothing much.' My voice was much higher pitched than normal and Meredith looked at me and raised one eyebrow. I flapped my hand at her and turned to the kettle. 'Drink, darling?'

'Yes please, if you've got time. Are you sure you're OK? You look a bit flushed.'

I forced a smile.

'I'm good thanks, darling, and I always have time for you. Why don't you go and sit in the conservatory and I'll bring the tea through?'

A few deep breaths in through my nose and blowing air out through my mouth seemed to help calm me and I arranged some chocolate digestives on a plate. Then I carried the tea tray through and chatted to my daughter as if everything was perfectly normal and my past hadn't just caught up with my future.

* * *

Meredith was in a funny mood today and I felt like there was more to it than she was letting on. She was asking me lot of questions about how I coped with the menopause and I explained that I'd been with my fourth husband during that time. He had always said I was the most neurotic and high-maintenance person he knew. I was unaware, therefore, of whether much of that was down to my age and the reality of what my body was going through or how much of it was the way he'd made me feel completely mad through his insinuations. A trip to a consultant gynaecologist who prescribed HRT made me feel normal again.

Meredith was clearly asking for a reason though.

'Is everything OK, darling?'

'Yeah, I'm fine thanks. Nothing I can't sort out myself.'

The deep guilt I felt every time she made a comment like this never got any easier. This daughter of mine was so fiercely independent and I only had myself to blame. Whilst we were growing closer, I couldn't expect her to forget the past and instantly be my best friend. That was a position I was aiming for, but one that I knew I had to earn gradually and was working at.

'You can talk to me anytime, you know. I'm here for you now. Not going anywhere ever again.'

'Thanks, Mum. But I'm good.'

I was waving as she pulled off the drive, wondering how I could get to the bottom of what was wrong with her without intruding, when I glanced across to notice another car at the bungalow next door. One of the reasons why I loved living at Bay View Cottage was because I never felt alone. My neighbour was close enough for comfort but we weren't on top of each other. If I ever needed help, I knew that Celia, who had lived in the house next door for over forty years and had been a neighbour to the previous owner for most of those, was just a message or a phone call away.

Celia appeared from the side of her house and waved.

'Yoo-hoo! Lydia, do you have a mo?'

Celia was a similar age to me. We had a lot in common and often had a cup of tea together sat in one of our gardens, or even a glass of wine at times, while we put the world to rights. She was a wonderful soul, salt of the earth, and seemed to be totally unable to say no to rescuing animals in need, currently being the owner of two beautiful chestnut horses, Eric and Ernie; four white and very affectionate goats, James, Gino, Gordon and Fred; and about twenty rowdy chickens, which gave us both a constant supply of freshly laid eggs.

I was sure that my face must have answered before my

mouth did. It wasn't that I didn't want to chat, it was just that I didn't want to do it right then.

'Can I catch you later instead? I've just got to do something.'

'It won't take a moment. I promise.' She came bowling over, and in tow was another lady. 'I just want to introduce you to my sister.'

'Pleased to meet you. I'm Dianne. Two n's by the way. I'm Celia's much younger and more attractive little sister.' Her high-pitch titter was a sound that dogs from the neighbouring town could probably have heard.

I went to offer my hand for her to shake but it took me totally unaware when she pulled me close and gave me a hug. Speechless, I tried to pull away and she took the opportunity to air-kiss me. Not just once. Twice!

'Oh, err... Nice to meet you, Dianne.'

'Sorry, Lydia, Dianne never did have any respect for personal space. My much more annoying younger sister, I always say. She's been living in Australia for a few years but has decided to make some big changes in her life too.' They both grinned at each other, clearly very at ease in their relationship and jesting in that way siblings do. Celia was practically hopping from one foot to the other and I could see that she was bursting to tell me something.

'Dianne is going to be your new neighbour for a while. Remember that round-the-world trip we talked about last week?'

'I do!'

'Well, inspired by your daughter, buying a lighthouse on a whim and it working out all right for her, I've bitten the bullet. I made sure it wasn't something that I dithered about for months and never got round to doing. I've booked my first flight and I leave next week.'

'Wow, Celia. That's quick.'

'No time like the present. You never know what's just around the corner in life, do you? We must do these things while we're fit and well enough to be able to enjoy them. No point finding out you're dying and then putting it on your bucket list and being that ill you don't get the full experience. So, next week, I'm jetting off to Thailand to start a six-month trip. I don't know how long I'll be staying there or where I'm going after that yet. I have a week to work something out but I'm staying with a friend for the first three nights – someone I used to air hostess with – and then I'll have the option to stay longer if I'd like to and I'm just going to take it from there. See where the mood takes me.'

I'd never been so stunned in my life. Celia was quite a quiet, some might say meek, character and this was something that had really surprised me. I never knew that she used to be an air hostess and would never have guessed in a million years.

I looked from one to the other. You would never say she and Dianne were related. They were so unlike each other. Celia was softly spoken with a gentle character and her whole style understated, classy in appearance, managing to even look elegant when feeding the animals in her Barbour jacket and wellies. Dianne was everything that she was not; quite brash, overfamiliar, dolled up in animal print from head to toe, bottle blonde hair, scarlet lipstick and a golden glow from spending a few years in a sunnier part of the world.

'I'm going to have drinkypoos at the pub to say goodbye to everyone. Do say you'll come.'

'Try and stop me, lady!' I said. 'And good for you! How exciting!'

'Of course, I'll miss everyone, and the animals of course, but no one more than this little fella.' She dropped her hand to her side where her faithful companion Hobson stood. He was a very handsome tri-colour English Setter, in mainly muted greys and white, and he certainly kept Celia on her toes. 'That's why Di is moving in to look after the animals – and especially him – for me. I know he'll be in safe hands with her. And he can keep on going to his sessions too.'

Hobson was a real character, cheeky as hell, but so very patient and loving that he'd been trained and enrolled as a therapy dog. With Celia, he visited local residential and specialist homes, along with the hospital in Truro and a couple of nearby schools. Therapy dogs are trained to provide affection, comfort and support for people and he was the perfect dog to undertake those very important duties, utilising his empathic assets for the good of others.

'Right, we won't keep you if you've got things to do but I just thought we'd grab you when we saw you. I can see you two getting on like a house on fire. I'll drop you a text when we know what night the "do" will be. Byeee!'

People never cease to surprise me. It's amazing really when you think you know someone and then they do something so out of character, it surprises you immensely. Lovely in a way you never really know people or anything about their lives. It's one of the reasons why I love living here. Sometimes in life, it's nice to be around people who don't know everything about your journey, as they see you exactly how you are in the now.

2

_____

The alarm woke me from a deep sleep. The sky was slowly changing from night to morning, and through my open curtains, I lay in bed, watching the bay beyond, listening to the morning birdsong. I threw back the duvet. It felt heavy on top of me, reminding me of another feeling I'd been having for a while now. Something that I had to deal with sooner than later. I couldn't keep pushing it away, much as I wanted to.

Wandering into the kitchen after I'd got up and dressed, as the kettle boiled, I ran my hand over the box that had been delivered the day before. It held so many memories and I knew that once I opened it, they would flood out and hit me again. While I should and could do it now, instead I made myself a hot water, placed a couple of slices of lemon in the travel mug and grabbed my rolled-up yoga mat, which lived on a shelf by the front door, slid my feet into my slip-on trainers and headed out.

At the end of my drive, while Celia lived one way, the other way there was a path through the local farm which led to a secluded cove. One of my most favourite things to do in life was to watch the sun rise on the beach and do some yoga stretches. It made me feel grounded and connected to Mother Nature in a way that nothing else did.

When I arrived this morning, there wasn't a soul in sight and the only sound breaking through the peace was that of the sea gently lapping onto the shore. I threw my mat open on the golden sand and placed myself upon it and got comfortable, cross-legged, straight-backed, and closed my eyes. I focused on the sound of the water, and concentrated on my breathing and could feel myself immediately being grounded to the earth's core.

Stretching my body this way and that, in various yoga poses that I'd been taught on my retreat, for the next twenty minutes I felt my body and mind totally connected with nature. As I came towards the end of this meditation, I could hear seagulls cawing, and lambs bleating in the background, the deep rumble of an early morning tractor in the distance bringing me back to reality.

As I glanced to my right, I noticed the Driftwood Babes heading for their early morning paddleboarding session. Paddleboarding was something I'd never even heard of before Clem taught Meredith to do it, but then she discovered such a love for it that she had met a group of women who got up early each day and launched themselves and their boards in the sea. These days it seemed to be all the rage. She joined them from time to time and had tried to get me to go along but I wasn't particularly fond of being wet, let alone cold. Even though I loved living by the sea, it didn't mean that I had to go in it further than my ankles. My daughter was horrified at this statement, and said it was a waste of living by the sea, but I did say that when you were used to Floridian waters, the English Channel didn't quite have the same appeal.

To my left, I could see a figure walking on the beach. Glancing at my watch, I thought that it was unusual to find anyone else down on the beach at this time of the day, and I could feel myself frowning. It wasn't until they got nearer that I realised it was Martin. He waved at me from afar and started to wander over in my direction.

'You're up early, Martin.'

'Couldn't sleep. Thought I may as well get up and head down here. Mind if I join you?'

'Of course not.' I shuffled over on my mat and patted the space I'd created. 'I'd have brought more hot water and lemon if I'd known I was to have company.'

He smiled and we both dithered a little, not quite knowing what to say, when suddenly, the sun rose gloriously and quite literally took our breath away as it cast a golden glow over the sea.

'I don't know how people don't want to live by the sea,' he said. 'How can anything in the world be more stunning than that?'

'I've lived in many places around the world and can't believe I used to live in New York. The city that literally never sleeps. I think I must have aged ten years when I lived there.'

He laughed. 'But it must be nice to be here now? With Meredith?'

'I love spending time with Meredith. It's my favourite thing to do. I feel like I've got a whole lifetime to make up for. I could kick myself for not being there for her all her life.'

'We can't change the past though, Lydia. You did what you did because it was what you thought was best at the time. All we can do is make the now that we have the best that we can.'

'Look at you being all philosophical.'

'I know, who'd have thought it? But it's true.' He looked down at the ground for a moment. 'When Miranda passed away, I spent so much time wishing I'd done things differently. Beating myself up for not noticing how ill she was. Not doing enough to help Clem through his grief while coping with my own. Some days, all I could do was get out of bed and into a chair. And other days, I couldn't even do that. She was my world, and I didn't know how to live in it without her.'

You don't always realise what some people are going through. I always saw Martin as a happy-go-lucky chap.

'About eight months after we lost her, Clem yelled at me, saying that she'd died and I hadn't, and that he'd lost one parent but felt like he'd lost two. It was then that I realised I still had my life ahead of me and that I could wallow and be miserable till I died too, or I could crack on and open up the business we'd created together and get on with life. Try to find other ways to make myself happy.' He nodded towards the sea twinkling away ahead of them. 'Just a view like that these days makes me feel contented.'

'Do you think it's because we're older and wiser that things have more meaning now? Like we always thought we'd have all the time in the world to do the things we've always wanted to do and now we're realising that maybe we don't?'

'Nah, I think it's self-preservation. I'll never have again what I had with Miranda and I don't want to. My memories are deep within me and no one and nothing can ever take them away from me. But now I get to create new ones on my own. Well, you know. With friends and family, I mean.'

I turned to look at him. Who'd have thought when I woke this morning that I'd be having deep and meaningful chats with my daughter's partner's father?

'We've got years ahead of us yet, Lydia, and who knows? They could be our best yet. Promise you won't laugh if I tell you something?'

'Of course,' I replied.

He stared directly ahead; I think probably avoiding eye contact. I had no clue what he was going to come out with.

'In those early days I was so lonely and I didn't know what to do with myself. So, one day, I sat and I wrote myself a list of things that brought me joy. Took me bloody ages to work out what did, but I sat and forced myself to remember.'

I pondered what I'd write on my list. There wasn't much that immediately sprung to mind.

'I think I've forgotten the things I've done over the years that have made me truly happy, Martin. Did it take you long to work it all out?'

'Not once I got started. Thought about things that hadn't occurred to me since I was a child. One of the main things was that I loved to tinker with things with my father. He was an absolute star and could mend pretty much anything. I think that's why I've spent the last few years just messing about with stuff. I know I had the shop but that was really Miranda's dream. The part I loved was when people came in and asked if we knew anyone who might repair something that was precious to them. That's what made my heart really sing. Knowing that by repairing something, it could really make a difference to someone's life.'

'That's beautiful.'

Martin smiled and looked across at me.

'I'll never forget the first time Geoff from the pub asked me to mend a clock that belonged to his late parents. Took me bloody ages to fix it. Fiddly little bugger it was, but I meticulously took it to pieces and managed to get it working again. When he came to pick it up, he was in tears, telling me that it meant the world to him because it had been gifted to his mother and father on their silver wedding anniversary and they'd passed it on to him. Brought a tear to my eye too.'

'I love that story. What a gift you gave him.'

'It's why when Gemma mentioned about extending into my shop, I realised it was the right time for me. There wasn't enough space to set up a workshop in there and when Reverend Rogers told me that the church space was up for grabs, I knew it would be perfect.' He looked to the sky above. 'It was almost like someone intervened and made everything happen at the right time. As if it was meant to be, if that doesn't sound daft.'

'Not daft at all. I'm a bit of a believer in divine intervention these days! Since I've been older, and more accepting, I've had so many things that have happened to make me think that there's something way more than us out there with a bigger plan.'

'I've got a bit of a name for myself now too so if you ever need anything mending, I'm your man. But that's a long-winded way of saying: you must find those things that bring you joy, however big or small, while you're still here and do more of them. Like sitting on the beach and just being.'

Looking out to sea, to the vastness before us where the sky met the sea... it reminded me of the life ahead of me. You didn't know how far away it was, but you could enjoy the journey along the way. Find those things that made you happy.

'Are you still lonely, Martin?'

He sighed, hesitating just slightly before answering.

'Sometimes. But I'm lucky, Lydia. I have wonderful people in my life that keep me company. Living in a place like this means that there's always someone around to chat with. Sometimes too bloody many and you can't even pop out to the mini market without bumping into everyone you know and what should have been a five-minute dash turns into an hour-long trek.'

I laughed, knowing exactly what he meant. Living somewhere like this had taken me some getting used to. When I lived in New York, no one really had time for you unless they wanted something. It was all quite superficial. When my husband was away on business, I felt particularly alone. Florida was better, but it was nice to be somewhere like this. Part of a real, genuine community.

Martin huffed and puffed as he stood and his knee clicked.

'Jeez, was that you?' I asked.

'Not as flexible as I once was.' His eyes crinkled when he laughed. Age hadn't stolen his looks; his craggy suntanned face was still handsome even though he was a similar age to me, and his salt and pepper hair swayed gently in the wind. He must have been a real looker in his day. On the occasions we'd all spent together when Meredith and Clem had invited us both round, he was entertaining, funny, and good company. More than anything, he was kind and a good man. A wonderful friend.

'I should do group stretching sessions down here for the locals. Stop all that creaking and groaning.' I laughed.

'You should. I'd be well up for that. I know Vi said the other day that she would love to be more flexible too. Since her fall, she's not as sprightly as she was even though she's coping better.'

'Maybe I will. I'll ask around. See if anyone else is interested. It's best to do it early though. Might be too early for some.'

'Us old 'uns don't sleep much anyway. It's all that getting up in the night to take a pee. This time of the morning is the best part of the day in my opinion. Sunrise yoga classes. Sounds pretty perfect. I'll ask around too. I bet the Driftwood Babes would come. Only do it if group yoga brings you joy though!' He winked at me. 'I'll leave you in peace, m'dear. Same time tomorrow?'

'It's a date.'

'God, haven't had one of those for a long time.'

We both laughed.

'Glad those days are behind me.'

'Me too! See you tomorrow.'

3

'Good morning. Is it OK if I call you Lydia?'

I nodded as I took a seat, scanning the untidy desk in front of me and not wanting to meet his eye.

'So how can I help you today, Lydia?'

Saying the words out loud, that I'd kept inside me for a few weeks now, was painful. But come on, Lydia. They're just words. Even if they are powerful and painful. It's just a very small sentence and you just have to say it. How can it be this hard?

'I've found a lump.'

'Ah OK. Would it be OK with you if I take a look?'

Mortification. That's the reason why I didn't want to do this. This man-boy person in front of me, who felt way too young to be standing in a doctor's surgery, having to manhandle a flabby breast which used to be one half of a pert and magnificent pair. I wasn't quite sure who of the two of us – him, fresh out of medical school, and me, old enough to be his grandmother – was the most embarrassed.

Hoping that he hadn't noticed the tear that had rolled down my left cheek, I looked away.

'Please try not to worry. You've done exactly the right thing by coming to get it checked straight away.'

I swallowed the lump in my throat. Ridiculous that the thought of this being such an ordeal could put you off getting something potentially so huge and life-changing examined.

'I can definitely feel something there, as you say. I will refer you to the hospital immediately and we'll get them to do a biopsy. They'll insert a needle into the lump and take away some of the cells for testing. Does that sound OK for you?'

I nodded, words failing me at that moment.

'I know it's easy for me to say but try not to stress. Most of the time these things are what is called fibroadenoma, which is non-cancerous tissue growth, or even a build-up of fluid forming a cyst. But until we do those tests we don't know. What I don't recommend is asking Doctor Google.' He smiled at me sympathetically. This poor lad. Having to deal with people day in, day out, giving horrendous news to one person one minute and amazing news to another the very next.

Despite this experience rendering me quite speechless, I had to find the words I needed to put my mind at rest.

'This will remain confidential, won't it, Doctor? I know you are new to Driftwood Bay but as soon as someone sneezes in this place, everyone knows about it. I don't want anyone to find out about this, not until we know more.'

'Of course, Lydia. Doctor–patient confidentiality is the first thing they teach us in medical school. All the staff here know how crucial it is, more so in a small village than anywhere else.'

I nodded, thanked him and left, trying to avoid the eye of the young receptionist as I headed towards the exit, hoping that she really did understand that rule.

It hadn't been until that morning that Martin's words resonated with me and I realised that there was a possibility that

I did have limited time left in the world. We all do really, when all is said and done, but getting older makes you realise it even more. But his words about finding the joy in life and doing the things that make you happy had really hit home and I knew, as I walked back to the cottage from the main beach road, that I had to do something about my issue. When I rang the doctor's and the receptionist said that they'd just had a cancellation, I agreed to get there straight away, knowing that if I could put it off for much longer, I probably would have.

So now, walking back from my appointment, not quite knowing whether I felt better for what I'd done or worse for what might come from it, I decided to pop into the new book-shop on the high street. Such a pretty little shop, run by Nancy, a young local lady, previously a teacher, who had come into some money and decided to make a go of this new business.

'Morning. Beautiful day.' She beamed at me from behind the wooden counter. 'Can I help you with anything in particular, or have you just come to have a browse?'

'I'll just mooch around if that's OK.'

'Perfectly OK with me. Just give me a shout if you need any help.'

On one of the stationery shelves, there was a beautiful gold-flocked embossed notebook twinkling away at me in the sunlight which was streaming in through the window. As I picked it up and stroked the velvet texture of the multi-coloured peacock on the front, I noticed that it also had sprayed gold edges. Then something occurred to me. Finding the things that brought you joy didn't have to be big things. They could just be small things like this exact moment. Finding a notebook that made you happy.

I took it over to pay and noticed the candles on the counter. I picked one up, breathing in the delightful smell. I turned it upside down to see how much it was and noticed that it was called Driftwood Dreams and was made locally. I loved supporting a local business so popped it on top of the notebook and handed them both over.

'So, how's life being a bookshop owner then, Nancy? Business booming for you?' I asked.

She flashed that great big smile again.

'It's wonderful. I've always dreamed of opening up a bookshop here. I can hardly believe that when I put my key in the lock each morning, and look around at all the books, that this is all mine. I get in early every day, excited for the day ahead, make myself a cup of coffee, sit in that big, winged-back armchair that looks over the bay and read for half an hour. When I can tear my eyes away from the bay that is. Then for the rest of most days I just wander around touching the books, still taking it all in. Don't even mind if I don't make a sale. Daft, aren't I?'

'You're not daft at all. I think it's wonderful.'

'There are plenty that don't. My mum for one. She thinks I was stupid to give up my job as a teacher, but teaching isn't about the future of our children any more. It's about the school and the grades and it's not for me, I'm afraid. This—' she opened her arms wide and indicated the space around her '—makes my heart sing and that's good enough for me.'

Isn't it funny how, when you have something on your mind, everything seems to connect with it?

'You know, parents just want what's best for their kids,' I said. 'She'll just be worried about you, Nancy.'

'Yes, I do know that. But it took me a while to work out that I had to do this for me. So that I didn't spend my life wishing I was doing something else. Regretting that I'd never tried to reach out and grab my dream. If we don't try things, how will we ever know if they work? One of the things I used to try to teach the children was that if you try and fail, then you learn. Most people wouldn't have tried in the first place.' She grinned, happiness radiating from her. 'And here endeth my sermon for today.'

I tilted my head at her. 'How did someone as young as you get so wise?'

'Mum always did say I had an old head on young shoulders.' She laughed. 'Oh, talk of the devil.'

The lady who came in through the shop door was clearly Nancy's mum. They were the image of each other. She nodded to me and said good morning. We knew of each other but I didn't know her well.

'So sorry to interrupt but you'd forget your head if I wasn't looking out for you.' She plonked a sandwich box onto the counter. 'Kids, eh?'

'Mum. I'm twenty-seven. Hardly a kid.' Nancy rolled her eyes but I could tell that these two had a wonderful relationship. They had a chemistry that was indisputable.

'I think it's part of being a mum. I know we're annoying. It's our job.'

I laughed. 'My daughter is just over fifty and I'm sure I annoy her most days.'

'I'd better nip and put this in the fridge. Won't be a sec.' Nancy meandered out to the back of the shop with the food.

'Your daughter's shop is beautiful. She's done a great job.'

'Isn't it? I'm super proud of her. Worried that it might not fund a good future like her teaching would, but it was starting to affect her mental health in a really bad way. Some days she didn't even want to get up and go to work and that really wasn't her. To see her smile again means more to me than anything in the whole wide world. Teaching used to do that, but not any more. And this place has so much potential. And Nancy's going to team up with "Five O'clock Somewhere" to have a fortnightly book club, so I think she'll be OK. I do hope so anyway.'

Nancy reappeared and, hearing her mum mention the book club, she handed me a leaflet. It was happening the following week. The title of the book leapt off the page at me: *You Are a Badass Every Day* by Jen Sincero.

'You should come along. It'll be fun, there's a few signed up already. We're selling the books here, just saying.'

She handed me a copy and I read the back cover: all about creating the life that you deserve.

If the message about living life with joy didn't get through to me today, it never would.

'I'll be there,' I said. 'And I'll take that too.'

'It's an amazing book. It's the one that kicked me into doing all of this.' She opened her arms wide, taking in her surroundings. 'My very first book club. I can't wait.'

She gave a little squeal and her mum laughed at her.

'It's so good to have my little girl back.'

I paid for my notebook, candle and book, leaving behind a very happy bookshop owner, and an incredibly proud parent. I pledged to myself that whatever the results of the tests were, I'd take a leaf out of Nancy's book and make sure that the time I did have left, whether it be a year or another twenty years, was going to be the best it could possibly be.

4

Compelled by the excitement of filling in my new notebook, I hurried home to start my list. Things kept popping into my head on my walk; fresh flowers were something so simple that I could have more of in my life. I never bought them for myself so only ever had them around if someone had gifted them to me. Pottering in the garden was a pastime I was particularly fond of; there was nothing better than potting up a tray of petunias, their vivid colours brightening up any day. Collecting shells on the beach was also something I could lose hours to, and over the years, when I was in Florida, I'd spent many doing this, wondering where in the world Meredith was and whether she might be doing the exact same thing.

Many years on, now in a much closer maternal role, I was finally building bridges, and more than that, we were becoming friends. I was so very lucky that my daughter had a forgiving nature and was giving me a chance to be the mother to her that I'd never been. But I still had a few demons of my own to slay.

'Cooo-eeee!'

As I approached Bay View Cottage, in a little world of my own, Dianne came tottering over in her fluffy kitten-heeled slippers. I mean, who wears those these days? She probably had a matching silky nightie and robe too, with fluffy cuffs. Surely slippers and nightwear are all about comfort, not glamour.

Don't judge, Lydia, I had to tell myself. Stay in your own lane and mind your own business.

Hobson appeared by her side and she stroked him behind the ears as he leaned into her.

'Celia's just about to take him out for a walk but she just asked me to tell you that her little "do" is at the Harbour House Hotel tonight. Around 8 p.m. She apologised for the short notice but said there's no time like the present. Do say you'll come. I can't wait for us to get to know each other better now we're going to be neighbours. In fact, I could come round to yours for a cuppa now if you like. I'm free.'

'I will definitely be there tonight. Thank you for letting me know,' I said. 'I've got some things to do now and don't have time for that cuppa. But maybe another day.'

I strode towards my front door with purpose and fumbled with the key, dropping it in my haste. Celia and I had an understanding. We both kept ourselves to ourselves – unless we needed each other, or wanted a bit of company. Even then, we always called or text first to see what the other was up to. My home was my sanctuary and I wasn't one for unexpected visitors. It was important to me to have boundaries and I didn't want Dianne to come crashing into mine, thinking she could drop in willy-nilly, which I had a feeling she might if I allowed her to. I needed to be firm from the start. Start as I meant to go on.

The cottage seemed so quiet today. I wasn't one for having the TV on for company and rarely had the radio on either. No reason why, it just wasn't my thing. But for some reason today I noticed it more than I normally did. Maybe it was because I was in a thinking mood. I made myself a drink and headed into the conservatory, and opened the French doors which overlooked the back garden and the bay beyond. It was shaping up to be a lovely sun-filled day and I wanted to make the most of it, so I took my coffee outside along with my notebook and handbag. I could always find at least five pens at the bottom of it.

Just looking at the sea and watching the ebb and flow of the gentle waves lapping the shore brought me peace. I opened the notebook at the first blank page and wrote the heading 'JOY LIST' in capital letters and underlined it. Then I added bullet points for watching the sea, followed by fresh flowers, gardening and shell picking. This is what Martin meant about them not needing to be big things. Just things that brought you peace and lifted your heart.

Some time later, the sound of a text message brought me to. I hadn't realised that I'd fallen asleep. Whilst I loved getting up at the crack of a sparrow's fart, by lunchtime I'd begin to flag, and most days, a power nap would see me through the rest of the day. In fact, if I knew I had a busy day ahead, I'd spend my waking moments wondering and planning when I might be able fit a nap in. If I hadn't had just had one, I'd have been in bed by 8 p.m. instead of going to the pub to celebrate Celia's impending voyage.

If you fancy walking down to the pub with Dianne and I later, let me know. We'll be leaving at about 7.45. See you later x

It would be lovely to do that actually. Whilst I was getting more and more used to spending time by myself, walking into a pub on my own was one of my least favourite things to do.

Thank you, Celia. That would be perfect, see you out front then. x

A long soak in the bath might be nice to start my getting ready to go out proceedings. Funny how years ago, I'd take ages to get ready. These days, a bath, a brush of my hair and slapping on a bit of make-up seemed to do the trick. I honestly don't know what I used to do for all the time I spent. However, I loved a bubble bath, and had splashed out on a huge claw foot tub when I'd had the bathroom refurbished.

I grabbed the list and wrote 'BATH' on it. When I lived with Peter, he would always bring me a glass of Prosecco when I had a bath. He'd sit on the closed toilet seat and we'd chat. Put the world to rights. But now, ever since I'd begun to live alone, a bath was more of a meditative pastime along with some soothing music.

Ah music, there was another thing for the list.

Years ago, music and dance were such a huge part of my life. Then along came the times that destroyed me – times when I closed myself off and wouldn't listen to the words or melodies; refused to allow my body or my mind to respond. I shut it all out and had done for years.

But maybe now it was time. Time to let it back into my life.

Celia, Dianne and I had a pleasant stroll down the hill. There weren't many cars in our part of the town, the narrow streets putting the tourists off, which wasn't a bad thing. Later, when we'd have to walk back up it the walk might not be so quick but we'd worry about that then.

It was a lovely clear spring evening, that part of the year when the whole of summer is still ahead of you. The morning and nights were getting lighter, lengthening the whole day and you just felt generally full of hope for what lay ahead.

There were cheers all round when we walked into the pub. On our walk Celia had said that she decided to have the 'do' sooner rather than later so she could introduce Dianne to the locals. And they'd certainly turned out for her.

I glanced around the room and saw Martin sitting in the bay window with Clem and Meredith, Jude, and Gemma. He waved and indicated that the chairs next to him were empty, so I made my way over, and after kisses and hugs all round, plonked myself down, making a mental note to stop making these odd noises which made me appear older than I really felt. All my life, I'd never been a hugger, preferring to keep everyone at a distance – probably both physically and mentally – but since I'd come to Driftwood Bay, to hug my friends seemed the most natural thing in the world.

James pushed through the crowds with Lucy following behind him.

'This is our first night out since the little man has been born. I'm excited and Lucy is frantic with worry.' He laughed.

'You look incredible, Lucy.'

'Thank you, but I honestly don't feel it. I didn't realise that boobs could hurt this much and my nipp—'

'Ew! Way too much information thank you, sis.' Gemma grinned, the love for her sister shining through. 'You really are an oversharer at times, you know.'

James leaned across and pecked her cheek. 'But we do love you.'

The call of 'speech, speech' came from Geoff, the landlord, and he took Celia's hand and led her to a stool which he helped her to stand upon.

Celia cleared her throat.

'Thank you, Geoff, I'm only going to say a few words. I wanted to introduce you all to my sister Dianne.'

'That's Dianne with two n's,' she shouted to the room.

Celia rolled her eyes in good humour. 'God forbid I forget the two n's of my darling sister.'

The crowd laughed at this.

'I just wanted to say that I hope you make her feel as welcome as you did me when I moved to Driftwood Bay forty years ago. And that I hope you don't miss me too much but also that you don't forget me.'

'You sound like you're not coming back!'

'Ha. Well, you're not getting rid of me that easily. I'm definitely planning to return at some point, but who knows what the future holds for any of us? Maybe I'll meet a rich man on a yacht in the Med who will whisk me away to a life that I never knew I wanted. Or maybe, I'll get homesick after three weeks of having Delhi belly and be on the next plane home, pining for my Hobson. Who knows? But I am going to take it all one day at a time and just see where life takes me. Thanks so much for coming tonight. Please do join me in having a celebratory glass of Prosecco and toasting each other in living our best lives.'

'Living our best lives,' echoed around the room. What a lovely sentiment to start her trip, I thought.

The evening was such a lovely one, but the early morning start and a couple of glasses of Prosecco were taking their toll on me and my eyelids started to droop. Martin offered to walk me home, claiming he'd got lots to do the following day and wasn't planning a late night himself. Before we headed out, my gaze panned over everyone in the room and I smiled, thinking of this lovely community which had welcomed me so openly and kindly into their world.

But as I scanned the room, my eyes fell upon a poster next to the bar. My heart began to thump and I had to ask Martin to repeat what he'd just said.

'I was going to talk to you about that. I've got a proposition for you.'

5

'Enter a dance competition?' I repeated. 'Are you having a laugh?'

'Well, I wasn't. Do you dance, Lydia?'

I breathed out a huge sigh and whispered, 'I used to.'

'But not now?'

'It's a very long story.'

'I've got all the time in the world if you want to tell me.'

Walking side by side with someone and pouring out your past felt totally different to sitting opposite someone to do the same. You couldn't see their facial expressions and somehow it made it easier to talk. The arrival of the box from America had stirred something within me which I couldn't explain. Almost restlessness. Maybe regret. A mixture of lots of emotions.

'So, you just stopped dancing when you found out you were pregnant?' he asked after I explained my story. 'Is that what you're saying?'

I nodded.

'It was when my life came crashing down. I had my whole life ahead of me. I was going off to university, was dancing in competitions around the country, then I went to a party, and ended up, well, you know...' I took a deep breath. 'When I realised that I was pregnant I knew that my life was going to be changed forever.'

'Gosh. That was a lot to deal with, Lydia. You were so young too.'

We reached my front door, but now that I'd started pouring my heart out, there was part of me that wanted to continue to talk.

It was only then that I turned to face Martin.

'Would you like to come in for a coffee or a nightcap?'

'That would be lovely, but only if you promise not to try to get me drunk and have your wicked way with me.'

'Ha!' I scoffed at the very idea. 'Sorry if this disappoints you but my days of seduction are well and truly over.'

'Thank goodness for that. Mine too. In that case, I'd be delighted to accept your kind offer, m'lady.' He pretended to take a bow and the ease in which we laughed with each other made me smile. It was nice to not have to wonder about whether something might turn into more. Whether more was expected of you. It was so relaxing to know where you stood with each other as friends.

On entering the house, I caught sight of the box on the kitchen countertop and the slither of crimson sparkly material poking out from one of the corners, part of my history invading my present. Maybe that was symbolic. Over fifty years after it had been banished from my mind, and after I'd been away on the retreat and worked through a lot of my issues, maybe it was time to dance again.

As we sat in the conservatory, side by side, overlooking the bay beyond, the streetlights of the harbour glittering away, it felt good to open up. Martin was a wonderful listener, his eyes full of understanding, not judging me in any way at all. Sometimes you just need someone to listen to you, not try to fix a problem. I felt totally at ease with him, discussing a part of my past which I hadn't talked about or even thought about for a very long time. I knew that it was something that would remain between us.

He turned to me. 'Can I ask you a question, Lydia?'

I nodded my response.

'Why didn't you dance again?'

'My mother once told me that if I'd never gone to that party, I wouldn't have got myself into that situation and ended up pregnant. She said that she wished I'd never started dancing because that eventually led to another time, when her little girl had to grow up. It wasn't until I did all that work on myself at my retreat that I realised I'd been hanging on to this for all these years.'

'And you've not danced since then?'

'No. Probably sounds totally ridiculous to you, doesn't it?'

'You feel how you feel, Lydia. It's all valid, but how have you managed to go through life and not dance again?'

'I just tell people I don't dance. It's been hard. When you go to parties everyone thinks you are a party-pooper. A bit like if you don't drink. I just avoid them now and at this age, it's not that difficult. Not many people have parties these days.'

'Oh, Lydia.'

'Yes, I know. Pathetic, aren't I?'

'God no! I would say the reasons you've just shared with me are justification enough. It just makes me sad to think that something you loved so much ended right then and there. Such a lot to go through.'

I knew he was being empathic; I could hear it in his voice, I couldn't bring myself to turn my head to look at him. The fact that I still couldn't see his face somehow made me feel not quite as emotional as I thought I'd be.

'Have you ever talked to Meredith about this? Maybe you should tell her what you've just told me. She is your daughter. She'd want to know.'

'I've never mentioned it to her. I just kept away from her really and that's one of the reasons that there was a massive rift between us. I didn't really want her to know that she's the reason why I stopped doing something that I had loved so much. I'd hate her to think that I've blamed her existence for the way I decided to deal with it.'

'She's your daughter and I'm sure that with some very careful wording she'd understand.'

I nodded. 'You're right. I should. I'll give her a call in the morning and see if she'll come over. But do you know what? Maybe this box turning up and that poster in the pub is the universe telling me to get over myself.'

'You could be right.'

We sat in companionable silence, each lost in our thoughts.

Martin's forced cough jolted me back to the present.

'How would you feel about showing me the dress?' he said.

I breathed deeply. Gosh. That felt incredibly huge. But the more I thought about it, the more I would probably find excuses not to. I jumped up, consumed in that instant by a sense of urgency, and carried the box into my bedroom, where I placed it on the bed. For a minute or two, as I removed the lid and unfolded the crimson dress, I forgot that Martin was in the other room. Feeling the fabric float through my fingers, I was whisked away to over fifty years ago, to the Lydia who was a young woman with her whole life ahead of her, with plans and dreams to dance her way around the world. As I held the garment up against my body, I breathed in the signature scent of my life then – the heady mix of Oscar de la Renta perfume mixed with a very faint smoky scent of cigarettes – remembering a time that smoking indoors was acceptable and even the norm. Unimaginable these days.

Glancing into the box, I removed the hardbacked journal which had been lying underneath the dress and slid it into the drawer next to my bed. I wasn't anywhere near ready to look at that. The next items to catch my eye were also red and sparkly, the exact same colour as the dress. I picked them up and ran my fingers across the tops. Even though, there were gems missing from the front, and the ankle strap had broken, they were still my favourite shoes in the whole wide world.

When I slid my feet into them, surprisingly they fitted perfectly, just as they always had. A memory of the time my mother had taken me to buy new shoes flooded back, her pointing me in the direction of some black Mary Janes which she said would go with everything, yet it was the red ones in the window that caught my eye. I prayed that they had them in my size, knowing that I'd be devastated if they hadn't and when they did and I tried them on, I begged my mother to buy them for me, promising that I'd pay her back with my very first pay packet.

That very first pay packet ended up being so very different to the one I had intended, of qualifying as a lawyer after university. Instead, I worked in the corner shop, around the corner from our family home; a two-up, two-down terraced house, saving every penny of my wages.

The gemstones on the dress caught the light and sparkled at me, and in a split-second decision, I grabbed it before I ran out of courage. As I wriggled out of my linen trousers and threw off my floaty chiffon blouse, I decided that it was now or never.

I slid the dress over my head, unsure as to whether it would still even fit me, but I was lucky that I'd remained the same slender size I'd been as a young woman. It fitted like a glove, skimming my ankles, not quite full-length. I noticed that it was a little frayed around the seams, but even with its faults, I bloody still adored this dress.

The woman staring back at me in the mirror was a stranger to me. But fifty years on, the girl that I had hated so much, who I had always blamed for stealing away my future, became someone that I quite liked again. How ridiculous that I'd held a grudge with myself for so long. So much so, that it had debilitated me at times and made my life an absolute misery.

Martin was a man to be trusted. I had worked this out in the short time that I'd known him. If I didn't do this now, I never would.

Straightening my spine, lifting my shoulders, and holding my head high, trying to reclaim that gracefulness that I once had, I flounced back into the conservatory.

A wolf whistle greeted me and Martin stood, taking my hands in his and forcing me to turn around.

'Lydia. You look sensational.'

I twirled underneath his raised arm, enjoying the glee of the moment as the dress sashayed behind me, falling back into place a second behind me.

'Even with my tatty old dress, and my poor old shoes?'

As I asked that, the strap snapped open on my shoe. I tutted.

'My broken shoes.'

'Especially with your frayed edges and your vintage shoes. They're things that can be fixed. Oooh, wait!'

He fumbled in his pocket and removed his phone, tapping away on the buttons, and a few moments later, I could hear the dulcet tones of Audrey Hepburn singing 'Moon River'. I slipped off my shoes and we danced a few steps, then he spun me gently, and dipped me backwards. I wasn't as flexible as I was at the age of eighteen, but I didn't think I was too bad considering.

'You simply must enter the dance competition with me,' he

said. 'I'm no twinkle toes, but I'm a quick learner, and I reckon if we practise, we could do it. We don't have to win; we can just take part and have some fun. What do you think?'

I pulled myself up straight and pondered. Could I do this? Did I want to do this? There was a little fizzle of excitement in my tummy – and these days, these feelings were few and far between.

'But where would we practise? We need somewhere with a decent-sized room. Bay View Cottage doesn't have a dance floor, you know, and I presume your house doesn't either.'

'No, it doesn't. But I know somewhere that has. Tell you what. After yoga tomorrow morning, keep an hour or so free and I'll share my ideas with you. Say yes, Lydia. Go on. Put dance at the top of your joy list and dance with me.'

Running my hands over my hips and turning this way and that, even with my broken shoes, I could see that this outfit had done for me today what it had done over fifty years ago. It made me happy. I'd had fun.

I nodded. 'OK. Let's do it.'

It was time to reclaim my life.

6

The emotions of the previous night seemed to catch up with me and I slept like a log. Feeling a little discombobulated at waking up later than intended, I dropped Martin a text saying that I'd be there in ten minutes and quickly splashed my face with cold water to wake me up.

When I arrived at the beach, I laughed to see Martin with a huge stick in his hand, completing a rectangle shape in the sand.

'Your dance floor, m'lady.' He waved to the space that he'd made. 'The audience will be over there—' he indicated to the back of the rectangle shape '—and the judges—' he swung around to indicate a space at the side '—will be over there.'

He moved across to where his phone was connected to two large speakers and pressed a button on the screen, and swing music began to fill the air. 'The band will be here. And finally, Claudia and Tess will be here. And here you have our rehearsal studio. Big enough for you? What do you think?'

'I think you are a complete and utter nutter. And I love it. This is brilliant.' I had certainly woken up now. Laughter first thing is a wonderful way to start the day. 'Although, I don't wish to be a negative Nellie but I'm not sure a beach is the best place to dance. You really need a more solid floor so your feet can glide. There's no chance of doing that on a sandy beach.'

'Well, let's give it a go. Even if it's not the best, perhaps it'll just give us some experience of dancing together. And we can always find somewhere else if it doesn't work. We've got a lovely floor in the church that might be more suitable.'

The beach wasn't the most glidy place in the world to dance, but it was certainly the most beautiful.

'So, Lydia... I hope you don't mind, but I've been doing some research and I have a list of dances. I know which ones I'd like to do but what do you think we should do? I think we should choose two and then pick our favourite one from the two. How does that sound to you?'

'Ah OK. Well, a waltz is the easiest. It's slow, smooth, and only uses six steps and three counts. It's all about the timing. A foxtrot is a four-step dance. Reminds me of Fred Astaire and Ginger Rogers. Gorgeous! Oh, what about the cha-cha-cha? It's a Latin style dance with five steps but you'd have to get those hips loosening up, Martin.'

Martin grinned back at me. 'I'll have you know there's nothing wrong with my hip action thank you very much.' From the rucksack by his side he produced a flask and two bone china mugs. 'Coffee?'

'Oooh, yes please. I normally have hot water and lemon first thing but beggars can't be choosers.'

'Duly noted!'

He carefully laid out the mugs on a flattish rock and poured the drinks. I shook my head when he held up a sugar sachet, and he passed my coffee over.

'Don't spill any on the dance floor please,' he said. 'We don't want to be slip sliding all over the place and break-dancing when we should be doing ballroom.'

'So, there's the mambo, the merengue, the tango. Gosh, so many choices! I'll have to have a little think but I suppose some of it depends on your experience. Have you ever danced before at all?'

'Erm, not really. And when I say not really, I mean no. I'm a proper beginner but I'm a quick learner. And I'll be an excellent student, miss. Honest!'

He was funnier than I'd given him credit for. He had a super sense of humour that I didn't know existed.

'So, I reckon the waltz and the cha-cha-cha. Yes, they'd be perfect. Do you think you could find some music for those?'

His face lit up. 'They were the exact ones I was going to suggest. Brilliant. So, here are my musical choices.'

He handed me a list. So organised.

After much deliberation, and obviously taking into consideration the huge difference in our musical tastes, fifteen minutes later we had a list that we were going to try out. 'What the World Needs Now' by Jackie DeShannon was Martin's waltz choice and 'Perfect' by Ed Sheeran was mine. I might have been the wrong side of seventy but I loved his music and thought it would be a good way to get the younger members of the audience voting for us. For our cha-cha-cha choices, we had 'Save the Last Dance for Me', Michael Bublé's version, as Martin's suggestion and 'Kiss' by Tom Jones was mine.

The next half an hour was filled with super music, singing, much hilarity, and the knowledge that my toes would be black and blue when I arrived home, because Martin had stood on them so many times. However, I couldn't remember the last time I'd had so much fun. Martin was such easy company and the fact that I knew we weren't interested in each other apart from being each other's dance partners added a whole new layer of friendship and simplicity.

A further cup of coffee, two croissants, and another half an hour of dance practice and I thought that we'd done enough for one day.

'Martin, you know this isn't working on the beach, don't you?'

'Well, I thought we were just crap to be honest.'

I laughed. 'We are definitely not crap but the floor just isn't right. While it's a lovely place to dance, we need somewhere else to train. Could we maybe try the church? You said before that you thought the floor might be better.'

'We can. We could try the sanctuary – the part at the top near what used to be the altar. I don't know why, but at some point, the original floorboards were all sanded down and refurbished. We could definitely try there instead. Why don't you come up later and have a look? See what you think.'

'Perfect. Are you up there today?'

'I sure am. I've a full day of repairing stuff ahead of me. I think the residents of Cornwall are all having a rethink about life and recycling and are reusing and upcycling their old items, rather than buying new. I suppose it's good for the universe really and we should all think about doing it more.'

My inquisitive mind was interested in finding out more.

'What sort of things do you do?'

'Well, a variety really and no two days are the same. Today for instance I'll be working on two carriage clocks. I've got someone coming in to drop off an old fob watch. Not sure why I'm suddenly the local expert on timepieces at the moment. I've done all sorts really. People ask me to do the most random of things. Last week I upcycled an old writing bureau for an author. And I had someone last month come in and ask me if I could repair an old trumpet that belonged to his father. It's an honour really, that people put their trust in me. Repairing and restoring people's memories and treasures is something that's such a privilege. It's not just about repairing things. It's about bringing these cherished items back to life and unlocking the stories they hold.'

He continued to wax lyrical about restoration. He was clearly very passionate and took his new role very seriously. I asked him about when he started to do these things.

'I've always been a tinkerer – if that's even the word. I always had a – what do you call it these days? Man cave. At the bottom of the garden, it was, and Clem and I used to make things. He loved working with wood even from an early age and it was just nice to spend time with him. He used to love making little presents for his mum and she'd love it when he gave them to her. Even if they were bloody awful and she couldn't quite work out what they were. But she was so kind to him, telling him what a clever boy he was and how she'd treasure what he'd made for ever.'

He smiled, clearly remembering a lovely time gone by. I could literally see him swallow the lump that had clearly formed in his throat.

'When she died, and we were sorting through some things of hers, we found a box of his gifts up in the loft. There was Clem and I thinking she'd thrown everything away years ago but she'd carefully wrapped them all up in tissue paper and packed them away. Unbelievable really. That brought some tears about, I can tell you that much. The day we found them was the day that broke Clem. I've never seen him so upset. He adored her. And she adored him right back. They say mothers and sons have a special bond, and don't get me wrong, I love him to bits, but they always seemed to have a relationship that we never had. I suppose that's why I did the wood working with him, to try and build something especially for us. Bless him. He was always such a kind boy and now he's turned into a wonderful man. I'm so proud of him.'

'I hope you tell him that, Martin. If life has taught me anything, it's about saying what you think. I spent years not telling Meredith how I felt about her and she grew up thinking I never loved her, even though in my heart I thought I was doing the best thing for her – because I loved her too much. Sorry, I don't mean to preach but don't let it ever be too late to say the things you want to say.'

He looked pensive, lost in his thoughts.

'Sorry, I went off on a bit of a tangent there.'

I smiled at him to let him know it was OK.

'When Miranda and I opened the bric-a-brac shop, people would come in for a mooch about and they'd say, "I've got one of those but it's broken" and I'd tell them to drop it in and I'd take a look. I just learned that I'd got a knack for things. And patience. An awful lot of patience. It just kind of happened really. Went on from then. A hobby, I suppose, that turned into a business. And now Gemma's taken the shop over and I've moved up to the church, there's so much room. I can have all my tools over the place and don't have to keep putting stuff aside to do other stuff. It's perfect.'

'How interesting,' I said, but my mind had wandered to my own life, thinking about all I'd achieved – or more like, failed to achieve. Martin seemed to pick up on my thoughts.

'What jobs have you had in the past? What are you good at?'

'Nothing really. I was quite good at finding husbands, to be honest, but not so good at keeping them. Not such a great hobby, I suppose. I stopped at husband number five. I'm done now. No more husbands for me.'

'So, you've never had a job?'

'No. I've always married people who didn't want me to work,

so I've mainly stayed home and played house. Made beautiful houses with their money. Yes. Maybe that's what I'm good at.'

I tutted, thinking how ridiculous it sounded to have never had a job. How shallow to have gone through life without a purpose. I stared out to sea, wondering why I'd never really asked this question of myself before.

'I'm quite handy with a needle and thread or a sewing machine. Oh, and dancing. I was good at that. You know, before everything changed.'

I didn't want to get maudlin thinking about the past again. The retreat and my time in therapy had taught me that no good could come from just going over and over the things that you could do nothing about.

'Right, best shake a leg and crack on. I'll pop into the pub then and put our names down for the competition, shall I? Last chance to say no! No hard feelings.'

I took a deep breath and then shrugged. 'I can't see any reason why we shouldn't go ahead.'

'Great stuff. And you know, it doesn't matter if we win or not. It's all about having fun. It's the taking part that counts, Lydia. And the money for charity. No pressure at all.'

'Sod that, Martin,' I said. I'd forgotten how dancing brought out such a competitive side in me. 'If we're doing it at all, then we're in it to win it! Bring it on!'

7

Celia's leaving day had arrived and it appeared that most of Driftwood Bay had turned out to wave her off. When it was my turn to bid her farewell, she gave me the hugest of hugs and murmured into my ear.

'She might appear brash and loud, but Dianne is dealing with a lot at the moment. She's working through some issues and is very fragile. Way more than she looks. I nearly cancelled my trip but she insisted that she'll be OK and that, if necessary, I'll only be a day's plane ride away if she needs me.' She held me at arm's length. 'I hope you and she become good friends, Lydia. Like you and I have. You are a good person and that's exactly what she needs in her life right now. I can't tell you why. It's her story to tell and maybe she'll open up in time. I just hope it'll all make sense at some point.'

So, it would appear that Dianne with two n's was a bit of an enigma. I would make the effort to get to know her better, I decided. I knew that at times I was quite quick to judge – it was something that we talked about at the retreat, it being something I could change if I wanted to.

Just before she got into the taxi, Celia ran back to Hobson, dropped to the floor, and clung to his neck, whispering into his ear. He leaned into her, sensing that this was a goodbye. He looked proper down in the dumps. As a setter, he had big soft eyes that looked sad at the best of times and my heart went out to him.

'Bye, everyone. Follow me on Instagram. I'm @Driftwood-Dropout.'

My heart dipped as I remembered what a social media addict I'd been until I went on the retreat.

When I think back to my time there, it really was life changing and I felt so much better equipped to deal with situations as they occurred these days. It would be great to have something like that here. Imagine a place like that in Cornwall. A beautiful venue where you could just forget about everything but work on yourself to make your life better. So many people could benefit from this type of therapy. Life is so ridiculously busy for so many people these days that they don't have the chance to sit down, take stock and evaluate their lives. All everyone seems to do is compare themselves to others, not even intentionally, but the constant scrolling on other people's social media posts where they're boasting about where they are, what they're doing, what they have and the like, can chip away at people. Without consciously processing, you're thinking: well, why am I not as successful, as thin, as rich, as happy? Why isn't my house as big, as tidy, as well decorated?

It's also such a time suck. I lost hours and days to meaningless scrolling then I'd think I didn't have time to do important things. In my humble opinion, it was no wonder that so many people are struggling with mental health nowadays. It's a spiral that I found it hard to get myself out of and was lucky to have some guidance. And I'm an oldie. It must be far worse for the youngsters constantly comparing themselves and feeling that they are not good enough. I only wish they knew how enough they already were.

'I'm really going to miss her, you know...' Dianne wiped away a stray tear that was rolling down her cheek as we waved Celia off in the taxi. 'I've only spent a week with her since I've been back from Australia, but we've reconnected so much in that time.'

My admiration for them both had grown over the last few days. We'd seen each other most days for coffee. I used to wonder what Celia did all day when I first moved in, but she was constantly busy with the animals, doing the morning feeds, the therapy work she did with Hobson and tending the small bit of land she had.

'Don't suppose you fancy a cuppa, do you, Dianne?'

I thought maybe a distraction and some company would be good for her. Hobson lay by her side, his head on his paws. He seemed so despondent with his big sad eyes. 'We could go to Five O'clock Somewhere and get Gemma to give us the biggest piece of cake she can find. And I'm sure she'll have some of those lovely doggy cupcakes that Hobson loves so much too. And maybe a puppuccino too.' His ears pricked up at the sound of that. 'Puppuccino, Hobson? What do you think?'

I was reminded of someone once saying that dogs have short memories and if they were fed, watered, exercised and loved, they'd be fine. Maybe they weren't the only ones.

I tucked my arm into Dianne's and we walked down the hill to the bistro. I would try to be the friend that Celia said her sister needed.

When we arrived, Vi was sitting at one of the tables that overlooked the beach, tucking into a hearty full English. Her Labrador Gladys was perched underneath in the hope that a stray bit of sausage might end up somewhere in the vicinity of her nose. Vi saw us and waved us over and asked us if we'd like to join her.

'How are you, Vi? Haven't seen you for a couple of days,' I said.

'The carbuncle on my left foot is giving me hell and I've got terrible wind but apart from that I'm all right, my darling, thank you. And I can blame the wind on the dog so it's not too much trouble.'

We giggled. She'd achieved her aim of entertaining us. She loved to make people laugh.

'My Dennis came to pick me up yesterday and we had a lovely day out,' she continued.

'What did you do nice?'

'Went to a funeral. Had a bloody lovely time.'

Dianne and I exchanged furtive glances.

'You had a lovely time at the funeral?' Dianne enquired. 'Whose was it?'

'A cousin of mine. Gertrude. Never liked her anyway. Miserable old bitch. No quality of life towards the end; lived in a nursing home but not sure what her excuse was for the rest of her life. I told our Dennis that's what would have happened to me if he'd made me go in one, like he very nearly did. Thank God your Meredith came along and turned my life around with her great big heart.'

My own heart burst with pride to hear again how my daughter had been fundamental to Vi's new lease of life. When Meredith had moved into the area, she'd befriended Vi and offered to help out with dog walks when Vi was incapacitated after an accident. Meredith was an incredibly kind and wonderfully warm person who would do anything for anyone if she could. She always used to say, 'Why wouldn't you help someone if you can.'

Dianne and I both nodded our approval.

'The food was amazing. So much so that I brought a load back with me.'

'That was nice of them to let you do that,' Dianne chirped.

'Oh, they didn't let me. I didn't ask. I just got my Tupperware box out and filled it as full as I could. It'll keep me going all week.'

Dianne's eyebrows nearly shot off her face and I had to stifle a grin as our eyes locked in disbelief.

'I'm an old lady, girls.' It had been a long time since I'd been called a girl. 'I've got to the stage of my life when I don't give a shit and people won't question me. I gave up thinking about what people thought of me years ago. It's none of my business. When that penny drops, I can assure you, it's a game-changer, especially when your yesterdays are more than your tomorrows like ours are.'

She winked at us both and went back to mopping up her baked beans with a slice of toast. Hobson had joined Gladys under the table and a huge string of slobber was dangling from his big flappy jowl. I watched as it landed on Dianne's sandal and inwardly heaved a little.

'It's a bit like my clothes,' Vi continued, evidently not noticing Hobson's exuberance. She pushed her chair back, stood and did a little twirl. It was only then that I really took in her outfit: a red and green tartan skirt, an orange flowery blouse and pink sparkly wellies. 'I'm comfy in what I'm wearing and I like it and that's all that matters to me. People can think of me whatever they like. I don't give a shit. I'm even thinking of having a tattoo. They can stick that in their pipe and smoke it.'

I laughed at this expression – it was one that my own mother used to use – and I imagined what it would look like for this fabulous octogenarian to get one of those tattoo sleeves that I'd seen on TV. Hopefully, if she was serious about it, which I couldn't quite make out, she'd have something a little more subtle. She did like a bit of attention and loved shocking people because she could. But Vi was right. She could do what she liked. I spent my whole life worrying about what people thought of me and the choices that I'd made. It had both encouraged me to continue and debilitated me at the same time.

Dianne was staring into space, and I felt that something in what Vi had said was resonating with her deep within. I had to say her name twice before she realised I was talking to her, snapping her attention back to me.

'Sorry, Lydia, what did you say?'

'Just asked what you'd like to eat and drink? My treat.'

'Well, in that case I'll have a small latte. And a piece of Gemma's amazing coffee and walnut cake would do just the trick, thank you.'

'Can I get you anything else, Vi?'

She waved her knife at me, narrowly missing Dianne's face who was sat next to her.

'Another cup of tea would be lovely, dear, thank you.'

I sauntered over to the counter, waiting for Rachel to finish taking someone else's order.

'Morning, Rachel, how are you? How's everything going?'

'We're getting there. It's not perfect but we're doing OK. And thanks again for helping me navigate through all these motherhood issues. I really appreciate the time you've given to me recently.'

Rachel had moved into Driftwood Bay at a similar time to me; me trying to make amends with Meredith and her trying to do the same with her daughter Occy and her ex-husband Jude, who didn't have the best opinion of her. We both needed to spend time repairing our relationships and were something like kindred spirits. We had sat and discussed our roller-coaster ride of a journey many times, sometimes over tea, and at other times over a glass of wine.

She was a nice lady, obviously still beating herself up over choices that she'd made, in a very similar way that I was doing, only she wasn't lucky enough to have had a three-month therapeutic retreat, so I was helping as much as I could, sharing tactics and tools I'd learned. I hoped that I could stop her making some of the ridiculous mistakes that I'd made which had given me high hurdles to jump over.

Rachel handed the card machine to me. 'Heard anything yet, love?'

She was also the only other person that I'd told about my health scare. She'd very kindly offered to drive me to the hospital while I had the biopsy, just so I didn't have to go alone. I didn't want Meredith to take on that role. She just needed to be my daughter right now and not my carer. And I didn't want her to worry about me while our relationship was doing so well.

'Not yet, I'm hoping no news is good news.'

She covered my hand with hers.

'Let's hope so, hey?'

8

The bistro door burst open, and Martin came stomping in.

I turned to see what the commotion was.

'All right there, Martin?'

'I am. I'm just bloody annoyed with myself over something and needed to get out to clear my head to see if I can think of a solution.'

'Can I help? Problem shared and halved and all that.'

'I could kick myself, Lydia. I've torn the fabric on the small footstool that I'm mending the legs on. It's really precious and I really wanted to get it back to its original state for the lady that brought it in. But now I think I've buggered it up completely.'

'Oh, that's a shame. Will she be gutted?'

'I think I'm more gutted than she will be. She said if I could save the material that would be great, but if I couldn't then she'd have to find someone to re-cover it instead.'

An idea began to form in my mind.

'Would you let me take a look at it, Martin?'

'You most certainly can. I'd love your help. It would do me a huge favour to be honest. You can either give me a solution or tell me what a blithering great idiot I am.'

'I'll come now, if that's OK with me leaving you, Dianne?'

'Yes of course. I need to get Hobson up to school anyway. It's his reading class in half an hour so I'll need to take him for a spin round the harbour first.'

As part of his job of being a therapy dog, Hobson also went along to local schools for the children to read to him. It helped with their literacy skills and their well-being as well as developing their confidence and interest in reading. When Celia first told me about it I thought it was such a sweet idea and when she explained the many benefits to me, even more so.

'Oooh yes, you don't want him shitting on the children.'

She giggled. 'Violet! You're incorrigible.'

We strolled back up the hill, Martin seeming a little calmer knowing that he now had a second pair of eyes on the issue. The workshop was at the top of Church Lane. Last year, Reverend Rogers broke the news to the community that they were closing down the church due to cuts and moving to a neighbouring town. I hadn't seen the space since Martin rented it out as a workshop and I was quite excited to see it.

He held the gate open for me as we entered the churchyard and then at the end of the pathway heaved open the heavy old oak front door.

The last time I'd been in here had been for the Christmas carol service and it sure looked different now. All the pews had been moved to the outside walls, creating a huge floor space and there were various workstations set up with an array of tools on them.

'God, Martin, this is a fabulous space.'

He grinned back at me.

'Yes, it's pretty cool, isn't it?'

'Does it not feel a little creepy being here on your own?'

'Far from it. It's peaceful and calm. I love it. And with the shop there were people wandering in and disturbing me all day long.'

I laughed. 'Customers trying to buy things, you mean?'

'Browsers too. Just come for a mooch with no intention of buying anything and interrupting me.'

'Perish the thought.'

I looked around, taking in the surroundings, and started nodding.

'This really would make a fabulous dance space. We should clear it all out to make it even bigger.'

'Another thing Miranda would have said, you know.'

'A woman of taste clearly.'

'You'd have got on with her like a house on fire, Lydia. I wish you'd had the chance to meet her.'

'Me too, Martin. Me too.'

Martin sat heavily on the nearest chair, as if he suddenly had the weight of the world on his shoulders.

'God, I miss her sometimes – so much that it takes my breath away.'

'Oh, Martin. I'm sorry.'

I touched his arm, not quite sure of what to say or do to make him feel better. He looked so sad.

'No, I'm sorry. I shouldn't have just blurted that out.'

'Do you want to talk about it?'

He paused before nodding. 'I do, but I don't really know what to say.'

Poor Martin. It seemed like he'd been bottling something up. I hoped chatting would help.

'Tell you what, I'll make us a cuppa while you have a think. Where's your tea stuff?'

I went through to the little side room he indicated, where there was a small kitchen. The old vestry I believe.

'Here you go,' I said when I'd returned to the main room. 'A nice cup of tea makes everything feel better.'

I handed him the cup.

'Don't know where that ridiculous statement comes from but it really doesn't, does it?'

I shook my head. 'No, not really.'

'Do you ever get lonely, Lydia?'

It was my turn to sigh before answering. 'I do. We have a wonderful community here, and there's always something on, but it's doing these things alone that I find the hardest to cope with.'

'Oh God, yes, it's that exactly; the being part of something. When you're in a couple, you are part of something. You are accepted more. You get invited to things that couples do. I'm sure people don't mean to, but you do get excluded when you are on your own.'

'That's so true. I never realised it until now really. I've always been in a marriage and had that someone by my side. Even if things weren't going that well, there was always someone there. I always had a purpose. Someone coming home to me, whatever the day had held. Sometimes it's when I get home from a busy evening out that I feel more alone than I've ever felt in my life.'

We both sipped our tea, lost in thought.

'I don't particularly want another relationship,' I said. 'I'm enjoying discovering who the real me is. In the past, I always thought I needed a man in my life to complete me. I know now that I don't but I do really miss that company. It would be nice sometimes to have someone to do nothing with. Sometimes it's so quiet I could scream.'

He murmured in agreement. 'Yeah, I hear you!'

'Gosh, listen to us. What a miserable pair.'

He sniggered at that. 'Maybe dancing together will give us both something to focus on. A bit of a purpose.'

I raised my mug. 'To friendship and freedom.'

'I'll drink to that.' He mirrored my gesture and we smiled as our eyes met, feeling a little bit closer as friends than we did before.

'Right, let's take a look at this footstool then,' I said, placing down my mug.

He brought it over and I appraised it. The footstool was small and had turned wooden legs. It matched a wing-back armchair in the same material, which Martin had already repaired and was positioned next to a long bench. Sadly, the part on the stool where the studs fixed the material to the base had come undone and it looked as if it had been stretched and torn in the process.

'Please don't make me feel any worse than I already do, by telling me I shouldn't have tried to stretch it.' He laughed and his eyes crinkled up again. 'I know I'm a silly old sod. I'd love to know if you think it's fixable.'

Martin took the empty cups back into the vestry, while I had a look and assessed the situation. When he returned I had a solution but wasn't sure it was one he might approve of.

I could take the main part of the fabric, which didn't have the tear in it, and put a contrasting fabric around the outside as a frame. And then I could make a matching cushion for the armchair too. I knew Meredith had tons of material in her garden room and I was sure that in her vast collection I'd be able to find something perfect. When Martin said he thought it was a grand idea and could work, I was delighted. He said that he felt the lady would be very happy with the compromise. When I left shortly afterwards to head to Meredith's, I was feeling quite excited about having a new little project to think about.

* * *

Every moment I spent with Meredith since I'd lived in Driftwood Bay seemed like a bonus to cherish and I adored being in her company. That day was no exception. When I'd first come to stay here, we were both quite prickly around each other, but our relationship had developed into something incredibly special. Mooching through her stash of fabric and just chatting with her about nothing in particular, was pure delight; one of my favourite things to do. I was so relaxed that I decided to be brave.

'There's something I should tell you about, but you need to promise not to laugh.'

'Oh, yes? Tell me more.'

'Well, Martin and I are going to be taking part in that dance competition for starters and he's asked me to help him out with a couple of the restoration projects he's working on.'

Meredith's eyes widened.

'I don't know what to comment on first. The fact that you just said you are taking part in a dance competition, or that you are going to be working with Martin. You seem to be getting on rather well these days.'

'We do and we're good friends. That's all. At my time of life, friendship is exactly what I'm looking for. I've done my time with husbands and trying to make someone else happy and hope that in turn makes me happy. It's taken me a while to realise that's all down to me. However, I'm loving dancing again and getting involved with these projects is something that really does lift my heart.'

'That's great to hear, Mum, but I'm still getting over that you will be dancing.'

I laughed. 'I used to be very good.'

'You're a blooming dark horse. How did I not know this about you?'

'There's a lot you don't know about your mother, you know...'

'If you are going to be smooching cheek to cheek with my potential father-in-law, there's probably a lot I don't need to know either.'

We both laughed.

How could I spoil this easiness we had together by telling her about my health worries? Also, not saying them out loud made them not seem real and I could pretend they weren't happening for short spells at a time.

* * *

When I returned a few hours later, Martin helped me bring the things in from the car, taking the sewing machine with a box of accessories while I carried a couple of rolls of fabric, and another box containing some different-sized glue sticks and a staple gun.

As Martin worked on a couple of other items, I made a start on the footstool. A companionable silence fell between us, with just the odd glance and smile across the room as we caught each other's eye and only the radio as background noise. I hadn't felt this comfortable for years.

I completely removed and cleaned up the old material with a mix of vinegar and water and gently wiped a cotton cloth over the surface. It came up a treat. Once I'd managed to sew the old piece onto a new piece and then fix that to the original framework of the stool, I was delighted with the result. I'd have been very happy if it was going in my house. When I looked up at the clock, I noticed that three hours had flown by.

Martin's voice broke into my silence.

'Oh. My. God. Lydia.'

My heart sank.

'You hate it? I've spoilt it, haven't I?'

'You haven't spoilt it at all. Not only have you repaired it, but you've made it look so much better than before. It looks fresh and brand new. And the colours perfectly complement each other. How have you done that? You're an absolute genius. Although I have always thought you were pretty amazing, you know.'

He winked at me. If I hadn't known better, I'd have thought he was flirting with me. More than that, the little skip in my heart was telling me I probably would have enjoyed it too.

Smiling at his lovely compliment, I realised how much I'd enjoyed the last few hours.

No one really needed me these days. Meredith had her own, busy, fulfilling life and obviously she had Clem. The last year or so had been the first that I'd been alone. I wasn't required to ensure the smooth running of a house, keep myself looking good or be entertaining to my husband and any guests. The feeling I had at that moment was the same as in domestic science at school when I made my first cushion. I knew back then that it was something I loved and my mother had scrimped and saved so she could buy me a sewing machine. I'd left it behind when I left for the US. The surprise I got when I saw it in Meredith's workshop a few months ago had really humbled me. Especially when she admitted to me that it had made her feel closer to me when she used to use it.

One of the first things I bought when I moved to Driftwood Bay was a modern machine and I'd been determined I was going to make my own soft furnishings, but I hadn't got quite round to it yet. Maybe that was something else I needed to remedy.

'Did you know that I was watching you while you were working?' Martin asked.

'I didn't. I zoned out, completely focused on my task. Why?'

'You've spent the last three hours with a dirty great smile on your face. It's been so lovely to see you so happy. In fact, I'd go as far as saying full of joy.'

I laughed.

'Something else to add to my list. I honestly can't tell you how much I've really loved doing that.' I beamed at him. 'I've had such a lovely afternoon. Thanks so much for asking me to get involved and for your, well, company.'

'You're a natural. As for the company, we've hardly spoken.'

'Yes, but that's what's been so nice about it. We never needed to.'

Martin held my gaze and chewed the inside of his lip. If I didn't know better, I'd have said he looked a little bashful.

'While you're here, I don't suppose I could trouble you to have a look at some other soft furnishing projects? I've a couple I could do with another opinion on.'

I grinned. 'What you got?'

'There's an old doll, which I know might sound a bit weird but she's not one of those creepy old dolls. She's donkey's years old and very pretty. She used to walk and I think I know how to get her going again. Let me grab her.'

He walked to the back of the room and opened a trunk. He took something out and brought it back over to me. Wrapped in tissue paper was a beautiful doll, the size of a small toddler.

'They always have a story, don't they?' I said. 'I wonder what hers is.'

'Now, I do know the story, but I think I might save it until we can get her looking amazing again. That OK with you? If you can trust me on it, I promise it'll be worth the wait. All I can say is that it would mean the absolute world to the lady who brought it in. Think you can do anything to help?'

Intrigued even more now, I took a closer look at the doll's clothes. Her antique lace dress was mouldy in places and in others had been eaten away by something. I reckoned though that with a bit of searching I might be able to create something similar and just as beautiful. A shiver of excitement ran all the way up my spine. There was no way that this was slipping through my fingers.

'You could always leave your stuff set up on that workbench,' Martin said. 'There's so much room here that it won't be an issue at all. What do you think?'

'Try and stop me!'

9

When I moved in here, I vowed that every day of my life, I would walk on the beach at least twice a day. What's the point of living by the beach if you don't make the most of it? It wasn't something I wanted to take for granted.

Since I saw her yesterday, the little doll's faded face was firmly etched on my mind as I sat on a bench overlooking the bay, gazing out to sea. I wondered why it was so important to the owner and why she was so desperate to have it restored to its former glory. However, I knew with all my heart that I wanted to be part of the restoration process to bring her back to life. Everyone has a story to tell and I was eager to know not just the history of the doll, but I was also fascinated by the history of the person who it belonged to.

I was so much in a little world of my own, I was surprised when a voice cut into my thoughts.

'Hi, Lydia. Are you OK?'

'Hello, Lucy, my love, how are you? And how is this little one?'

I peered into the pushchair to see whether he was awake but trying not to frighten him if he was.

'Oh he's absolutely perfect but...' She sighed loudly. 'You know how it is with a newborn. You're so utterly in love with them that you feel like your heart might burst open! At the same time, you are so bloody exhausted from getting no sleep that you don't know how you'll survive the next few days let alone the rest of their life.'

I remembered when Meredith was a baby. There were times when I couldn't stop staring at her, beside myself with worry, always watching and making sure she was breathing. Other memories far worse came flooding into my mind. Years of practice had taught me to keep the heartache from my face and the hurt from my heart.

Lucy continued, oblivious to my internal pain.

'It's blooming scary being a first-time mum, isn't it? You've never done it before, and are trying so hard to make sure that you're doing everything perfectly. You're so full of emotion that it's overwhelming and you don't know how you'd ever live without them.'

I felt my eyebrows raise before I could try to stop them.

'Oh, Lydia, I'm so sorry. I think I might have been bottling that all up.'

'Don't apologise, my lovely. I don't want you to filter how you are feeling with me. I, of all people, understand how it feels.'

I'd hidden my own pregnancy for months before my mother found out and it was then too late to do anything about it. It was no secret that when Meredith was born, I couldn't cope. I was a single mother, Meredith the product of an unfortunate drunken night when I was taken advantage of. I was young and hadn't got a clue what I was doing. What I didn't realise was that I had been suffering in silence with post-natal depression. It wasn't until I met someone that I realised how bad it had got and I felt like things might be getting better. He was wonderful and swept me off my feet, offering us both a new life in the United States.

Excited about having a new start I went out there to set everything up, leaving Meredith behind with my own mother until we were ready to send for her. But then I discovered that I was pregnant again. Just when everything was wonderful, I lost my little boy in the most excruciating circumstances. When depression set in again, even worse than the first time, I decided that I clearly wasn't fit to be a mother at all. I left Meredith in the UK while I stayed in the US, thinking that it was the best thing for her and feeling that she'd have a better life without me.

It was a decision I made when I was ill and I couldn't blame Meredith for thinking so little of me because of it. It was something I had and would regret for the rest of my life. It had such an impact on us all and the reason why I'd come back to live near her now. I'd vowed to spend the rest of my life making it up to her.

My mind was both reminiscing about the past and wandering into the future and my right hand instinctively went to my breast and panic rose within me. What if this did turn out to be cancer? What if the time I had left wasn't enough to repair the damage from the decisions I'd made while I was ill?

'Lydia, are you OK?'

Her words cut into my thoughts and brought me back to the here and now, pushing away my fears and closing them down for the time being.

'I'm so sorry, Lucy, I drifted off for a moment then. Let me look at your beautiful little boy.'

I leaned into the pram. I'd purposely kept away from Lucy and her family, pretending to give them space, but really it was because I needed to give myself distance instead. I don't know how I did it but I'd managed to avoid babies as much as I could for most of my life. Avoidance seemed to be my speciality.

As I peered down into the pram and saw the little boy grinning back at me, I couldn't help but let a smile spread across my face. God, he was perfect. Absolutely perfect. His little pleading face and the slobbery bubbles and little gurgles coming from his mouth were delightful. Instead of being sad and wondering whether my little boy might have looked like him, for the first time in my life, I felt happy to be around a baby.

'Oh, Lucy, he's just the sweetest little boy.' I looked at her face and could see how exhausted and worried she was. 'But I do know that however you feel, you should tell someone. It's so important that you do that. If I can help in any way, then just let me know. I'm a great listener.'

'Would you...?' A little bit of hope appeared in my heart but she stopped herself. 'No, ignore me.'

'Would I what?'

'I don't suppose you might like to, well, you know, hold him?'

I felt a whoosh of emotion from my head to my toes, but instead of them being negative emotions, they were overwhelmingly positive.

'I would love nothing more,' I whispered, surprising myself.

Lucy picked him out of the pram and handed him to me gently as if he was the most precious jewel in the world. I supposed he was to her.

'Hey, little man,' she said. 'This is your aunty Lydia. She's going to hold you.'

Our eyes locked and I could understand her pleading look: please take care of my baby. My nod in return promised that she could trust me: I would be more careful than I'd ever been with anything else.

I felt nervous but excited as he nestled into the crook of my arm. He gurgled again and wrapped his little fingers around my thumb.

'Hello, little Taran. Aren't you a little stunner?'

His eyes fluttered. He was clearly close to sleep, comfortable enough in my arms to be starting to drop off. His eyes closed completely and my heart leapt with raw emotion. The only time I saw my own little boy was after I'd given birth to him; his eyes were already shut tight by that point, and that vision has forever been etched in my mind.

I closed my eyes, trying to push away memories from the past when I could hear Taran gurgling at me.

I gently sat back down on the bench. Lucy laid her hand on mine as she rested her head on my shoulder.

'I'm so tired, Lydia.'

'Being a new mum is a shock to the system, isn't it?'

'It is. God! I wish my mum was here.'

'I know you do, darling. People will say that she's watching from above and they mean well, but it's not the same, is it?'

'No, I just wish she was here to share this amazing time in my life.' She forced a laugh. 'A bit of babysitting from time to time wouldn't hurt either.'

My mind started to work overtime and an idea quickly came to me that I thought could help.

'Lucy, I know I'm not your mum, and you can tell me to bugger off if you like. I won't be offended if it's a no, but if you ever wanted someone to give you a little bit of time to yourself, I'd be very happy to help, you know. Time is something I have way too much of and Meredith's over fifty so I'll never get the chance to be a grandma. I know it's too late to do that now, but maybe I could do something to help you instead.'

Lucy raised her head from my shoulder and looked at me.

'It's a rubbish idea. I'm sorry. I'd never try to replace your mother and it was insensitive of me to even mention it. Do forgive me.'

'A bit like a surrogate grandma! I love that idea. I'd, well, we'd be honoured, Lydia.'

'Really?'

'As long as Meredith is OK with it. I'd hate to upset her.'

'I'm sure she'd understand. We can't change the past, can we? But we can use what we've learned to shape the future.'

'I love that. It's making the most of a situation that neither of us thought we'd be in.'

She leaned into me again and I whispered, 'Thank you,' into her hair.

'Do you think she'll mind?'

'Only one way to find out.'

As I passed Taran back to his mum, he gurgled again and his little face lit up with a beam. Then he let out the almightiest trump and closed his eyes once more.

'He takes after his father.'

We both laughed, the relief from quite a heavy conversation flooding through us both.

'Taran means thunder, you know,' she said. 'Little did I know when we chose that name, it would relate mostly to his backside.'

I giggled as Lucy laid him down in his pram.

'Let me know how you get on with Meredith.'

'Will do, darling. See you soon.'

I decided to go and have a walk round to the lighthouse.

No time like the present.

I wish I'd taken that approach years ago. Sitting and mithering about things had wasted literally hours of my life. This was one of those situations that could go one of two ways.

10

Every time I saw my daughter, my heart skipped a beat. When she was born, being a parent was something that I didn't adapt well to. But being a parent now later in life meant that I'd had time to learn what I needed to do and I constantly hoped Meredith would recognise that – that I wanted to make up for lost time.

Inside the lighthouse, sitting on the balcony, I looked around at everything she'd done. She had such a good eye for decor. Everything was classy with just the right amount of colour to look lavish and not garish. I was so proud of everything she'd achieved. She'd turned her life around and refurbished this property, with Clem's help of course, and between them, they'd done an incredible job, falling in love during the process.

Her decision to stay in Driftwood Bay was one of the best ones she'd ever made and my decision to follow her was equally as positive for me. Meredith had welcomed me with open arms and over the past twelve months or so our relationship had flourished. We were in a really good place.

I wanted to tread carefully to make sure that what I was

about to propose to her didn't dent this new happiness we'd carved out for ourselves.

'Pinot OK for you, Mum?'

Every time she said the word 'mum', it reminded me of what a huge heart she had. Someone who could forgive me for all my faults and love me for the person that I was today.

I smiled back at her, wondering how to approach the topic. But even then she helped me out.

'I saw you in the harbour with Lucy a while ago. How's she doing? I've hardly seen her since Taran was born. There's a fine line between interfering and wanting to be a help, isn't there? I must make the effort to go and see her.'

'Actually, it's funny you should say that.' Her head snapped round to face me. 'There's something I wanted to run by you.'

'That sounds quite ominous.'

'Not really but there is something on my mind; an idea I've had but it's important to me that you are fully on board.'

'OK, spill.'

'I'd like to help Lucy out. She's not got a mum of her own to help her and I know that it makes her sad, but also, she's missing out on so much physically too. Someone to help her and James with practical things.'

Meredith lowered herself onto one of the wrought-iron benches, adjusting the cushions to make herself comfortable.

'Go on…'

'Meredith, I know I was never the mother to you that you wanted me to be—'

'Mum, if I've forgiven you for that and moved on you have to forgive yourself for it too.'

'I know and I thought I had. When I came back from Bali, I felt so much more in control, but recently all these feelings have come back to me. I think I just have too much time on my hands, so helping out Lucy with the baby is a good solution for us both.'

'And why does this have anything to do with me?'

Her eyes bore into mine.

'Because I can't do this for you.'

There. I'd said it. Another little sentence that had a huge impact.

'Because I won't ever have children, you mean?'

I nodded in response. The tension in our words was almost painful, the only sound the gentle splashing of the waves as they reached the rocks below.

Meredith turned her head towards the sea. Today it was as calm and still as a lake. I could see that she was pondering my words. She opened her mouth to speak, then paused to collect her thoughts.

'I think I'm OK with that,' she said. 'Yes. I really think I am.' She smiled back at me. 'That's really kind of you, Mum, offering to help out. I know she'll really appreciate it. I know that Gemma wants to help as much as she can too, but with the bistro being busier than she ever thought it would be, there's only so much time she has to spare. I know they'll both value your help. I'll try and put some time aside too. Maybe we could do things together. That might be nice. Weird but nice.'

I scooted over and sat beside her on the bench.

'I would only do this if you were one hundred per cent OK with it. I wouldn't do anything to jeopardise our relationship. I hope you know that.'

'I do and it's definitely OK, Mum. I think it's lovely.'

Tears welled up behind my eyes as relief sank in. She reached across and squeezed my hand, confirming for me once again that this woman before me, my daughter, had the biggest heart of anyone I knew.

'Thank you for asking me.'

'You are the most important person in the world to me, Mere, and if you hadn't liked the idea, then it would never happen.'

'It's much appreciated that you asked me. Anyway, while we're chatting, what's with that mysterious box you were hiding from me last week?'

A moment's hesitation from me got Meredith narrowing her eyes, as she realised she'd caught me unawares.

'Just some stuff that Peter sent over. Nothing much, but I promise I'll show you next time you come round.'

'Do you miss him, Mum?'

I'd formed a habit of twisting the gold St Christopher ring on my little finger. It was my mother's; she'd given it to me when I left to go and live in America. She said when I touched it, it would give me strength and an invisible connection to her, even though there was an ocean between us. So that she would always be with me in spirit if not in person.

'I miss having someone to look after. I've never been very good at sitting still. I didn't realise that I would feel quite so lonely on my own, though I'm not sure if that's about Peter or not.'

We both gazed out to sea.

'You can always come here if you're lonely. You're always so busy; I didn't think you felt loneliness.'

'Thank you and I do know that. But it's not that type of lonely, Meredith. It's not the company I'm missing. It's hard to explain.'

What I missed was having someone who was there all the time. Someone to cook for, to watch TV with. To comment to when a track came on the radio. Living on my own gave me a lot of time to think. Too much sometimes. To reflect on my past and contemplate my future. To realise that there was still so much more life left within me, but that I might not always be around and well enough to do the things that I wanted to do. I know I needed to push myself to do those things alone.

There was a part of me that wanted to make a to-do list and work my way through it as quickly as I could, but there was the other part that cried myself to sleep at night, wondering what I would be leaving behind if the news was bad. I knew that the scare I'd had was nothing compared to what some people faced but it was still new to me and much as I tried to think myself lucky for what I did have, it still affected me.

'When my fifth marriage failed, it really messed with my head. Another failure in my life. But I realised that even though I thought I loved Peter, we were only together because we were afraid of being alone – not because we were in love. That's why since all my therapy I've decided I'm better alone. I'm just finding me again now and have to find a way of enjoying all the things I'm doing now on my own.'

Meredith's brow furrowed.

'It makes me sad to think of you being unhappy, Mum.'

'I'm not unhappy, darling. I'm happier than I've been for a long time. Just sometimes I feel lonely.'

'I'm sorry, Mum. I thought you were OK. You always said you were OK. I'm always here for you, I hope you know that.'

A piece of hair was dangling free from her topknot and in the gentle breeze was wafting across her face. I tucked it behind her ear.

'Thank you,' I said. 'That's really kind of you but you can be surrounded by people every minute of every day but still be lonely. Sometimes it's even lonelier than being by yourself. But that's on me, not you. It's not up to others to fulfil me. It's up to me. Up to me to find a purpose in my life; I think that's what I feel is missing. Maybe I've never had that because of giving you up when I should never have done.'

'You were ill, Mum.'

'I know. But it still happened.'

'That makes me sad too. I'm sorry that you feel that way.'

'Don't be, darling, honestly. I'm working on it all. It'll get better and I'm only telling you because you asked and because my therapist said that if people ask you how you are, they're asking because they care and want the truth. Bet you wish you'd never asked now though.'

She reached out to me and gave me the warmest of hugs. After everything, I was so lucky to have her in my life.

'Maybe helping Lucy will give you the purpose that you need.'

'There is that. It could help us both maybe, but we'll never know until we try. Thank you for giving me your blessing.'

'I just want you to be happy, Mum.'

'I'll be fine.'

I knew I would be. This could be the turning point that would change everything.

11

There was nothing that the Driftwood Bay community loved more than a committee. There was one for the spring picnic which was looming, one for the late summer party and now there was another for the dancing competition. And of course, as a lady of leisure, I was on them all.

Vi had asked me to call for her on the way to the community hall where the first meeting about the competition was being held. She asked me to wait for her on the corner as she had a very quick errand to do. I watched her as she walked over to the red plastic box on the harbour wall, lifted the lid and popped something inside. She pulled a face and when she returned, she was still wrinkling her nose.

'It's a bit bloody whiffy. I think I might report it to the postman when I see him.'

'Vi darling. What were you doing then?'

'Posted another letter to Dennis, you daft bat. He keeps saying that he's not receiving the things I'm sending him. I might report that too.'

'You posted a letter to Dennis? In there?'

'Yes, keep up, Lydia!'

'In that red box?'

'Yes, what do you think I did?'

'Vi, you do realise that's a dog poo bin, don't you?'

She swung round to face me. 'What?'

'It's a dog poo bin.'

'Bugger off, it is!'

'It is, my lovely. Did you not see the picture of a dog on the front?'

'Well, of course I did. My cataracts aren't that bad. But I just thought it was for decoration. I wondered why it didn't have a slot like a post box. No wonder it smells of shite. I'll bloody kill that young man who told me it was the new post box.'

Tears were literally streaming down my face. Why was no one here to share this moment with me? Thank God that Vi saw the funny side and she started laughing too.

'Are you sure he didn't say poo box?'

'Oh Lord. Maybe he did. I'm a silly old bugger, aren't I? Should probably wear my hearing aid more often. Don't you be telling anyone I did this now, will you, Lydia? I don't want the headline on the Driftwood Bay Bog to be "Daft Old Bag Mistook Poo Box for Post Box" now, do I?'

That just made me laugh even more and I tried to explain that it was a blog not a bog, but she was having none of it.

We were strolling towards the community centre, arm in arm and still giggling, when Gemma came out of the door of the bistro, also heading for the meeting.

'Who's been tickling you two?' she asked.

'Oh, we can't say. Too embarrassing.'

I knew, however, that she'd never be able to contain herself. I was right.

'Oh, go on then, I'll tell you if you promise not to tell a soul.'

Gemma and I looked at each other and grinned. Vi didn't have the nickname of Loose Lips for nothing. Gemma was also in hysterics when she heard Vi retell her story but we made her promise not to repeat it.

We didn't rush to the hall. No one rushes in Driftwood Bay, instead, taking in the prettiness of the seaside setting; the turquoise waters of the sea and the blue skies above, a sharp contrast with the golden sand. The pastel-coloured harbour houses and the boats bobbing on the sea, along with the narrow, cobbled streets really were a glorious sight to see.

When I moved here, the thing that struck me more than anything else was the pace of life, which was so much more relaxed than anywhere else I'd lived. Shops opened and closed as and when they felt like it, and people quite happily waited in queues, passing the time of day without a care in the world. Certainly very different to the life I lived in the United States.

Even though the church wasn't open any longer, the centre was still well used by the locals. There was crochet club, play-group, youth club, dog training... You name it and we probably got it. And if we didn't, we'd create it. Basically, anything that couldn't be done in the pub happened in the community centre. I'd gone from living in America, where you didn't know your neighbours to living here, where you couldn't sneeze without it going on the Driftwood Bay blog. Occy, Gemma's stepdaughter – or would be so when Jude and Gemma were married – had dreams of being a journalist, so had decided to create and launch a blog, and share everything that was going on in the community.

What she didn't realise was that not all things that happened had to go in the blog. It wasn't till she wrote about some of the locals complaining about Dylis putting her prices up in the minimarket, and got a telling off that she realised that she would have to censor some of her content.

Occy was the first person that we saw when we arrived.

'Hi, Vi. Come and sit over here and I'll get you a cup of tea and some biscuits. You can sit by me at the front.'

Occy had blossomed into a lovely young woman over the last year, since Gemma had become a fixture in her life. And with her own mother, Rachel, now playing a more dominant maternal role too, she was flourishing in her role as community journalist. Now she'd calmed down a bit, and was really getting involved with everything that was going on, she'd risen to the role of deputy chair of the committee.

'I meant to ask you, Vi,' she continued, 'do you have your hearing aid today?'

She held her hand out and showed Occy her aid.

'Yes, here it is.'

'Should it not be in your ear?' Occy shouted at her.

'No need to shout, dear. I'm not bloody deaf.'

Gemma and I grinned again over her head.

Vi winked at me. Age certainly hadn't affected her sense of humour.

Over the next ten minutes, the rest of the committee meandered in and when we were all seated and had been given our drinks, Occy rang the bell to get everyone's attention.

'Welcome, ladies and gentlemen.'

Vi's hand shot up.

'Yes, Vi? Do you have a question?'

'I'd like to say that I don't think you should say "ladies and gentlemen". I've been reading up on gender equality recently and I don't think that it's politically correct.'

Gemma laughed behind her hand.

'OK, I apologise. You're right, Vi. I'd like to change that to "everyone". Welcome, everyone.'

'Can you make sure you put that in the minutes please?'

Occy smiled. 'I will, Vi. So, the first item on the agenda is—'

Vi's hand shot up again.

'Yes, Vi? Another question?'

'I do yes. What about the lesbians?'

Occy looked totally puzzled. 'Lesbians?' she repeated.

'Yes, lesbians. It's when two women—'

'Thank you, Vi, I'm very well aware of what a lesbian is. In what respect are you referring to?'

'Well, does the word "everyone" include lesbians? And the gays of course – what about the gays?'

'I think the word "everyone" includes all people, Vi,' Martin, who was sitting on the other side of her, cut in, 'so how about we let Occy get on with it, shall we now?' He patted her hand.

'Just wanted to make sure we were being fully diverse and inclusive. Thank you, Occy. Do proceed.'

Thankfully, Vi settled down at that point and allowed Occy to work her way through the agenda, all of us agreeing on our designated jobs to ensure the smooth running of the competition. When she asked if that completed all the items on the agenda, Vi yelled out at the top of her voice.

'Balls!'

'You OK there, Vi?'

'We need balls. Big shiny disco balls. You can't have a dance competition without big shiny disco balls.'

'That's true actually. I'll add it to any other business. Thanks again, Vi.'

'Good job I was here today,' she grumbled. 'Don't know what you'd do without me.'

Occy muttered something under her breath, which sounded

remarkably like the words 'just imagine'. Then she took a deep breath and declared the meeting officially over.

I headed her way and congratulated her on her handling of the meeting and said that she deserved a medal. She beamed back at me at that.

Gemma said that she would walk Vi back home while I had plans to pop into the workshop. I told them a little while lie and said I had something to pick up and arrangements to make with Martin.

Overhearing me say this, Vi winked and in a very loud voice said, 'I bet you do too, you saucy little minx.'

She really was incorrigible. I blushed and so did Martin. Somehow, she'd managed to turn something so totally innocent into something that people were now wondering about. Let's hope Occy found something else happening in the neighbourhood to report on to take the focus away from us.

It had been a couple of days since we'd practised our dancing and the competitive streak in me knew that if we wanted to win, we'd really have to put in hours of training. My dance skills were certainly rusty and Martin's technique left a lot to be desired. But earlier that day, as I'd been shimmying around my kitchen while mopping the floor, as well as realising how much I was missing dancing again, I'd had a brainwave. It wasn't something I wanted to discuss in front of the others, so that's why I made the excuse about fetching something from the workshop.

What I hadn't bargained for was Martin's reaction.

12

'Cinema? You want me to go to the cinema?'

'Yep!'

'I've not been to the cinema for years. In fact, I can't remember the last time I went.' Martin scratched his head while trying to remember. 'Probably when Clem was a boy.'

'You mean that you never took Miranda?'

'I don't think I did. God, how can I have never taken her? She used to go with her friends. But we never went together. In all our years.' Martin hit the heel of his hand off his forehead forcefully. 'What a terrible husband I was.'

'I'm sure you weren't. But I'd really like you to trust me on this and just come with me.'

Martin was having trouble understanding why I wanted to go. I was refusing to tell him what I wanted us to see.

'Look, I just want it to be a surprise. I promise you will like it and it will help our dancing.' I nudged his shoulder with mine. 'Go on. Say yes.'

'You're a mean woman, Lydia. I don't know why I'm agreeing to do this but OK, I'll come.'

I could feel the smile widen on my face.

'Pick you up at four o'clock. Wear something smart but casual and your dancing shoes. I'll see you later.'

* * *

The nearest cinema to us was in Truro and they showed an eclectic mix of films.

Martin grumbled as he got in my car.

'You might even have fun, you know.'

'My idea of fun might be very different to yours.'

'Good Lord, Martin. At our age, you don't think I'm going to make you go zip lining or hang-gliding or anything, do you?'

'Oh jeez, I hadn't thought of that.'

I patted his knee as he did up his seat belt and I turned the music up.

'Don't worry, I'll look after you.'

We pulled up in the car park and he was still grumbling a bit about not liking surprises as we walked towards the doors, stating that at his age, he couldn't do a long journey without needing the loo.

'Great idea, Martin, we've got two films to watch so we might be a while.'

When he returned from his quick dash to the gents' and saw the title had appeared for the film that we were queuing for, he grinned and turned to me.

'*Dirty Dancing*. Really?' His face had lit up and his eyes were bright with glee. 'I bloody love this film.'

'Seriously? What a relief!'

'It was Miranda's favourite ever film you know.'

'Oh, will you be OK watching it?'

'Yeah, I think so. I've seen it since she passed so I'm pretty sure I'll be OK. It just holds very happy memories for me. I'll apologise now for quoting the lines before they happen. She always used to tell me off for doing that.'

The film was pure delight. I wrapped my arms around me, welling up with joy when the main male character, Johnny Castle, taught the older ladies to dance. It was one of my favourite scenes and out of the corner of my eye I could see Martin watching me. I playfully nudged his shoulder and we turned to each other and smiled before going back to the screen.

Mesmerised as always with that film, we took a short break and brought drinks and popcorn back to our seats before the title of *Strictly Ballroom* loomed large on the screen in front of us and he patted my hand.

'You are a good surpriser, Lydia. I approve.'

'Well, I don't want to say I told you so, but...'

'Yes OK. I've learned my lesson.'

Once more, we sat captivated and it totally got us into the dancing vibe, and as we left the cinema room, Martin shimmied across the foyer to the door before holding it open for me.

'Oh, Lydia, I feel like I just want to go back and dance now. I'm right in the mood.'

'Funny you should say that because the night is far from over.'

He peered at me suspiciously before shrugging his shoulders.

'Now just remember,' I said, 'you did say I give good surprises!'

'Do your worst.'

After a short car journey, we pulled up outside a warehouse in the middle of a dark and virtually abandoned industrial estate. There was only one other car in the car park apart from mine. Martin frowned as he read the letters above the roller shutter door: 'Strictly Yours'.

I banged three times on the door, and moments later, it opened and there in front of us stood a man who looked the spitting image of Freddie Mercury.

'Leed-eya I presume? And you must be Mar-teen.'

'Err yes I suppose we are.'

'I am Miguel. Come, come!'

He waved us in via a small office and through into a warehouse where the sight before me led me to gasp out loud.

If Vi could see this, she would have been beside herself with delight as there must have been at least twenty big shiny disco balls hanging from the high ceiling, along with rails and rails of sparkly dresses and sequinned suits which shimmered at us from across the room.

'Now, Mar-teen. Stand on this mark, hands on your hips and legs slightly apart.' Miguel kicked gently at the insides of both of Martin's feet to widen the space between them. 'Better!' He circled Martin slowly, his eyes appraising every inch of his body from his head to his toes, made a kissing sound with his lips then turned abruptly. He shouted over his shoulder. '*Perfecto!* I have just the thing. Wait!'

He disappeared towards the rails and came back with a black sparkly suit and a pair of shiny black shoes.

'That won't fit me.'

'I'll decide what will and won't fit you, Mar-teen. You listen to Miguel. Yes?' He didn't give Martin time to answer. 'Now, go behind that screen and put that on.' Martin nodded, scared to death to refuse. 'And, Leed-eya, you have brought your dress? So it's just shoes for you.'

'Yes, sadly my very old dance shoes broke.'

'Ah, maybe you have them repaired. My *amigo*; he might be able to help. Bring them to me. Yes?'

'Thank you. I might just do that.' I could feel myself frowning. He seemed to swap to very British phrases from time to time.

'I'll grab some shoes for today then. You go and put your dress on behind the other screen.'

When I came out from behind my screen, wearing my lovely crimson dress, I was greeted by Martin in his tight-fitting spandex suit. He was looking awkward with his slightly portly tummy resting on top of a very tight waistband. I don't think I've ever seen him look so uncomfortable, although he didn't look at all bad. Quite dashing in fact.

I wolf-whistled.

'Don't, Leed-eya.' His eyes sparkled at me as he mimicked Miguel's voice.

'Oh, it's like that, is it, Mar-teen?' I grinned back at him.

'It's OK for you. You look gorgeous while I feel like I'm wearing a wetsuit. What on earth have you done to me?'

He looked like a truculent teenager whose mother had chosen his clothes. Endearing really on a man of his age. I turned to the mirror, but instead of seeing the vibrant young woman of fifty years ago, I saw an ageing woman with blonde streaks trying to disguise the grey in her hair and bingo wings. And the dress, which had been magnificent back in its day, now felt like a tatty, faded red dress with frayed edges. The words 'mutton' and 'lamb' sprung to mind. The excitement that I previously had when we arrived was waning fast. Had I done the right thing by bringing us here or was I just setting us up for disappointment? Could our self-esteem take it? Mine was still quite fragile as it was. I hoped that the little angel sat on my one shoulder telling me 'You've got this, Lydia,' would be stronger than the devil sat on the other saying 'What are you doing, you silly old woman?'

The tip-tap of dancing shoes and the sharp clap of hands brought me back to the present.

'OK, lovebirds. You both look fab-u-lous! Now, I want you to stand facing each other and take each other's hands. Women on top, Leed-eya. Always the women on top.'

Martin's eyes crinkled and his mouth twitched. I shot him a warning look.

'So, watch me first,' Miguel continued.

He performed a series of overemphasised moves while simultaneously counting out loud and barking instructions. As he did so, my mind struggled to keep up. I looked across at Martin who looked simply dazed.

'Christ alive!' Martin grimaced.

'Ees OK, Mar-teen. I will teach you. That's what I'm here for.' The way he rolled his 'r's threatened to give me a fit of the giggles and I struggled to pull myself back to the task in hand, not able to look Martin in the eye.

Miguel took his place and showed him again, making Martin follow behind until it sank in and he was ready to take his turn. Then he stood behind Martin, holding his hands to his hips. I could see at first that Martin was quite uncomfortable with this – their proximity was incredibly close – but as he relaxed into it, we discovered it was quite necessary to get the desired effect. It was most helpful when Miguel did the same with me. His hands pushing and moving my hips to the music, getting the most out of the dance, put a whole new perspective on our dancing abilities. Gosh, I was going to need yoga in the morning to stretch these joints.

'Yes! You've got it. And again!' He clapped enthusiastically.

He then threw in a move called the 'New York', where we did

a half-turn to the side and back to the middle, followed by an
'Around the World' which Martin eventually mastered after a
few times of trying where he ended up facing the wrong direction on the opposite foot. But practice made perfect. We were
soon repeating it faultlessly, Miguel clapping and yelling,
'Again!'

Miguel pressed a button on the amplifier behind him and
the sensual sounds of Spanish guitar music filled the air.

'And now we do it to music. Let's dance!'

Martin counted the numbers out loud as we danced, but for
me, the moves came naturally, as if I'd been doing them all my
life. Maybe it was muscle memory but I knew every movement I
made was the right one and I drifted off into another world.

* * *

'Christ, Lydia, I'm bloody knackered!' Martin was gasping for
breath as we headed back to the car. Miguel had certainly put us
through our paces this evening.

'Me too. I need a bloody big G and T!'

'I can honestly say that, ahem, tonight was the time of my
life, Lydia. And that's all down to you.'

'If I wasn't so shattered, I'd laugh at that. Even more if you'd
got the words right.'

'Old snake hips Miguel was brilliant, wasn't he? What a
performer. Although I'm sure I heard a Brummie twang in his
voice at times. Where did he say he was from again?'

'Can't remember the exact name but he said that the village
was on the southern coast of Spain. And with those swarthy dark
looks and his mop of curly black hair, he's definitely got some
Spanish in him.'

'Must have imagined it then. Great guy though and he clearly knows his stuff.'

Miguel had been an incredible teacher, first dancing with me to show Martin how to imitate him and move his hips and then swapping sides and doing the same for me.

'Seriously, Lydia, even though I wondered what the hell you were getting me into tonight, I've had the most fun I've had in ages.'

Under the glare of the security light outside the warehouse, I could see that he was speaking the truth. His eyes were twinkling and his cheeks flushed. And my own heart was full to bursting with happiness and joy. I'd laughed more tonight than I had for years and when that rhythm reverberated through my body, I had truly let go of all my inhibitions and danced like no one was watching.

I thought ahead to the competition. I hadn't wanted something this much for ages. It felt good to have a focus again. Something to aim towards. At this time in my life, I wasn't sure what my dreams were any more. Maybe this would be the thing that would kick-start me. Life is too short to sit and stagnate. Life was for living. He was right, it was the most fun I'd had in ages also.

'Me too, Martin. Me too.' I jangled my car keys at him. 'And I'm glad you said that because I've booked for us to come back again next week.'

'God! You are competitive, aren't you?'

'You'd better believe it! That glitter-ball trophy has got our name on it! We need to up our game. Come on, twinkle toes, let's go home!'

13

Because we'd had a late night, we decided not to do early morning beach yoga and to have a bit of a lie-in. However, these days it didn't seem to matter what time I went to bed, I still woke up reasonably early.

I was certainly feeling every one of my seventy-something years, aching in places that I didn't know I had. As I swung my legs over the side of the bed, I gazed out at the bay beyond, feeling blessed. Waking up to this view was purely enchanting and I considered myself to be incredibly lucky.

A lazy morning was a treat for me and I sat in bed propped up against my pillows just gazing out of the window. The low cloud made me smile. When I first moved here, and commented to the farmer at the end of the road on how unusual a sight it was, he took his woolly hat off and said, 'The angels are flying low in the valley this morning.' What a delightful thought that was.

In the distance, I could see the paddleboards of the Driftwood Babes gliding through the still sea. In my early days of arriving here, they'd invited me to join them, but it wasn't for me.

Whilst I had heard that sea swimming was invigorating and maybe one day, I'd pluck up the courage to be brave and try it out, watching was enough for me.

I saw Karl, the postman, out of the corner of my eye and my heart was in my mouth as I waited to see if he had anything for me. He hesitated at the end of my drive, checked his bag, and then walked on by to drop some post in to Celia's house before continuing on. Another day with no news made me hopeful. Surely if the results from the biopsy contained bad news, I would have heard by now.

My normal breakfast of fruit and yoghurt wasn't really cutting it; tiredness always made me feel like a full English but I knew that if I had one, I'd be feeling too full afterwards to work and today was an important one.

To get to Martin's, I walked past the field with Celia's animals in it, calling out 'Morning, boys,' to the goats and horses, and headed into the village centre and back out again. I could have walked a shorter route, but it wasn't as pretty and I loved walking down the hill towards the sea. It literally lifted my heart each time, like I was seeing it for the first time. Even on winter days when the weather was awful, I made sure I walked twice a day.

A flutter of excitement was still running through my tummy as I got nearer to the church. Last night had been so lovely, the only part missing really was the romance between us, but it was also nice to be comfortable in someone else's presence who was just a friend. To know that your friendship and enjoyment of the moments were enough.

The doll that Martin had mentioned to me had been on my mind for a while and I was looking very much forward to working on getting her back to her former glory. She was clearly very precious to someone for a reason, and I couldn't wait to find out the story behind her. I'd been able to source some vintage lace, similar to the existing dress and so I felt I would be able to create something that the owner would be happy with, while also keeping some of the original fabric and essence of the outfit.

Martin greeted me with a cup of hot water and lemon, his speakers playing from a playlist that was based on Cuban dance music. Miguel had told us that the style of music needed to be embedded in our memories and that we should play it at every opportunity, to almost implant it into our souls. According to him, we would perform to our maximum possibility if we did this. Anything was worth a try at this stage if we wanted to win.

Time passed quickly as we both focused on our respective tasks in companionable silence, stopping only occasionally to chat. Martin had been working on researching how to repair the mechanism for a couple of days and was nearly finished. I glanced over at him a couple of times, noticing how he chewed the inside of his cheek while he was concentrating and it made me smile. We all had our little foibles. Mine was biting my lip, sometimes to the point of making it bleed.

He made me jump when he exclaimed, 'I'm done!'

He was beaming, clearly delighted with himself.

'Amazing. Show me!'

'No. You have to wait until she's properly ready. How long do you think you'll need to finish your part?'

I straightened my body. Sitting bending over the machine had made my back ache a little. 'To be honest I'm not sure. I hadn't really thought about a timescale. Do you need to know?'

'They said there was no rush so it's not a problem. I'm just excited to see it. Tell you what, let's go down to the bistro and grab a sandwich and then we can come back and finish off for today.'

My stomach rumbled. I hadn't realised how hungry I was until I heard it and we both laughed.

'I take it that's a yes then?'

The short meander down the hill to the bistro was always a pleasant one. I wondered how I ever lived without it featuring so prominently in my life. While we ate, we discussed what we had left to do to get the doll finished and we made a good plan for the afternoon.

While Martin was in the gents', Gemma headed over to clear the table.

'You and Martin are getting on well.' She raised her eyebrows at me.

'Oh, blimey. You're as bad as Meredith. He's a lovely man but after five husbands already, I can assure you that I'm not looking for anything more right now.'

A cough from behind me indicated that he had returned.

'And as you know, Gemma, I'm a widower and am certainly not looking to replace my Miranda, thank you very much. Not that Lydia isn't wonderful and stunningly attractive for a woman of her age.'

This time it was my turn to raise my eyebrows.

'You know what I mean. That was meant to be a compliment and sounded much better in my head. I'm making a right pig's ear out of this, aren't I?'

'Yes, you are.' Gemma and I laughed.

Martin turned to me with serious eyes. 'Lydia, if you were looking for husband number six, any man would be lucky to have you. It's just that it won't be me.'

'Well, that's settled that then.' Gemma huffed and walked away.

'Come on, you. We've got work to do.'

'See? That's why I don't need another wife too. I have enough women in my life to nag me already.'

We chatted easily as we made our way back up the hill,

taking in the lovely scenery and the gardens coming into glorious technicolour bloom, our walk up slower than our walk down. Much as it was lovely to have wonderful views, Driftwood Bay was quite hilly and I wasn't as spritely as I once was, despite my early morning yoga sessions. I hoped that age was the only factor in my recent tiredness and nothing more sinister. I tried to push the thought to the back of my mind again. I was quite good at compartmentalising but this one was harder to ignore, sometimes popping out and scaring the living daylights out of me.

When we got back and I was happy with the outfit that I'd repaired, I called Martin over. I couldn't wait to see the doll back to her former glory.

As Martin began to dress her in what I'd made, I realised that I didn't know if she had a name. An object that was being restored like this was surely going to have a name.

When Martin was done, my heart caught in my mouth when he introduced me to a nearly mended Dottie. I couldn't wait for the owner to see her when she was finished.

* * *

The following day, when I arrived at the church and Martin suggested sitting on a bench in the graveyard to drink our morning drinks, I thought he was making fun of me.

'You want me to sit in a graveyard?'

'Yes, but it's OK, they're dead so no one will bother you.'

'Erm, well, I suppose so but...'

'It's the best view in the village, Lydia. I promise you that much. And before you ask, Miranda is not buried here.'

I heaved a huge sigh of relief. 'That would have felt a little strange, if you don't mind me saying.'

'Not at all. She's here.' He fiercely patted his heart, and then waved his hand around the graveyard. 'Not here. In fact, she's out there somewhere.' He pointed his finger out to the bay. 'Clem and I went out on his boat and scattered her ashes into the sea. That's what she wanted. She even specified we should be drinking from a bottle of Taittinger champagne, which was her favourite. That's how she wanted us to say our final goodbye.'

He wiped a stray tear from his eye and gazed out. I patted his hand and we smiled at each other.

As I held his gaze, I knew that my friendship with this lovely man was a very special one. My husbands, every single one of them, had tried to change me, and with them I became someone that lived in order to please someone else instead of myself. Yet Martin just accepted me for the person I was. That's what true friendship is about.

14

The next morning, I woke with a slight headache and much as I tried to shift it naturally by drinking water and getting fresh air, I needed a little help. As I opened my bedside drawer to grab some ibuprofen, the journal I had hidden there previously caught my eye.

Perched on the side of my bed, I pulled it out and sat with it on my lap wondering whether I was yet brave enough to open it.

The clank of the letter box broke my thoughts, and I slid it back into the drawer to go and collect the post. Maybe reading it would be something I'd feel up to later tonight. I'd no plans that evening, so with a little Dutch courage from a large gin and tonic, I'd put on my big girl pants and tackle it.

Nothing again from the doctor.

Martin joined me for yoga that morning, which was enjoyable, and although the forecast had threatened rain, we were lucky that it stayed dry.

'Fancy a cuppa at mine? I'd love to just catch up on some dancing stuff with you.' Despite spending most of the previous day with Martin, we never seemed to be short of anything to say and I always remembered stuff that I meant to bring up.

We speed-walked back along the beach path to the cottage and as we got two hundred yards from my door it started to hammer down. We were soaked just in that short time.

Martin filled the kettle while I went to get changed. I returned with my dressing gown kimono, which I offered to Martin.

'I know it's not very manly, but it's about the best I could offer you. If you want to pop this on while I chuck your clothes in the tumble dryer? At least you won't have to sit in wet clothes.'

'Do you mean, you don't want me sitting on your furniture in soaking wet clothes?' He took the robe from me with a grin and headed for the bathroom.

There was a knock at the front door and I opened it to find Dianne standing there with a piece of paper in her hand.

'Thought I'd just bring this over. Had a lovely email from Celia and thought I'd let you know what she's been up to.'

The click of the kettle grabbed her attention.

'Perfect timing. Has the kettle just boiled? I'm gagging for a cuppa. Tea, two sugars for me, darling. Thank you.'

I laughed at her boldness as she flung herself onto one of the kitchen chairs, but grabbed another cup from the cupboard. I was pouring the hot water in when Martin waltzed back in through the kitchen door, doing a very theatrical twirl, not realising we had company.

'Not sure it's really my colour. What do you think?'

He stopped abruptly when he saw Dianne and she raised her eyebrows at him.

'Oh! Good morning, Martin. Actually, I think red silk suits you very much.'

For some reason, although it was all quite innocent, both Martin and I blushed. I know I should have given up worrying what people thought of me years ago, but I hadn't.

Martin stumbled over his words as he tried to tell her why he was in my kitchen in my dressing gown first thing in the morning.

She held up her hand. 'No explanation needed on my account. You're both consenting adults as far as I'm concerned. Entirely up to you, what you get up to.'

'But, but—'

'I'm winding you up, lovey, don't worry. I believe you.' She winked at him. God knows if she believed us or not, but it also hit me then that I was seventy-one years of age and that if I wanted to 'entertain' a gentleman friend, in any capacity whatsoever, I could do exactly what I wanted to.

From the letter that Dianne read out, Celia appeared to be having a total ball. She'd been gone just over a fortnight and it sounded like she'd seen all the sights she'd wanted to in Thailand and was now moving on to Cambodia, somewhere she'd always wanted to visit. She really was having the time of her life and I hoped that it would continue. How brave she was to take on a trip like that alone. I'd never been on holiday by myself. Maybe it was something I should consider. The thought of it made me feel a little uneasy but I wondered whether I should push myself out of my comfort zone more.

Dianne's next question broke into my thoughts.

'Are you both going to the beach picnic later? I hope it stays dry for it. It's that time of the year when it changes from one minute to the next. There's more technology around than ever before, and we never really know what the weather is doing until we're in the moment.'

'Wouldn't miss it for the world. It's going to brighten up this afternoon too according to the forecast but who knows. Not like fifteen minutes ago, eh, Lydia?'

'God yes, I've not seen rain like that since I've been back in the UK. Are you going, Dianne? It'll be a great opportunity for you to spend time with everyone and get to know them. You can walk down with me. I'll be going about ten to four if you do. And you can bring Hobson. Everyone else will be taking their dogs.'

'Go on then, that would be great.' Dianne smiled. 'I'll feed the goats before we go in case we're late back.'

'Oh, you can probably assume we will be. It's normally a late evening. It'll be lovely to have you with us.'

Even though Dianne appeared to be quite confident, I wondered if there was a little bit of it which was bravado, and that underneath she was actually quite nervous about being in a new place.

'What shall I take?' she asked. 'Oh, crikey, I don't know what I've got in. I'll have to go shopping. I can't go empty-handed.'

'I wouldn't worry, Dianne. There's always so much food there, no one would notice. There'll be plenty. Do you have a bottle of wine you could take maybe?'

'I'll definitely have one of those. Maybe I could throw something together this afternoon. I'll see what Celia has in her cupboards.'

'Don't stress though. I want you to look forward to going, not stress about it. I have plenty in. You can just say we've brought it along between us.'

'Thank you, Lydia. You're very kind and I'm very lucky to have you as my neighbour. In time, maybe even my friend.'

The high-pitched bleep of the tumble dryer sounded.

'And I suppose that means that my clothes are dry now too,

so I can make a move. Can't believe we got caught out in the rain like that.'

I noticed Dianne wink at Martin.

'If you say so...'

Embarrassed again, he asked if he could go through to the bathroom to change. When he'd left the room, Dianne grinned at me.

'I love winding him up. He's so cute. You're not actually together, are you? Oh God, tell me I didn't interrupt something going on here?'

'Of course not. We're just friends.'

'He's a right hottie though. A proper silver fox. You'd make a wonderful couple. You're very...' she indicated speech marks with her fingers '...easy with each other.'

'Oh, get off with you. With him being my daughter's future father-in-law, he's practically family.'

'Yeah, but he's not actually related, is he? Oh, what a lovely story that would be.'

'Dianne. Really, there's nothing going on. We're just dancing together.'

'Intimate though, isn't it? Dancing close together. Bodies moulding against each other. Mmmm. Sexy.'

'Stop it. You're incorrigible.' I swatted her gently on the arm.

'You know what they say. The couple that dances together, loves together.'

'Who says that?'

'Me!'

'You're so bad, Dianne.'

'Just teasing. See you later.' She slipped out the door giggling to herself.

Moments later, Martin appeared fully dressed and we agreed

that later on in the afternoon he would walk round our way and escort both of us to the picnic.

Waving him off at the doorstep, I watched him walk across my front courtyard.

Yes, this was not the first time that I'd noticed he was rather handsome.

15

The turquoise sea twinkled in the bright sunlight, like tiny little diamonds dotted on the surface. The contrast with the golden sand made my heart do a little skip. It filled up my joy meter. As we headed down the hill towards the beach, I smiled as I saw the red and white lighthouse standing proudly in the distance. Meredith had done a wonderful job of renovating it, with the help of Clem, who was so incredibly clever with his hands, and I was immensely proud of what they had both achieved. I was so impressed by my daughter and her ability to switch careers, and to now be an expert interior designer, something she clearly was fabulous at, and adored as a job. She and Clem made a formidable team, joining forces on many local projects.

'Over here, Mum,' I heard her voice call out and we headed towards where she sat, spread out across a couple of large picnic rugs, with Jude, Lucy, James, and baby Taran. Vi was looking very comfy on a deck chair with Gladys by her feet, holding up her cup to us and saying cheers. I presumed she was already on the sherry.

Meredith stood and kissed my cheek.

'Remind me to talk to you about Vi when we get chance, Mum.'

My heart lifted every time she called me Mum. There was a time when I thought I'd never have her in my life, and I couldn't be happier now to be playing a large part in hers. I would spend the rest of my days making up for how I'd behaved in the past and I felt like we were getting there slowly but surely. There was hopefully no rush, although just thinking that thought made me put my hand to my chest and pray that I got some answers soon about this lump in my breast. I couldn't bear the thought that now our lives were coming together, I would be cruelly taken away from her. Surely the universe wouldn't be that unkind to us.

'OK, darling. Is everything all right with her?'

'I'm not sure. Give me a few minutes and maybe we can go for a little walk, and I'll tell you my thoughts.'

Dianne and Martin got settled into the deck chairs next to Lucy who was struggling with Taran. He was a little bit grouchy, which Lucy had said was down to the fact he was due a sleep.

Desperate to know what was on Meredith's mind, I offered to see if we could get him to nod off by taking him for a walk around the harbour. Lucy looked glad to have a break and James said he'd love to have his wife to himself for half an hour too.

'Everything OK, love?' I asked when we were far enough away from the group, lest Vi hear me.

'I'm not sure, Mum. The last few times I've been to pick Gladys up to take her for a walk, I've got the feeling that Vi doesn't want me in her house.'

I stopped walking to look at her. 'What's made you think that?'

A squawk from the pushchair made us continue. 'OK, Taran, we'll keep moving.'

'Well, she keeps meeting me at the door with Gladys's lead,

whereas she used to leave the door open so I could let myself in. Now the door is always locked and I have to knock on it.'

I chewed the inside of my cheek, worrying that there was something going on that we needed to get to the bottom of.

'Do you still have her grandson's phone number? Maybe he can have a word with her or throw some light on it.'

'That's a good idea. I'll ring Dennis tomorrow. Not sure why I didn't think of that.'

'Why don't you and I take her home later and we'll see if we get an invite in. Maybe we can work out what's going on.'

'Perfect. Yes, let's do that. Thanks, Mum. I knew you'd know what to do. I don't know why, but I just have a funny feeling. Something feels off.'

'I'm glad you thought I could help, even if it was just to listen to you.'

She smiled. 'Of course.'

She had already made my day. This time two years ago, I never thought for one minute that I'd be so present in my daughter's life. I'd been blessed with an amazing opportunity and loved every day that I got to spend living in close proximity to her.

I tucked my arm into hers and we walked along in silence, both lost in our thoughts. I couldn't say what Meredith was thinking, but the things that struck me were that I'd never done this with my own mother and again how much of Meredith's life I'd missed out on. I'd neglected her so much and while I couldn't go back and fix it, it still made me sad. My other thought, as I glanced across at my daughter, was that we were doing this with Lucy's baby and not Meredith's. I wondered whether she regretted that she'd not had children, or whether she'd ever tried. There was still so much I was learning about her and it wasn't something that I felt confident enough yet in bringing up with her. It was way too personal and we'd built so many bridges recently that the thought of them being knocked down again did stop me raising certain topics. Maybe in time this would change, but it felt a little like we'd built a wonderful house of cards but that with an ill wind, they could topple over at any time and we'd have to start rebuilding all over again.

We heard a loud snuffly snort come from the pushchair and realised that Taran had finally fallen asleep, so we headed back along the promenade to the beach, both quiet and reflective.

When we returned, James put his fingers to his lips as he pointed at Lucy who was lying on the picnic rug, her head on his jacket under a blanket. Her baby wasn't the only one who had fallen asleep.

The picnic was a wonderful community event although there were a few moments where I wondered whether I was imagining a bit of an atmosphere around Meredith and Clem. She'd snapped at him a couple of times and he'd glanced my way and shrugged. They just didn't seem to be their normal laughing selves with each other. I hoped that all would be OK between them. Maybe they'd just had a tiff before coming along. Life wasn't a bed of roses one hundred per cent of the time and we all had our off days.

It was nice to see that she did lighten up a little when Gemma arrived. She could only spare a couple of hours before heading back to the bistro, although I had caught her and Meredith with their heads together a couple of times, looking over at me while I was trying to give Lucy a hand trying to give her and James a bit of a break. I thought I saw Meredith brush away a tear at one point, but I was sitting on the other side of the group so couldn't be certain.

When Lucy woke she was startled to know that she'd fallen asleep with fun and shenanigans happening around her, but the power nap seemed to do her the world of good and all the parents in the midst sympathised with her need for grabbing some shut-eye while she could.

More and more of the locals joined us and overall the atmosphere was one of joviality and I looked around at the scene before me and smiled. My heart was contented and I felt at peace amongst my friends and family.

Clem and Martin were on barbecue duty, handing round hot dogs and burgers to everyone. The food was a little on the singed side but a barbecue wasn't a proper event without a burnt sausage or two.

* * *

Vi was ready to go home at around seven o'clock, so Meredith and I offered to walk her back. And sure enough, she was very cagey about letting us in the house, allowing Gladys in before her and not accepting our offer to help her in and get her settled, even when Meredith pretended she was bursting for the loo. There didn't seem to be any way that Vi was letting anyone over her doorstep.

'What do you reckon then, Mum?' Meredith asked when we'd turned back to the road. 'I'm not imagining it, am I?'

'No, darling, I don't think you are. Maybe Dennis can throw some light on the situation if you give him a call.'

'Yep, I'll do that tomorrow.'

We meandered back down to the beach, passing through the harbour.

'Are you OK, Meredith?'

'Me, yes I'm fine.'

'You don't seem yourself. You and Clem seemed a little off with each other. Are you sure you're OK?'

'Nothing that a good night's sleep won't sort out. I'm having about as much sleep as Lucy and James but it's not down to a baby keeping me awake. More like my body temperature is going through the roof and I keep waking up with a pool of sweat around my neck.'

'Ah, that could be an age thing, you know.'

'Yes, I know. I'm trying some natural remedies that I saw on the internet.'

'You might need some medical support. Best thing I ever did was go on HRT patches. Sorted me out pretty much immediately. I went from waking up four times a night to sleeping right through.'

'God, I can't remember the last time I slept through the night. What a treat that would be. Poor Clem. I've not been staying at his much because of it and I can't tell him the real reason why. What would he think?'

'He'll think that you are going through something that all women do and maybe you're struggling a bit and might need some help.'

'You think? I reckon it'll just remind him of the age difference between us and scare him off even more. He's already commented that the honeymoon period is over. And not just the honeymoon period, if truth be told. Periods in general in my case.' She stopped walking and looked down at the floor, twiddling with a tissue which was in her hand. 'I'm not sharing that sort of information with him thank you very much. It's hard enough saying it all out loud to you.'

'Meredith, sweetheart, you can say anything to me. I've already been there. When I went through the menopause, I lost my libido completely and I remember wondering what the hell the matter was with me.'

'Can we leave it there please, Mum? I love you, but I don't need to hear about your libido if you don't mind.'

I laughed. 'It's all perfectly natural. It's like puberty. All women go through it; some sail through and others don't. It's only the talking about it that normalises it and makes you not feel like you're an alien from another planet. I'm not going to push you but I'm always here for you to chat to.'

'Thanks, Mum. I'll bear that in mind.'

Moments like this were priceless and I thanked my lucky stars that my daughter was kind enough to let me back into her life.

16

We soon arrived back at the promenade, the sky starting to turn a slightly darker shade of blue, the night rolling in and the odd star appearing in the sky. We celebrated our togetherness by opening a few bottles of Prosecco. When I handed a glass to Meredith she refused and had sparkling water instead. In my fifties if I drank anything that contained bubbles, from Diet Coke to Dom Perignon, it kept me up all night with awful palpitations and I had to stop drinking it. Bizarre how the body works. I wondered if this might be the same for her. I wondered how my mother got on through those years of her life. It wasn't something that we talked about and she was probably so busy bringing up my daughter, at a time when we hardly spoke, that she was hardly likely to call me up and have a chat about her midlife crisis when I was going through a permanent one.

As I sat and looked out to sea, I wished more than ever that I could turn back the clock. But as I learnt in my retreat, you can't change the past. You can influence the future though and watching Meredith now, who was in turn watching Clem bounce baby Taran on his knee, laughing, and making silly noises at him, I vowed to do all I could to help her through this difficult time as smoothly as possible.

Dianne and Martin were sat shoulder to shoulder and he was laughing at something she said.

I stood, suddenly feeling quite alone.

'I'm going to head back now, folks. See you soon.'

Martin stood. 'I'll walk you back, Lydia.'

I held up my palm.

'No. I'll be perfectly fine. You two stay and enjoy yourselves. I'm feeling a little bit tired and I'll be home in no time.'

Clem handed Taran to Meredith. 'I'll walk you back. I'm not taking no for an answer.'

I smiled. Such a nice man.

'In that case, how can I refuse? Night, everyone.'

We strolled away from the beach towards the bottom of my hill.

'It's lovely to see you with the baby, Clem. He's such a sweetie, isn't he?'

'He is. But I couldn't do it full time. God! It's exhausting. I once thought that I'd love kids but honestly... I'm so glad now I met someone who doesn't see them in her future either. It's quite refreshing. Although I've been meaning to get you alone for a while.'

'Oh, Clem, I'm not that type of girl you know.'

'Ha, I'd be flattered if you were, Lydia, but you know I'm a one-man woman.'

'Glad to hear it.'

'But seriously. I'm a bit worried. Meredith is acting a bit strange lately. Do you know if everything is OK with her?'

'As far as I know. She's not really said anything to me. I know she's tired and not sleeping well.'

'Yeah, I noticed that she'd not been stopping over as often as she did and she's not really invited me to stay at the lighthouse either. You don't think she's... well, you know... going off me, do you?'

'I really don't, Clem. She adores the very bones of you, I know that much for sure. Just give her a bit of time and space. Maybe there's changes going on in her body that she feels a little uncomfortable about.'

I didn't really know whether to say any more.

'Oh God, I hadn't really thought of that. I remember Mum having a terrible time when she was a similar age. She even threatened to kill Dad a few times. He used to take himself off to his shed and ignore her.'

'Ha. I think that's how men handled things in those days. Good that times are changing really.'

'I'll do a bit of research and see if I can find anything useful.'

'You're a good man, Clem.'

'I try.'

I could honestly say that I think Meredith had won the lottery with Clem. He really was a lovely man and I knew that he adored her.

'You don't have to try, love. You just are. And I love that you're there for my daughter.'

'I won't let her down, Lydia. I promise you that. A love like ours doesn't come round many times in a lifetime and I'm so lucky. I will do anything for her. For us.'

I tucked my hand into the crook of his arm and patted his hand with mine.

'She's a lucky lady.'

He made sure I was safely inside, before giving me a big bear hug and kissing my cheek. Men like Clem were hard to find and I hoped that Meredith wouldn't push him away because she was too proud to ask for help.

The evening and the chat with Meredith had brought back several memories for me, so it felt like the right time to finally face my journal. I made myself a cup of tea, got into bed and removed the diary from the bedside table. It was the first time that I really felt brave enough to bring back the past.

As I turned back the front cover, I breathed deeply and knew that it was the right time.

OMG, Mum is going to kill me. How can I have allowed this to happen? I knew that my body was changing but I didn't know why. I have no one I can tell. What on earth am I going to do? I can't tell her; she'll be so disappointed in me. I'm so disappointed in me. I need to think of a plan. If only I had a friend now who could help. Maybe I should have spent the time I was learning to be the best dancer I could, being the best friend I could instead. I don't have a single person I can turn to right now. My stomach is starting to be noticeable. And I thought it was only the mornings that were meant to be awful but I'm being sick all through the day. It's only a matter of time now before Mum finds out. I can't hide it for much longer.

My heart pounded as I remembered how I felt in those early days of pregnancy. The days that I tried to hide everything from everyone. At home, I sat in baggy jumpers, my skin starting to lose its pallor and my hair greasy and lank. I knew that I wasn't eating properly, certainly not enough to nourish a baby as well as myself and Mum was worried that I'd got an eating disorder – but that was preferable to her learning the truth. If it wasn't for my dance teacher, Miss Gibson, cottoning on to my condition I honestly don't know what I would have done.

'How far gone are you, Lydia?' she asked out of the blue one day when I was having extra dance tuition.

Stuck for words as she had stumbled across the truth, I couldn't speak. She put her arms around me and kissed my head.

'You poor child. What are we going to do with you?'

I'd always looked up to Miss Gibson. She was the most elegant person I knew, tall, willowy, with long chestnut hair which she always wore tied back in a ponytail. Stunningly beautiful with a perfectly symmetrical face, her body naturally graceful with every move that she made. If I could be anyone in life, I'd have chosen to be her. Women adored her and men were dazzled by her, yet she was oblivious to it all. Her love was dance.

Her kindness, as she held me close and rocked my body against her, and the release that someone finally knew the truth of the secret I'd been holding on to burst through my body and I was wracked with sobs, falling into a crumpled heap on the floor. I don't know how long we sat like that for, her stroking my hair and whispering, 'It'll be OK. We'll sort it all out somehow,' was just too much for me. I felt like neither my body nor my mind could take any more.

It had been Miss Gibson who had held my hand and sat with me in our front room as the mortifying truth came from my mouth as I broke the news to my mother.

She shouted and she screamed at me. I ducked as she threw a framed photograph of our family at the wall above the fireplace.

'I'm glad your father isn't alive to see his little girl turn out this way. He would be turning in his grave. He'd be so ashamed of you.'

I had never ever in my life been so embarrassed about anything and I felt so worthless, but finally she calmed down.

I could remember her words still to that day.

'You, lady, are a Robinson. And Robinsons don't give up. Yes,

I'm furious at you right now, but you are also my daughter and I love you and we will get through this. Together.'

The sound of laughter and the slamming of a nearby front door jolted me back to the present. I put the journal down and got up and looked out of the window. Lights were on in Dianne's house and I saw the silhouettes of her and Martin in the kitchen. I pulled the curtains shut tight and went back to bed, pulling the duvet over my head, shutting the past outside of my mind as much as I could. I frowned as I was tried to process why I was feeling a little bit uncomfortable about this. My initial emotion was a slight pang of jealousy, but I reminded myself that we were just friends, good ones. He can spend time with whoever he likes.

I pushed these thoughts away and eventually fell asleep.

17

The next few days flew by and it was soon time for our second lesson with Miguel. As we pulled up outside of his industrial unit, I was just about to knock the shutter door that he'd told us to use, when I heard a harsh loud Birmingham accent talking behind it. Martin and I looked at each other, puzzled expressions on our faces. He must have someone with him, but we could only hear the one voice. Very strange.

Martin bit the bullet and knocked. There was a cough from behind the door and we could hear the click of the shutters starting to rise. A very flustered Miguel appeared, stroking down his hair. He seemed to have a shadow of stubble on his face, but instead of it being dark and swarthy like his mop of curly black hair, there was a definite ginger tinge. Wondering if he dyed his hair, I said hello and he ushered us in, in his thick heavy Spanish accent.

Martin shook his hand and came right out with it. 'Thought I could hear a Brummie then. Someone here with you?'

'Ah no, I was on the phone with a friend of mine. He lives in

Birmingham. Always got plenty to say. Must have been him you heard on speakerphone.'

He waved his phone at us, and then hid it away in his back pocket.

'Hope you've remembered everything from last week,' he said as we entered the dance space. 'And hope you have done your homework.' He emphasised his h's and rolled his r's in the way that lots of European people do. He had such a lovely sing-song voice. I could listen to him for hours but we were here to dance so dance we did. This time we'd gone over our competition dances and Miguel had also given us a square tango for a change too.

More than anything, it had been fun. We'd laughed till our sides hurt and we came out grinning.

I imitated Miguel as we walked back to the car.

'Mar-teen, stop counting out loud and stop looking at your fleep-ing feet.'

Martin chuckled good-naturedly. He was able to laugh at himself too. A lovely quality in a person in my humble opinion.

'If I stop counting I go wrong and if I don't look at my feet I go wrong too. I'm rubbish, Lydia. Maybe you should have had a different partner.'

'Ah get off with you. You're not rubbish at all. You're actually very good once you relax into it. Remember when Miguel told you to close your eyes and just feel your way around the floor.'

'God yes. I was better when I did it that way. How does that even work? Maybe I should just dance blindfolded all the time.'

I reached out to touch his arm.

'You'll be great, you know. It's just all about practising. It'll soon be second nature to you. Don't forget when you watch *Strictly*, they've been practising all day every day for a week before they do their Saturday night show.'

'Very true. I am blooming enjoying it though, Lydia, are you?'

I took a deep breath, and cleared my throat, my voice thick with emotion.

'I am absolutely loving it. I feel a little obsessed if truth be told. Dancing is definitely my happy place. I'm so glad you persuaded me to allow it back into my life. It's such a great way to spend time. I really do feel like a different person. Thank you so much, Martin.'

He winked at me and to my surprise my heart gave a little skip.

'Hey, what are friends for if not for treading on your toes and making you laugh when I go wrong?'

Fun and lots of laughter was back in my life for the first real time in years. With a vengeance. And maybe a little something else which I wasn't sure what to call. It felt more than friendship but fondness didn't seem to be enough.

We were exhausted and quite quiet with our own thoughts in the car on the way home. I looked across at Martin, who was concentrating on the road, and it felt like the natural time to mention the events of last night.

'The picnic was fun, wasn't it?'

'It was yes. Were you OK? It's not like you to sneak away early.'

'Fine, thank you, yes. Just a bit tired. It's these early mornings. Were you late home?'

I hadn't meant it to be, but this would be a good test of whether he was going to admit to being at Dianne's.

'Not too late. I walked Dianne back up here actually. Two birds with one stone. I wanted to make sure she got back OK, and just wanted to make sure you were OK too, but there were no lights on at yours so I didn't disturb you.'

'That's kind of you, Martin.'

He held my gaze and gulped before continuing. 'That's what people who care about each other do, isn't it, Lydia?'

I nervously fiddled with the straps of my handbag which was perched on my knee.

'Dianne would have sat up chatting all night I think, but I excused myself after a nightcap.'

'She's nice, isn't she? Glamorous. Vivacious even?'

'She is nice yes, but she never shuts up.' He laughed. 'Although she's definitely quieter when she's not got an audience.'

Funny he should say that. I'd noticed the same recently when she popped round for a coffee. I wondered whether it was a confidence thing with her and sometimes she was quite loud and boisterous to cover up the fact that she's actually not all that confident after all.

I could feel him look across at me, as I kept my eyes on the road ahead.

'It's a shame really that she feels like she has to do that. True friends shouldn't have to do that with each other, should they? We don't and we're perfect. As friends I mean.'

I tried to cover my smile. And felt a little relief in my heart at the same time as hoping I wasn't being mean towards Dianne.

I waved to Martin as his car drove away and fell into bed that night and slept through till the following morning without waking once.

* * *

I decided that once I'd got myself moving, I would make a start on potting up some of the summer bedding plants that I'd been cultivating in the greenhouse. Even though I was admitting it myself, and there weren't that many things that I felt I was skilled at, being green-fingered was one of the gifts I was blessed with and one of my favourite things to do was to potter around in the garden. The radio kept me company and I hummed along making up my own words when I couldn't quite remember the original ones, glad that no one could hear me apart from the goats in the field beyond.

'Good morning, Lydia. Beautiful day.' Dianne gave me a little wave as she went down to feed the goats. They were hilarious, bleating like crazy when they saw her open the gate and skipping around her legs as she chattered away to them before heading down to the far corner of the field towards the chicken shed.

There were a couple of heavy grow bags that needed emptying out and I managed to drag them over to the potting bench where I sat on my stool looking out to sea, taking the plants out of the smaller terracotta pots, and making them part of an arrangement in both the empty hanging baskets and the larger floor-based pots. When finished, I stood and stretched my back and groaned out loud. It was hard work and the bending over was really making my back ache, although I was determined it wouldn't get the better of me.

'Here you go, angel. Some nice fresh eggs for you.' Dianne placed a plastic bowl on the wall between our two gardens.

'Thanks, lovely. Very kind of you.'

'Kind of you to take them off my hands to be honest. They're churning them out quicker than I can eat them.' She gave a little tinkly laugh. 'I'll have egg rash if I'm not careful. I'll pop some round to Martin later too. We said we might meet up for a little drinkypoos later.'

Strange that Martin hadn't mentioned that when we were discussing her last night. That funny feeling in my tummy was back again. I wondered why he hadn't said.

Martin had offered to put the hanging baskets in place when I was ready, but I had my stubborn and strong-willed head on me today, determined that I didn't need a man to take care of me and ready to prove that I could do anything that I wanted to. I knew there was a pair of stepladders in the garage so I went and unlocked the garage door, eager to get the gorgeous baskets up. Some were full to the brim with scarlet geraniums, trailing fuchsia and white lobelia. Others had vibrant pink, purple and red busy Lizzies, a favourite of mine.

I'd potted a couple of tall pots up for Dianne too with the leftover plants. I knew she couldn't have low down pots because Celia had them off me every year and couldn't understand why they weren't lasting when mine were still full in bloom, until she saw Hobson cocking his leg up on them one morning. Yep, that'll do it.

Watching Dianne and Hobson pack themselves up and into the car, made me smile and she beeped the horn and waved again as they left their drive heading off for the day. Today was one of their busiest therapy days of the week when they did school readings in the morning, visited a care home over lunch and went to do more reading at a school a little further afield in the afternoon.

I turned up the radio and danced along to the music, grinning to myself. It struck me how happy Dianne looked today, and she and Martin were on my mind while I climbed up the stepladder. My balance wavered when I reached the top and I realised that maybe I should have waited for someone else to be here after all, but I was up here now. On the climb down I made sure that I was extra careful.

I stood back and looked at my handiwork. The baskets looked gorgeous and I was rather proud that I'd managed to get them up without any help. I clearly didn't need anyone after all.

I moved round to the back of the house with the ladders to get those sorted too.

There was just one more basket left and I had promised myself the reward of a cup of tea and a piece of cake. It was a stunning day and I was looking forward to sitting on my garden bench, looking out to sea.

As I hung the final basket, and went to climb down the first step, I completely lost my footing and fell down the whole thing. I screamed out loud as I hit the deck. The pain that shot through my ankle was absolutely excruciating.

'Shit!' I gritted my teeth and tried to pull my leg round, but my ankle throbbed with the piercing pain that seared through it. I could immediately see that it looked twisted and it was already turning a strange colour. I called across to next door.

'Dianne. Help. I'm a bit stuck. Dianne!'

When I managed to drag myself back up into a seating position, rubbing my shoulder which also felt extremely tender where I'd fallen against a pot, I remembered that Dianne wasn't in and that the house next door was empty. I glanced at my watch and realised that she and Hobson would be out for a good while yet.

I reached around to my back pocket for my phone and then realised that I'd left it on the kitchen table.

'Damn.'

I honestly had no clue of what to do, or when someone might come by to rescue me. Maybe the postman would be along soon. Surely it couldn't be that long.

I shivered, the shock of the fall starting to hit me. I tried to push myself up, but the stones on the ground made it hard for me to get any traction and both of my arms hurt. I couldn't put any weight on one.

After a few minutes, a vehicle engine and loud music could

be heard in the distance. Thank God. It sounded like someone was coming up the road. I could see the sign on the side of a white van – it was the nice young man who had delivered the box from Peter a couple of weeks ago. I'd flag him down and see if I could get him to help me.

I waved frantically. Through the car window, I could see he was singing his head off.

'I need help!' I yelled at him.

But he sailed right past, both the engine and the sound of his music dying down to nothing as he approached the farm at the end of the road. My only saving grace was that I knew he would be back soon. There was no other way out of the farm so I'd just have to wait patiently.

Every time I tried to move, the pain in my ankle was agonising and nausea washed over me. I tried again to move myself but couldn't. Panic started to hit me. What if I couldn't help myself? How long would it be before someone found me?

After another five minutes, while I was trying to breathe deeply to make the pain bearable, I heard the familiar rumble of the engine again. He was coming back. Hurrah! I waved again frenziedly. It wasn't easy because my shoulder hurt so much but I raised my arm as high as I could.

And the young delivery driver just drove right on past once more.

'Arggghhh! Bloody idiot!' I wasn't sure whether I was referring to him or me at that point. I was cold, I was frustrated and I was in so much pain, and I had no clue how I was going to get myself out of this ridiculous mess. So much for being able to do things for myself. I was such a silly old fool.

I could hear my phone ringing in the kitchen but even though I tried to drag myself across the stones on my bottom, I couldn't budge. I'd just have to wait here until someone else came past. I knew Dianne should be back around 4 p.m., so it looked like I was going to have to stay here till then.

I had never felt so alone.

The sun was starting to get hot and I didn't have any sunscreen or a hat on. Could this day get any worse? I tried to move myself again as I was so uncomfortable lying on the stones. A tear rolled down my cheek as pain shot through my ankle once more.

After that, I think I must have passed out.

18

The next thing I knew, there was a big wet sandpaper textured tongue licking my face. Hobson. In the distance I could hear a voice shouting, which was getting nearer.

'Come back here, you big daft dog. Oh, my goodness, Lydia. Whatever have you done?'

'Oh, Dianne, thank goodness.'

'Look at the state of your foot.'

I looked down and my ankle was twice the size it should be, red as a tomato and the throbbing had started again. It felt like it was on fire.

'Yes, ambulance please. Bay View Cottage, Sandy Lane, Drift-wood Bay. As quick as you can please? Neighbour has had a fall and has been unconscious. Not sure how long for.' I could hear Dianne's voice but it kept coming and going and I couldn't focus.

'Can you get here now? There's been an accident. She's OK but I think we need you.'

There was a droning noise in my ear and I just wanted to sleep but Hobson kept nudging me with his nose.

'OK, I'm back now. Drink some water, Lydia. Come on.'

Dianne put a glass of water to my lips then draped a light blanket around my shoulders and put another over my knees. I didn't realise how thirsty I was.

'Thank you,' I whispered.

Just having someone nearby made me feel a whole lot calmer along with my vision getting clearer. I turned to look at Dianne and winced at the pain in my shoulder and neck.

A siren in the distance was getting closer and closer.

'Oh, Dianne, you didn't!'

'I blooming did. God knows how long you've been lying here.'

'What time is it?'

'Twelve thirty. Thank goodness I forgot my ID card and came back home. He can sense it, you know. The minute I opened the car door he was out like a shot and came straight round here. If he hadn't have done that and I hadn't come to get him, I wouldn't have seen you on the floor.' She patted him on the head. 'Clever boy, Hobbo. Clever boy!'

The dog lay by the side of me with his head on my leg. The warmth from his body was finally warming me up.

An ambulance had pulled up at the end of the drive and soon two paramedics were jumping out with bags and heading over. Another car door slammed and Meredith came running.

'Oh my God, Mum. What's happened?'

'If you could just move aside, so we can assess the situation please?'

Meredith moved slightly back, her hand over her mouth. She and Dianne began to talk in low whispers, Dianne filling her in on what she knew.

'What's your name, love?' the paramedic asked me.

'Lydia. Lydia Robinson.'

'Do you know where you are?'

'Yes, I'm at home in my garden.'

'Can you tell us what's happened?'

'I just lost my footing on the ladder while hanging the planters. Fell to the floor.'

'How old are you, Lydia?'

'How rude are you?' I shot back with a grin. 'Don't you know you should never ask a lady her age?!'

He smiled.

'I take it you're feeling a little better now?' He looked over at Dianne and Meredith. 'Did one of you find her?'

'Well, the dog did to be honest.'

He looked over at Hobson and patted his head.

'Good lad! Bloody clever, aren't they? Never cease to amaze me.'

'I just followed him round here to find out where he'd gone running off to and found Lydia on the floor. I rang you straight away.'

'I'm perfectly sane, you know,' I said. 'You don't have to talk about me like I'm not here.'

Meredith came round and held my hand. 'They're just doing their job, Mum.'

'Sorry, love,' one of the paramedics said, nudging Meredith out the way. 'Can you tell me where it hurts? Can you stand? And do you remember if you banged your head at all?'

After I listed everywhere that hurt, and we worked out that I couldn't stand without help, the two men rolled me one way, to put a plastic stretcher under my bottom so they could get me on it fully, and then the other to straighten me up.

'Right, let's get you off to get checked over at the hospital.'

I groaned. What a silly old bugger I was getting myself into this state just because I wanted to prove that I was independent.

'Meredith, would you just grab me my phone. I think it's on the kitchen table. And could you lock up for me please?'

'Could you just hang on for two secs please, guys, and I'll ride in the ambulance with Mum if that's OK with you?' She headed towards the door.

'You don't need to come with us, Meredith,' I shouted out to her. 'I'll be fine. I'm sure you've got enough to be getting on with.'

'I'm coming and that's that.'

I was secretly relieved at this, and once Meredith had locked up and jumped in the back of the ambulance, she waved to Dianne and Hobson as the doors were closed. As we headed to The Royal Truro Hospital, Meredith held my hand and a tear ran down my cheek.

* * *

'Six to eight weeks!' I shrieked. 'I have a dance competition in eight. I must be better for that.'

'Mrs Robinson, in all probability, you won't be taking part in a dance competition for a very good while.'

'I have to. Surely if it's only a sprain it'll be better.'

The young doctor lectured me on how a sprain can sometimes be worse than a break.

'Some sprains can take three to four months to fully recover, especially in—' he coughed '—older people.'

I looked at Meredith in complete disgust, not knowing whether the fact that he put me in the 'old' category was worse than how long he'd predicted a recovery would take. Meredith smirked as I explained to the doctor, who didn't look old enough to have even left school, let alone been to university and qualified, that I did daily yoga and was as fit as a fiddle.

'It doesn't even hurt that much.'

'That'll be the medication, Mrs Robinson.'

'I suppose I'd better ring Martin and tell him I won't be able to do dance practice tonight then.'

'I've rung Clem and he was going to ring his dad. Don't worry, Mum.'

'I could kick myself, you know. I was so hell-bent on not being a burden to anyone and wanting to be independent that I couldn't wait for help. I'm so annoyed.'

'We'll help you anytime you need it, Mum.'

'I know, but I'm not very good at asking for help.'

'Really?'

We both smiled.

A nurse appeared with two crutches and a wheelchair. 'Here you go.'

I knew I was rolling my eyes at her; I couldn't help myself.

'Is this totally necessary?' I asked. 'It's all a bit dramatic, isn't it?'

'If you want to walk again, then yes, it is. There's a risk of further damage if you don't take this seriously. After two weeks, your ankle should start to feel much better, and the swelling should have gone down, but you must avoid strenuous exercise for up to eight weeks. And maybe you should think about having one of those alarm pendants around your neck in future.'

I put my head in my hands and groaned. I was seventy-one not ninety-one. Surely it was all too early for this. This was just an unfortunate mishap; it could have happened to anyone.

'The good news, Mrs Robinson, is that most ankle sprains heal well, so with the correct treatment, you should be up and running in a few weeks' time.'

I needed a glass of wine. That was the sort of treatment that would make me feel better.

'One more thing. Avoid drinking alcohol too.'

Damn.

'Drinking can slow down your recovery and mask your symptoms, so steer clear for a while.'

'Oh, Lord.'

'Cold compresses, lots of rest and you'll soon be back to normal.' She pulled the wheelchair round. 'Scoot over to this and we'll get you back out to the taxi rank.'

'I'm not going in that! I'll walk!'

'Well, you can either go in the wheelchair, or you can try the crutches but it could take a very long time. Or obviously, there's a third choice.'

I swung round, and wished I hadn't, as the sudden pain in my neck made me flinch.

'You could have a nice little stay here with us for a few days. The food is amazing. It'll be just like being in a five-star hotel.' She smiled over-sweetly as the man in the cubicle to my right yelled out in pain and swore at the doctor who was evidently doing some sort of stitching to a wound on his arm.

'You might end up on the same ward as someone like him.' The nurse nodded towards the curtain.

I shuffled myself over to the edge of the chair and let the nurse help lift me into the wheelchair.

'Do you have some help the other end?' the nurse asked Meredith as she handed a bundle of papers over. She nodded her assurance.

'Yes, we do. We'll be fine thanks.'

'Bye then and take care.'

* * *

By the time we got back to Bay View Cottage, dusk was settling in. Clem was waiting on the drive when we pulled up. Together, he and Meredith got me out of the car and into the house but it took a while. I'd had the most revolting cup of tea at the hospital, milky and weak and couldn't wait for a proper cup of tea. I was absolutely exhausted.

'Do you want some dinner, Mum? You've not eaten for hours.'

'No thanks, darling. I just don't feel like anything.'

They put me straight into my bedroom and Clem made himself scarce as Meredith helped to get me into my nightie. I'd never felt so useless in my life. Fancy having to have your daughter help you get undressed. What a state I was in. All because I was too stubborn to wait for help. So much for being independent.

Meredith left the room to get me the tea that Clem was making and I heard voices in the kitchen. There was a timid knock at the door.

'Hello, sweetie. How are you doing?'

'Oh, Dianne.' I burst into tears.

She sat on the bed and rubbed my hand.

'It's just a little setback, Lydia. And I'm just next door and can help you at any time. I've written my mobile number for you.' She tucked a piece of paper under the bedside light. 'I know you have the landline number, but just in case I'm out. We're all here to help you. And you must accept it. Do you hear?'

I nodded, but I had honestly never felt so deflated. What a mess.

'Tea and toast for the patient.' Meredith came in with my china mug and a plate of hot buttered toast. Dianne sat beside me while I ate. Despite not thinking I was hungry, it went down an absolute treat.

'Thanks for everything, Dianne. What a stroke of luck that you had to pop back home.'

'I know, I'd forgotten my ID card for the school, so I had to come back to pick it up. Do you know, I thought twice about it too, thinking that they'd let me in anyway but then I decided that I'd come back anyway as I had a bit of time. I'm so glad that I did. But it was all Hobson, really. I'd forgotten – don't ever tell Celia this – to attach his lead to the frame in the car and he jumped out as soon as we got back. Came straight here, he did. It was like he knew there was something wrong.'

'Thank God for you! And Hobson. What a little star. First kiss with tongues I've had in years.'

Meredith caught this as she came back into the room.

'Ew, Mum. Must you?'

'Sorry, darling.' I yawned, a wave of tiredness suddenly sweeping over me and I blinked back tears, suddenly feeling quite sorry for myself.

Dianne patted my hand. 'I'll leave you to get some sleep. And I mean it, Lydia. I'm just next door. It'll take me seconds to get here. Call me if you need anything.'

'Thank you.'

I was so grateful that she was living in Celia's house. If the place had been left empty, then I might not have been found for hours. Maybe at some point, someone would have noticed that I wasn't answering my phone and would have come up to look for me, but it didn't bear thinking about.

'Come on, Mum, you need to sleep.'

'I do, but I need a quick wee first.'

But a quick wee seemed to be something that wouldn't happen for a long time. I had to put up with the humiliation of Meredith and Clem helping me to get out of bed and into the bathroom, then they had to wait for me while I... did what I needed to – it was just awful.

When I finally got into bed, I slept for hours.

19

Whatever was in the tablets that Meredith gave me knocked me right out. The bedside clock must have stopped because it was showing up as 11.30. I could hear someone clanking around in the kitchen which felt odd. I wasn't used to having people in my house.

'Hello?' I called out.

'Good morning, sleepyhead. How are you feeling? Fancy a cuppa?'

'What time is it, Meredith?'

'Eleven thirty. You've slept for over thirteen hours. You clearly needed it. And the doctor did say that you should rest. It's your body's natural way of repairing itself.'

'Oh, my goodness. Eleven thirty. I need to get up.' I moved but the pain in my foot stopped me in my tracks.

'Maybe you just need to stay where you are.'

'I can't do that. Firstly, I have things to do today and secondly, I'm dying for the loo!'

'OK, well the loo we can sort out. But I don't think you are going to be doing much more today.'

'What about the competition and all the dance practices? What are we going to do? I need to think.'

'Martin knows about your fall.'

'Oh, Lord. Don't tell people I've had a fall; it makes me sound old.'

'You did have a fall, Mum.'

'I fell, that's not the same as having a fall. Very different in fact.'

'If you say so.'

'I do say so. Now please help me up, darling. If I don't get to the loo soon, we'll be clearing up more than we bargained for.'

Meredith managed to manoeuvre me into a standing position and she handed me the crutches that we'd been given in the hospital.

I shook my head, but she insisted.

'You're going to have to get to grips with them, Mum. I can't be here twenty-four hours a day. I don't mind for the first few days but I don't think I can do it for much longer than that; I have appointments to get to.'

'You don't have to stay with me, love. I'll manage.'

'We'll see about that, shall we?'

I half shuffled, half hopped to the bathroom – thank goodness it was close by.

I stared at Meredith.

'You can go now. I'm sure I can manage from here. I'm not a child.' I slammed the door behind me and heard her mutter something under her breath – something like 'well you're behaving like one'.

Charming.

'Let me know when you've finished and I'll come and help you off the loo.'

I was pretty sure I could cope with getting to the bathroom

myself but I did wonder how the hell I was going to manage in the shower. I didn't even have the energy to think about it let alone attempt it. I tried to push myself up off the toilet seat, but my shoulder was still really hurting me and I couldn't put weight on my ankle.

'I've finished,' I mumbled reluctantly.

I could hear Meredith shuffling around in the hallway.

'Did you say something?' she called out.

'I've finished!' I yelled and then started laughing at a memory that popped into my mind.

She knocked the door and came in and helped me up.

'What's so funny?'

'When you were a little girl when you were potty training, you used to sit on the toilet for hours and when you were done you used to yell "I've finished" really loudly and proudly – in a little sing-song voice.'

'You've never told me that before.'

'I've only just remembered. Mum and I used to find it hilarious.'

'That's the first time you've ever implied that any part of my childhood was something to laugh about. I thought you hated being a mother.'

I shook my head and smiled.

'Aw, there were lots of times, darling. I'll try and remember some more to tell you.'

'I'd really like that. Now, do you want to go back to bed?'

'I'd rather sit in the conservatory if possible.'

'OK, let's get you out there. Let's see how you manage with these crutches.'

I shuffled my backside to the edge of the bed and tried to swing my legs round to a sitting position. Even that was exhausting.

'What time did you come back round this morning? I was out like a light.'

'I didn't leave. I stayed in the spare room.'

'What? You didn't need to do that.'

'Well, I think I did. What would you have done if you'd woken up and needed the loo, or a drink?'

'I'm not sure.'

Meredith tutted.

'Also, the hospital only agreed to let you out if someone was with you last night. They wanted to keep you in but I thought you'd be better off at home, with me.'

'Thank you, darling, that's very kind.'

I patted her arm as she tried to help me up.

'I'm your daughter, Mum. That's what families do. And you could hardly come and stay in the lighthouse.'

'Well, I still appreciate it very much.'

It took a while but we eventually made our way into the conservatory and I plonked myself in an armchair with a big sigh. Mission accomplished.

'So, cup of tea and some brunch? You must be starving. You hardly ate anything yesterday. Fancy a bacon sandwich?'

'Oh, gosh, I normally only have granola, yoghurt and fruit for breakfast.'

'Well, I'm your nurse today and I'm prescribing you a bacon sarnie.'

I grinned. 'Don't suppose you could do me an egg on top too...'

She grinned back and it suddenly hit me how like me she was when I was that age. I'd never really noticed it before. It was comforting. I wasn't sure how she'd take it though, so didn't say anything.

'Thank you, Meredith.'

'For looking after you? No problem.'

'No. For being my daughter. I love you.'

I watched her closely as she swallowed a lump in her throat.

'I love you too.'

I hadn't realised just how hungry I was and I managed to polish off my sandwich quite quickly. Meredith collected the cups and plates and I heard her load them into the dishwasher.

'Martin said he'll be round later to see how you are.'

'Oh God, look at the state of me too. Does he have to?'

'I know he wants to. He thinks the world of you, Mum, and I know he wants to talk to you about the dance competition.'

'Oh that. I've just been thinking about that. I reckon that if I rest this for a few days, I should be OK to get back to practising next week.'

Meredith shook her head and reminded me that the doctor said not to do anything strenuous for at least eight weeks. The competition was in eight weeks' time. I'd have to think about how I could get better quicker. That's all there was to it.

She also told me that the district nurse had called that morning to see how I was and to see if there was anything they could help me with.

'She offered a walking frame and a commode and said to let her know whether you needed either or both.'

'A commode. Really? Was she joking?'

'Deadly serious. I told her I didn't think you'd want either but that we'd call her back. She left her number and said to let her know.'

'I hope you told her that I was seventy-one and not ninety-one.'

'Of course. I even told her you'd say that. You're very predictable, you know.'

'Why thank you!'

'Well, it's true. And talking of stubborn old buggers...' She grinned at me.

'Watch it. You're never too old for a cuff round the ear, you know.'

'Ha, in your state it would take so long for you to get to me, you'd have forgotten what you got up for.'

'True. So, who else is a stubborn old bugger then?'

Meredith went on to tell me that she'd been in touch with Dennis and had been quizzing him about Vi. He said that strangely, she'd been discouraging him from visiting lately, making excuses every time he said he'd pop round.

'Something's not right, Mum, I can feel it.'

'I think you're right, darling. I wonder if she's getting in a bit of a mess in the house and she's a bit embarrassed. She might need some help. She is in her eighties.'

'She and Dennis have had a bit of a falling-out apparently. Last time he went in, he said that she'd got two mats in the hall and they were all ruckled up. A falling hazard for an old lady he thought, so he suggested she get them up and she got quite shirty apparently, shouting that he had to stop telling her what to do.'

'Oh dear. That doesn't sound good. Maybe I'll give him a call. Not sure I'll be doing much else for the next few days, so it'll give me something to do with my time.'

'I'm sure he'd appreciate it. I know he works all hours and doesn't get much chance to get over here. That was why, last year when she had her accident, he wanted her in a home near him, but she didn't want that to happen. Thank goodness I was able to help out when I arrived and she was able to stay in her own home and keep the dog.'

I could feel myself dozing as Meredith pottered around in the kitchen. I closed my eyes for what I thought was a few minutes and the next thing I knew I could hear Martin's deep jovial voice in the other room.

'Mum, if you're OK for an hour or so, I need to pop back to the lighthouse to do a couple of jobs. I'll also get some bits and pieces together to bring back. I've been in these clothes since yesterday. Martin is going to sit with you so you're not on your own.'

'Darling, it's very kind of him but I'm sure I'd be perfectly fine.'

'Well, no bother, I'm here now so... We need to talk about the dance competition too.'

'Indeed, we do, Martin. I've been giving it lots of thought already. I reckon that if I can find someone to fill in for me for the next week, then I'll get a complete rest and then I'll be back on my feet and we'll be fine.'

'Well... Actually Lydia, I've...' Martin tried to speak, but I was on a mission and interrupted him.

'I suppose we could ask Dianne. She's got plenty of time on her hands. Shall we give her a call now, Martin, and ask her?'

I wasn't sure about Dianne and Martin being put in a close proximity situation like this but couldn't really see an alternative. I sighed and turned to get the phone. Maybe throwing them together would let me see for myself if there was anything going on between them. Even though that pang of jealousy had just reared its head again, it was better for me to know the truth.

'It will only be temporary. Until I'm able to get back to it. Shouldn't be too long and then I'll be able to dance again as your proper partner.'

'You can't possibly do that, Lydia. It's not practical. You won't be well enough. Anyway, it's already taken care of. On our behalf I've withdrawn us from the competition.'

20

'Noooo! We can't pull out, Martin. It's the one thing that's kept me going for weeks. Please let's not. It'll be fine! I'll be fine. They were just being overdramatic at the hospital.'

'Lydia, look at you. You can hardly get to the bathroom alone. There is no way that you're going to be able to practise dancing next week, let alone participate in a competition in a couple of months' time. I can see in your face how disappointing this is for you. I know this is hard for you to accept.'

'No, Martin, I don't think you do. This competition, it meant everything. It's the start of a new life for me. One that I've not lived for over fifty years. Dancing with you has made me realise that this is what I was born to do and what I want to do until my dying day. I haven't had as much fun in literally fifty years. I gave it up once and I don't want to give it up again.'

'No one is asking you to give it up. We're just saying that you can't do it right now. You're not well.'

'Martin, I can't go back to that time – that time I last gave up dancing. That period of my life is one I never ever want to repeat.

I spiralled into depression and ended up leaving my daughter to be brought up by someone else. I can't go back there, I just can't. It'll be like history repeating itself.'

Martin came and knelt next to me, removing a white hand-kerchief from his pocket with which he wiped away the tears that were now freely flowing down my cheeks. He pulled me close to his chest to soothe me but I was practically hyperventi-lating and tried to pull away.

'Please don't cry, Lydia. We'll sort it all out.'

'How can we sort it out? We either dance or we don't.'

'Maybe we can get involved in the judging or some other way.'

'I want to dance. I don't want to be involved in some other way. We must think of a way.'

At that point, Meredith walked back into the room and as she asked me what on earth the matter was, it was as if a light bulb had gone off within my head.

'I've got it,' I shouted.

'Got what, Mum?'

'You could do my practice sessions for me.'

It seemed like the perfect solution to me and put my petty jealousy at ease again if he was dancing with Meredith instead of him spending even more time with Dianne.

She looked at me and screwed her face up. Something else that she got from me. It made me smile again even.

'You can practise with Martin. I'll tell you what to do and you can do it. It's the only way and I know it'll work. You always used to love dancing as a little girl. It's in your blood. You'll be great. Yes, it'll work.'

The more I thought about it, the more I knew that it was the perfect solution. She was the exact same height and weight that I was, which meant that we were onto a winner. Martin would be ready; I'd be at every practice without actually doing anything to damage my ankle further and then I could step in at the last minute and do the competition evening.

'I think those tablets are addling your brain. It's ridiculous. I'm no dancer. Also, I have a life of my own, you know. If I wanted to enter the dance competition, I would have.'

'Oh, go on, darling. Please. This will mean the world to me. I don't think you understand.'

'Why does this mean so much to you, Mum? I'm sorry but I don't know why this is bothering you so much.'

'Meredith, I haven't talked much about this and only really opened up about it myself recently. To Martin in fact. Briefly, and I promise I'll tell you about it properly when we're alone, but when I found out I was pregnant with you, I was due to take to part in a dance competition. I was favourite to win but pulled out because I was pregnant. I've not danced properly for fifty years.'

'It's preposterous, Lydia. I'm sorry, but I'm not dancing with Meredith.'

'Thanks a lot, Martin,' Meredith griped back. 'What have I ever done to you?'

'Sorry, love, no offence meant. But it's a daft idea. You're nearly my daughter-in-law. I can't be dancing intimately with you. It's not right.'

Meredith and I looked at each other in shock and she turned back to him.

'Why ever not? It's only a dance. And you do it with Mum.'

The heat started to rise up my neck as Martin and I glanced at each other and quickly looked away again. I'd not really thought about it before. Dancing with Martin just felt right. Lovely in fact.

'But it's not just dancing, is it? It's bodies touching bodies and it just feels a bit bloody weird. I'm sorry but no. It's not happening.'

I laughed. 'Perhaps he's worried that he might get an erection, with a nice younger model like you.'

Meredith pretend heaved.

'Charming!' Martin muttered under his breath but loud enough for us to hear.

'How do you think I feel?' I continued, trying to make light of the situation even though all I could think about right now was Martin's body pressed against mine. 'Clearly, he doesn't think he'll get one when he dances with me so that's OK.'

I was enjoying winding him up now. He was going quite red in the face.

'I am here, you know!'

There was a rat-tat-tat at the door.

'Yoo-hoo! It's only me, can I come in? The door was partly open.'

Dianne peered around the door.

'Hello, Dianne, how are you? I've had a fabulous idea. Listen to this.'

'Don't listen to anything, Dianne,' Martin said. 'These pair are raving mad.'

When I explained my suggestion, her little face lit up.

'I'll happily be Meredith's understudy too in case she can't make any of the training. I've done a bit of dancing in my time and I'd be very happy to dance with such a handsome silver fox. What a splendid idea, Lydia.'

She was definitely very flirty around Martin and the way he laughed back at her really made me feel uncomfortable. They seemed to be way more familiar with each other than only recently made friends.

Meredith put her head in her hands.

'God, I wish I'd just gone home when I said I was going. I'd have missed all of this and you'd have had the job, Dianne.'

I could see she was wavering and made sure I took advantage.

'Meredith, my darling. Please do this for me. I'm an old woman. I might not have much time left in this world and it would mean the world to me to finally win a dance competition. Pretty please. Do it for your poor old mum.'

'Mum, you are not poor and you keep telling everyone that you are not old. Stop being such a drama queen. You can't pick and choose when to turn it on and off, you know.'

A smirk appeared. I needed her to commit to this. Despite being laid up with a badly sprained ankle, this could be the answer to everything. I would get to relive my dream. Fifty years after entering a dance competition, I could have the opportunity to enter another and this time, I could even win it. We, I should say, not I. We could be winners. Dianne broke the silence.

'So come on, Meredith, are you going to make your mum's dream come true?'

She groaned and flung herself on the sofa like a truculent teenager. Those years that I'd missed out on must have been just like this and it made me sad to think about it, but a little fire inside my belly was burning away. We really could do this.

'Please.'

She sighed and I knew in that moment that she'd accepted her fate.

'OK. But no erections, Martin. I draw the line at that. Any sign of anything and I'm off.'

'To be honest, Meredith, I think you two, between you, have put me off ever having one ever again. What if I don't want to do this. Do I get a choice or a say at all?'

Dianne, Meredith and I all chorused 'No!' and the four of us laughed.

'Are you sure this'll work, Lydia?'

'It's a little bizarre, Martin, I'll grant you that, but it's bloody genius. And it absolutely will work. Get back in touch with the people who are running the competition and tell them it was a mistake to withdraw. We're back in the game!'

21

_____

For the first day, Meredith and Martin danced together in the conservatory because it was drizzling outside and I didn't feel like leaving the house. The painkillers were making me really tired.

There wasn't the room to fully dance the routine that we'd choreographed so it was just the main steps. It would be so much better if we could go up to the church but even getting in a car was a trial. I was also missing the beach which I hadn't been to now for a couple of days. I did feel a little guilty that Meredith was giving up so much of her time but she assured me that she was happy to do it.

Once the initial awkwardness of dancing with Martin had passed, they made a good partnership. They'd need a lot of polishing – I felt like a judge on _Strictly Come Dancing_, shouting 'floppy arms' and 'hold your head up' at them both more than once. 'Your frame, Meredith!' and 'Again,' my most overused phrases.

It was lovely to see them laughing and joking together, and

enjoying what they were doing. A really lovely friendship was blooming – with not an erection in sight.

On day two, I was delighted to see that the weather had changed and there was a freshness in the air along with the sunshine and warmer temperature, which gave me a little hope. I was still struggling to get used to being on crutches but did manage to get out of the front door and walk a little way to the end of the lane and back. However, it was quite exhausting and I was worried about slipping and doing more damage.

I'd told Meredith that she should go home in the evenings. I could manage to get myself to the bathroom, and with a struggle, even managed to have a shower and wash my hair, leaving it to dry naturally instead of doing my normal blow-dry.

The Driftwood Bay community had absolutely pulled together to help and support me which was lovely and I had a fridge full of lasagne and cottage pies. However, my house was like Grand Central Station with people popping in left, right and centre and, to be honest, I was not used to having so many people around me. Time spent at home when the food-bringing visitors calmed down did give me lot of time to think and read more of my journal, revisiting my past which had been most cathartic, rather than upsetting.

Vi was also on my mind a lot. She was well into her eighties and I knew how difficult I was finding it with my mobility issues right now. She'd not long recovered from a tumble, with quite severe injuries, and her mobility apparently had never quite got back to how it was before. And with age, it would only get worse. The community had rallied around her at the time to keep her in her home, but when she was better, everyone had gone back about their busy lives. Meredith still walked Gladys most days, which was a huge help, but I wanted to investigate more about why she wouldn't let anyone in her house.

I had an idea, but I needed Meredith's help as I couldn't visit at the moment.

I looked at my watch. I was expecting Meredith and Martin at any minute. I heard an unusual little high-pitched peep-peep noise outside so made my way into the kitchen and looked out of the window.

I threw my head back and laughed at the sight that greeted me.

'Morning, Mum. Look what Geoff from the pub lent us. Martin had an idea to make life a little easier for you.'

'And what a great one it was too.'

I had completely forgotten that Geoff had a golf buggy which he'd bought a couple of years ago and used for the annual beach party to ferry Vi backwards and forwards so she could join in the celebrations.

Martin turned and patted the seat at the rear.

'Plenty of room on board for you. And you won't knock your foot like you would trying to get into a car. And it's great on rough terrain apparently, so we thought we could take you on a trip down the lane to the beach to see how we get on. Then we can zoom up to the church and get onto a better dance floor. You up for a trip out?'

I nodded, excited to be getting out of the house and have a change of scenery. After hobbling back to the kitchen table to grab my bag and phone, I locked the door behind me. Everything took twice as long with crutches but I supposed I should be grateful that I was able to walk at all and wasn't bed bound.

Meredith was staring off into space, a world away in her head, but smiled as I reached the buggy.

It was a bumpy ride and I yelped when we went over a pothole on the dirt track, but within a couple of minutes we were on the beach and even though it had only been a few days since

I'd been here last, I was mighty glad to see that beautiful sight before me, glistening in the sunlight of the morning.

'Are you sure you have time for this, Meredith? I know you said you had a lot of work on.'

'Well, what's the point of working for yourself if you can't have time off when it's needed? Family first and all that.'

A big lump appeared in my throat and I swallowed. I'd hardly been a good advocate of family coming first in the past but I was doing all I could to change that for the future. I wished I could think of a big grand gesture to show Meredith how much I'd changed and what she meant to me.

When we reached the sandy part of the beach, Meredith helped me off the back of the cart while Martin marked up the 'dance floor' with a big stick he found on the beach.

'Come on, Hopalong Hattie.' Meredith tucked my arm in hers. 'Let's get you perched in a chair.'

Bless her heart, Meredith had even brought a fold-up table for me to put my foot on. I'd been told to keep it raised at all times and was pondering on whether a paddle in the cold sea might be helpful and get the swelling down a bit.

She seemed a little down today. She was quieter than normal and I'd caught her just staring out at the sea a few times when she thought no one was looking. I'd try to get her on her own a bit later and check that everything was OK.

Out at sea, a procession of proud Driftwood Babes paddled past and all gave a synchronised wave, not batting an eyelid at all about people dancing on the beach. I loved that in this fabulous little community, no one judged you. They just let you be yourself. I'm not sure I'd ever lived somewhere like that before. In the States, my life was so different. You felt like you had to fit into a compartment, so you were either a golf wife, or a business wife, or on a committee somewhere. And you always had to be doing something. God forbid that anyone ever popped by and you looked less than polished. It was quite exhausting to be 'on' all the time. I even got dressed for dinner in our own house even if it was just the two of us. Our friends thought it was truly decadent and I was constantly told how lucky I was but it was like a constant pressure, never being able to just chuck on a pair of leggings and a T-shirt. If you did go casual, it was always a matching designer lounge suit. I always thought that I enjoyed that life, but it wasn't until I came to Driftwood Bay that I realised how unhappy I was, just drifting along to the tune of someone else.

I now knew that life was short, precious and even fragile – and Martin's reminder to find the joy had reminded me of that and how important it was to live life to the full. I loved that here, in Driftwood Bay, I felt free to explore life and find out what I enjoyed doing, but also felt part of something at the same time, even if there was still a tiny something missing that I couldn't put my finger on.

22

After about ten minutes of dancing, Meredith asked if we could stop for the day. Her eyes looked darker than normal, and a little puffy. She came and plonked herself beside me on a low rock with a big sigh.

'You OK, Mum?'

'I am, darling, thank you. But are you? You look tired.'

She frowned. 'I'm not feeling great today to be honest. I'm not sleeping well.'

'Something on your mind?'

She hesitated a little longer than I might have liked.

'One or two things but mainly it's these ridiculous surges in temperature I keep getting. They wake me up and I'm bloody roasting. I throw one arm out from under the duvet, then the other, then a leg, and then the other and then next thing you know I'm bloody freezing and wrap myself up again. Not sleeping makes me miserable and I then I forget things. I feel like I'm constantly walking around in a daze.'

'Have you been to the doctor? Maybe it's time you tried some HRT, you know.'

'I don't really want to go on it, to be honest. It's bad enough Clem being ten years younger than me, I'm sure he doesn't want someone with a bloody great patch on her arse to look at when he's getting all fruity.'

'I think they're quite small and discreet these days. There are also creams, for those who can't have patches. Maybe just do some research. It could really help you.'

'Yes I will. I did have a look but saw some horror stories.'

'There are also some amazing success stories. I saw a programme the other day on TV with Davina McCall and it said that thousands of marriages had been saved and also people who had been wrongly diagnosed with depression had been moved to HRT and it had changed their lives. Promise me you'll look into it, darling. There's no need to suffer if you don't have to.'

'I will. I promise.'

'Actually, I hope you don't mind but I have a little favour to ask you.'

'Another one?'

I decided that I wouldn't put any additional pressure on her right now. By her reaction, I could tell that she was obviously feeling a little frazzled and snarky. My mum always used to say that mothers had an instinct about how their child was feeling and whether they had something on their mind. I'd just cut her some slack and be there for her.

'I'm sorry, Mum. I seem to be snapping at everyone at the moment. What did you want me to do?'

'I just wanted you to walk with me down to the sea. I don't know how I'll manage on the sand with my crutches but I'd love to dip my foot in the water.' My ankle was still pretty swollen and the bruising was really quite a myriad of colours. I was sure that I'd read somewhere that ice baths were good for injuries. After all, professional sports people used them all the time.

'Of course.'

'I was rather hoping that it might speed up my recovery.'

'Don't run before you can walk, Mum. Or should I say don't dance...'

'I know, but I cannot tell you how much I want to be back in that competition.'

'Why does it mean so much to you?'

'It'll all become clear soon, darling. I have something for you to read. I'm not quite ready yet to hand it over but I will be. Soon. I promise.'

'Even after all these years, you still keep things so close to your chest.'

'I'm trying not to. This is more about not upsetting you than anything else. Nothing more than that. Trust me on this, darling, please.'

'Come on, let's get you down to the sea and put that cold water theory to the test. Sorry about stopping the dancing earlier than planned. I'm just not feeling up to it.'

'Of course.'

She was worrying me. Up until recently, she'd always been full of energy. It really wasn't like her at all to say that she's not feeling a hundred per cent.

'Martin!' she yelled. 'Can we borrow you?'

It wasn't easy but we made it, Meredith on one side and Martin on the other. There were some rocks to one side, so they guided me over to one of those and I sat down and dangled my foot in the cold water which was total bliss. Although I wasn't sure if it was the right thing to do medically, or that I couldn't feel the pain because I couldn't feel my foot because it was so cold, it did feel easier when I finally removed it. After being submerged in the cold water for so long there was every chance that I might now get frostbite, but even if I had, I would do it again. The relief was overwhelming. I won't say it was the most graceful I'd ever been in my life but I finally flung myself on the back of the golf cart, totally exhausted and feeling every single one of my seventy-one years. If Martin had the golf buggy indefinitely maybe he'd be able to bring me down each day. It would help us all.

I was still so blooming annoyed with myself for falling off the ladder. If only I could turn back time, I wouldn't be feeling like a silly old woman right now and would be enjoying my dance. I didn't realise how much I missed it. I loved the feeling that dancing gave me. Instead of tiring me, which I feared it might after all these years, it energised me and filled my heart with joy. I couldn't love it more and could kick myself for missing out on it for so long.

Meredith and Martin had done well in the short time that they'd danced together. There was definitely an improvement. Martin was holding himself more upright, and Meredith's footwork seemed a little lighter. She seemed bouncier. Perhaps it was the texture of the sand that helped. I knew that we'd have to take it to the church again soon, so they could get their feet gliding but in these very early days, practice anywhere was worth doing. I would do everything I could to be in that competition, but if for any reason I couldn't, while it would break my heart, I would do all in my power to make Meredith and Martin the best couple there and take home that trophy. Meredith offered to come back to the house with me.

'You really don't need to be watching over me all the time,' I said to her. 'I'll manage.'

'Maybe I want to be here for you. I'm enjoying spending time with you. I know we live in the same village now but we don't spend quality time together. It's been... well, you know... nice.'

'It's been lovely, darling; I just wish I could get about a bit more and not be such a burden on you. I'm sure you've got plenty of work you could be getting on with. Clem told me the other day that you'd put yourself forward for a big commission at Driftwood Manor.'

Driftwood Manor was a small mansion house on the outskirts of the bay which had recently been bought by a celeb but we had yet to find out who it was. Rumour had it, there was very likely to be a TV docu-series being filmed there soon, following its progress from ramshackle ruin to magnificent manor. It used to be known many years ago, all around the county, for its splendid, landscaped gardens which were open to the public and it was hoped that they would also be restored to their former glory.

'Yeah, it would be nice, but way too big a job for me, I think. If it was just me doing the re-upholstering, I think it would take me an age.'

'That's a shame, something like that would be wonderful for your portfolio.'

'Yeah, well maybe it's just not the right time for me. I honestly couldn't cope on my own. It's OK for Clem. He's got loads of mates in the same industry so they've put together a joint proposal.'

'That's a great idea. Who knows, maybe something will come of it for you.'

'Yeah, it would be amazing but I'm not holding much hope.'

'How's Clem? Is he busy?'

'Yeah, he's OK. He's spending a lot of time with James at the moment. To be honest with you, Mum, he's really quite taken with baby Taran. There's a bit of me thinking that he's regretting getting with someone who is too old to have children. He should really be with someone in the prime of her life, not someone who's never going to be able to give him a baby.'

'I thought you said he wasn't bothered about having children.'

'I didn't think he was but honestly, he's like a big kid himself around Taran. Sophie and Russell have had their baby too and he's always popping by to see them and drop off a present. He's obsessed.'

She was so dejected. She just wasn't herself at all. The only time I saw a flicker of joy was when she was dancing; where she seemed to cast all her troubles aside and just give in to the music. I knew it's said that dancing is therapeutic, and I definitely felt it for me, but it was evident that Meredith was also feeling it too.

'While we're talking about Clem, he told me to write a list of jobs that needed doing and he'd come and do them for me. Maybe I'll drop him a text and see if he can pop by sometime soon. Nothing massive, just some little things that I've been saving up. Unless you'd like to ask him to do them for me, darling.'

'It's probably best if you message him yourself, Mum. I'm not sure I'm his favourite person in the world at the moment.'

'Oh dear, I'm sure it's not that bad, is it?'

'Truthfully? I'm not sure right now.'

I really felt like I needed to keep an eye on her and would make sure that she was a high priority for me. I might not be able to physically help, but I was sure there was a lot I could do to mentally support her right now. There was nothing that I wouldn't do for Meredith. I just needed to work out what she needed from me.

'Anyhow, what's the plan to tackle Vi, Mum? Any ideas there?'

'Funny you should say that, I do have a plan, but don't think I haven't noticed that you've changed the subject.'

She grinned. That sense of humour was still there, it just wasn't getting much of an outing at the moment. We needed to remedy that. Vi wasn't the only one that needed a plan.

23

'She really upset me, Lydia.'

'I bet she did.'

I was feeling so sorry for Dennis. This didn't sound like Vi at all.

'It was like all she rang me for was to tell me I was fat and needed to lose weight. She didn't have anything else to say.'

Something else must be going on with Vi. I just knew it. And now, I was even more determined to get to the bottom of it. She was never one to mince her words, claiming that at her age she could say what she liked, but she wasn't normally so openly rude to people. Certainly not to those who she loved.

I was glad that I'd called Dennis; he sounded like he needed to offload.

'She told me that I'd clearly got a weight problem and needed to get a grip of it. Suggested things that I could do. I've never felt so humiliated and ashamed of myself in my life. An old woman fat shaming me. Whatever next?'

'Do you think there's something going on with her? Have you been inside her house lately?'

'Do you know, I haven't. The last time I went, she said that it was such a nice day she wanted to sit in the garden and have our tea out there. And she insisted on making the drinks herself and bringing them out. She wouldn't even let me in to use the loo, saying that it wasn't flushing and that she had a plumber coming out that afternoon. I did think it a bit odd at the time but then I didn't really think about it again. And after she rang me and was quite nasty, to be honest, I've hardly been in touch.'

'Mmm, it's a bit odd. Not really like her. She doesn't appear to want anyone in the house. After her accident, she seemed to be getting out and about more, but she seems to have retreated into herself again.'

'I feel awful. I don't get chance to see her as much as I should. Work is so busy. I'm being sent all around the world at the moment which I know sounds really glamorous but all I get to see are airports and hotel rooms and when I'm back in the county I'm knackered. I know I'm neglecting her but I'm not sure how to get a better work–life balance right now.'

Dennis's job was helping businesses to diversify to make them successful apparently. I was never sure exactly what that involved and he had tried to explain it to me once, but I still never understood. It went way above my head.

A bleeping noise came through the phone.

'I'm really sorry, Lydia, but that's an alarm saying I have to go into a meeting now.'

'You get off, Dennis, and as long as you're happy for us to interfere, we'll do some more digging and we'll keep you posted.'

'Thank you, Lydia. She's very lucky to have you in her life, you know. I don't think the people in my apartment block would even know me if they bumped into me in the street. To live in a community that cares about you is very special. I envy you.'

'I know what you mean, it was like that where I used to live in America. Look after yourself and stay in touch.'

Pondering on my next idea, I dropped Meredith a quick text and put my plan into place before the mammoth task of heading up to the church. I was so fed up of relying on other people to help me to get around I had decided to be brave and try it on my own. Dottie the doll hadn't been worked on for days and I was hoping to catch Martin to sort out what the next steps were to progress her restoration.

However, when I arrived, Martin was getting some things out of the back of his car and he immediately rushed over.

'Lydia, you look shattered.'

'I am actually, what seems like a short walk when I'm not on crutches is a bloody long way when I'm on them. Everything is such an effort.' He rested his hand on my back and guided me through the door and onto the nearest chair.

'You look like you could do with a nice hot, sweet cup of tea to give you some energy. I would have come to fetch you if you'd told me you were coming. You only have to ask.'

'I'm trying not to bother people.'

'Firstly, you're never a bother. Secondly, I'm not people. I'm your friend and want to help. In fact...' he lowered his head and wrung his hands, before nervously clearing his throat '...we're more than friends to each other, surely.'

My eyes widened and his expression softened.

'We're friends, family, dance partners and we work together. There isn't a name for all of that, but makes us have a pretty special relationship in my eyes.'

I rested my hand on top of his and looked deep into his eyes. 'We do.' We both smiled and after a moment of comfortable silence, he got up, mumbling that he would go and make the drinks.

When he returned, we chatted about Dottie and came up with a plan to work on her a little bit each day and I shared my thoughts about Vi with him. He was such an easy person to chat to and offered to drop me down to hers when I was feeling up to it. I would have been happy to stay with him all day but he had some errands to run so I messaged Meredith and said that I would meet her in the harbour where he dropped me off on his way out.

* * *

'Hello, Vi, how are you? Can we come in? I've hobbled for ages on these bloody things—' I wiggled my crutches '—and need a sit down.'

'Ah, well I was just about to go out actually.' Vi pulled the door behind her and much as I tried to peer into the hall, I couldn't see anything. Suddenly, there was a bark and Gladys appeared at the sound of Meredith's voice.

'Hello, beautiful.' Gladys had pushed the door open with her nose. 'Clever girl.' Meredith stroked her head.

There were boxes in the hallway, piled on top of each other. It must be like an assault course for Vi every time she walked to the front door. Taking the opportunity, Meredith gently pushed her way into the hall and headed for the kitchen.

'Please, Meredith, don't go in there. I... I...'

'It's OK, Vi, we're here to help.'

Vi hid her face in her hands and sat down on the bottom stair which was right behind her.

'Mum, I think you'd better come in here.'

When I entered the kitchen, towards where Meredith's voice was coming from, it all became apparent as to why Vi was shutting the world outside.

24

'I'm so ashamed.'

'Vi, come and sit down.'

As I led her through to the lounge through the mess, I couldn't help but look around. It didn't look like the house had seen a duster for months and it smelled fusty and damp.

'We're your friends, Vi. Sometimes in our lives, we need help more than at other times. Will you please let us help you?' I wanted to reassure her that we could stop her feeling so alone.

Meredith stood in the door, leaning on the door frame watching our exchange.

'You don't look like you are in any position to help anyone right now on those things.' Vi pointed to my crutches. 'I was just plucking up the courage to ask for some advice when you had your fall. I know what that feels like. When I was off my legs, it was awful. I've never felt so lonely to be honest and useless.'

'Yep, I do feel a bit like that, but we're lucky, you and me. We have friends and family who want to help us. Not everyone has that. We all love you and want to do what's best for you. And this —' I waved my hands around '—can't be making you feel good. I might not be able to physically do much right now, but I can help organise things to get you sorted out. But only if you'll let me. Tell me to bugger off if you want to.'

A tear rolled down Vi's cheek.

'How can I have let myself get into this mess? Look at all this lot.' She waved her arms around her. There really was a lot of stuff around. 'Please don't tell anyone else.'

'We won't but I do think you should let Dennis know.'

'Oh, my lovely Dennis. I think he hates me right now.'

'I can assure you he doesn't. I spoke to him a couple of hours ago and that's the last thing he does. He's worried to death about you.'

'Is he? I would have thought after what I'd said to him recently, he might not want anything to do with me.'

'Yes, he mentioned that.'

She put her head in her hands and began to weep.

'I couldn't help myself but I know I went about it the wrong way. He's clearly not looking after his health and the last time I saw him he was looking proper porky.'

Meredith's mouth twitched.

'Maybe I could have put it better,' Vi continued. 'Sometimes the words come out before my brain engages.'

'Welcome to my world.' Meredith sighed loudly.

I hoped that my next words might reassure Vi.

'My mum always used to say it's not what you say it's the way that you say it. Maybe just take a few seconds to think ahead of speaking. If what you are going to say is going to hurt someone's feelings, is it really kind to say it?'

'You're right, Lydia, I know you are. My husband used to say it to me all the time. I'll try. I can't promise to be better, but I can promise to try.'

I rubbed her back. Now she'd spoken about it, she seemed a little less upset.

'What I was trying to tell Dennis was that he's so important to me, the last thing I would want is for him to be poorly and miss out on so much in life. What if he became diabetic and had to live through having to inject himself every day?'

'I understand that you are worried about him. We always worry about our family, don't we? However old they are.' I looked towards Meredith who was gazing out of the window.

'But people are resilient, Vi. If that's what he has to deal with on a daily basis, he'd cope. Just like many other people have to. Right, let's stop wittering shall we? Sitting around chattering isn't helping the situation, is it? Shall we make a plan?'

Vi let out a huge breath.

'Yes please. I think we should.'

'OK, so first things first. Meredith, would you be able to have a look and see what cleaning stuff Vi has in the kitchen? And we can make a list of stuff that we need to get.'

I stood and tried to balance myself on my crutches to move across the room to where Vi was sitting. The rug on the floor made it difficult to step over. There was a big wrinkle in the middle.

'Do you really need this rug? Doesn't it make life difficult for you?'

'Yes it does. But it's been there for years and even if I wanted to, I can't get down there to get it up. My knees won't bend like they used to.'

'So are you happy for us to take it up? Do you have somewhere to store it at all?'

'It can go in the spare bedroom I suppose.'

'OK, I'll get Meredith to pop it upstairs in a bit. I bet just getting the rug out of the way will make things a little easier for you.'

'I hate being old, Lydia. I feel like I'm giving up and I don't want to. I've been independent since I've been on my own and I always wanted to stay that way. I feel older than ever now, not able to do things for myself. I feel like accepting help is me giving up. My mind is all there, but my body doesn't work like it used to. Bloody frustrating it is. Maybe it's my time to leave this world now and go and join my Albert.'

'Nonsense! You've got years ahead of you yet. This isn't giving up. This is giving you even more opportunity to enjoy life. Making life easier for yourself. It's only now that I've been off my feet that I've realised how difficult it is for people with mobility problems and I've found lots of solutions to help me out temporarily. It's just sensible.'

'I've never thought about it that way before.'

'Well, maybe you could try. None of us know how much time we have on earth. Life is precious and can be snatched away at any time, whether you are eight or eighty, so it's up to us all to make the most of it and enjoy it. And if we can help you to do that with a few tweaks here and there, then that's what we shall do. With your permission, of course.'

Meredith came back into the lounge.

'Yes, we're only going to do what you're happy with, Vi. We're here to help, not bulldoze you into doing things you don't want us to.'

'Vi, how do you manage with those steps down into the kitchen?' I enquired. I struggled myself.

Vi huffed out loud. 'Not bloody easily.'

'What about if I asked Clem to put a grab rail on the wall, would that help?' Meredith was always great at finding solutions.

'Oh God, yes. I did think about that only a few weeks ago and how helpful it would be to have something to hang on to.'

'That's something else we can do then. Make a list of things like that for us, things that could help you.' Meredith grabbed a pen and an empty envelope off the sideboard and asked Vi if she could use that.

Vi nodded and smiled at us both.

'You're so alike, you know, you two.'

Meredith and I locked eyes and smiled.

'I like that,' she whispered.

'Me too,' I replied.

25

When we came away from Vi's, we had a firm plan. Meredith and I would go back the following day. Meredith would start cleaning, and I would start to help Vi go through some paperwork and do a general declutter of her house to make life easier for her to manage. While I wasn't physically able to help much, and poor Meredith would take the brunt of all the hands-on work, I was determined to get stuck in.

I gave Dennis a quick call to update him.

'Oh, Lydia, thank you. You're so kind to help her in this way. I'll come over at the weekend too and get stuck in with you. Sod work. I'll tell them that I have a family crisis. This has made me realise that it's only there to pay the bills, and that working my socks off for a company and not spending time with the family that I do have, is not worth it. My family is too precious to not make them a priority. I'll get in touch with Lucy and James and see if they have a room free at the B&B. You're a star, Lydia. I'll let you know when I am planning to arrive.'

'Before you go, Dennis, I just wanted to pick your brains.

There was a really old tatty teddy bear at Vi's that she was quite loath to throw away. Do you know what I'm talking about?'

'Oh yes,' he replied enthusiastically. 'That's Theodore. He was a gorgeous old stuffed teddy bear, gifted to Nan from her parents on the day she was born. He's so old but Nan let me play with him when I was younger as long as I promised to be extra careful. Nan was livid and then upset when Gladys as a puppy, chewed one of its ears off. He's quite a sight these days as he only has one eye and he looks a little "naked" with his fur practically worn away in several places. Oh, I'd forgotten all about Theodore. Gosh, that brings back some memories.'

He thanked me again before ending the call and my mind was working overtime thinking about maybe restoring Theodore too.

I felt like I'd really done some good today. Helping others is a really good way to feel better yourself. I needed this as I was beginning to feel quite morose, being useless off my feet. More and more, helping people was making me feel that I could make a difference to others and that in turn was making a difference to me, bringing that joy factor back into my life that Martin had spoken of.

* * *

That evening I sat on a chair in the church, watching Meredith and Martin dance. It was painful to not be taking part, but hopefully, it wouldn't be too long before I was back on my feet again. At least I was able to make myself useful by operating the music on Martin's iPad and speaker system and keeping time out loud so they didn't have to.

Watching Martin twirl Meredith around the dance floor made me sad that it was her instead of me, but also happy at the same time. They had a wonderful relationship. He and Clem were similar in so many ways, in mannerisms as well as looks, although being older, Martin was craggier but in a handsome older man way. Some men aged well and others didn't. Martin was definitely in the former category.

I wondered what his wife was like. When anyone talked about her, it was with such fondness and love. Her family and friends all very obviously adored her. I must remember to ask about her more. A widow friend of mine in America used to say that her friends were scared to mention her husband, as if it reminded her that he wasn't there any more. She also said that she wasn't ever likely to forget and that it was more upsetting that people didn't include him in conversations. She loved talking about him.

There weren't too many disasters and Meredith seemed to be enjoying herself, with lots of laughing out loud when they got the steps wrong and lots of whooping when they got them right. We called it a day and when Meredith asked us to show her what we'd done on the doll so far, Martin and I acted like Dottie's proud parents. I mentioned Theodore and Martin said he would definitely have a look and see if there was anything he could do.

Martin invited us to the pub for a quick pint before dropping us both back, neither of us wanting to be too late as we had a busy day at Vi's the day after.

'Oh, you two, I could cry, honestly. You've made a massive difference already and Meredith, look what you've done to my kitchen! There were so many things on the worktops before. Where on earth have you put them?'

Meredith smiled. 'I've put the things that you said you use all the time in places where they'll be easier to reach and the things you don't use much in the cupboards which are lower.'

'Oh, Meredith, you're a genius.'

'Not really, but I am practical. I've bought you a mug tree, so you don't have to reach into cupboards and you can put your favourite mugs at a decent height. It's just little things like that. I hope you get on OK with it all. Just let me know if it's not workable once you start cooking and doing things in here though and we can rearrange them.'

'Amazing.'

'I should probably also tell you that I've thrown quite a lot of out-of-date food away too. I found a tin of corned beef that said it was best before 1987.'

'Oh I wondered where that had got to. It's only a recommended date, you know. I'm sure it would have tasted fine.'

Meredith looked at me and I rolled my eyes.

'Well, I'm glad to say there'll be no salmonella sandwiches on my watch.' She laughed. 'All the things that you said you didn't need I've put to one side and will give them to Gemma to take to the soup kitchen to see if they're of use to them. That all OK?'

Vi flung herself at Meredith.

'How can I ever thank you? I'm such a silly old woman. It's lovely to think that some good might come from my things, instead of me throwing stuff away.'

'You're not silly at all. I'm sure if you came into my house, you'd see things different to me.'

'Well, you can rest assured that I won't be going up all those stairs in your home until you put a stair lift in!'

'If I ever put a chair lift in there, I'll be charging admission fees and calling it a fairground ride, but you'll be first for a spin, I promise.'

As well as a long list of things that Clem could help Vi with –

putting shelves up, including grab rails here and there and even putting the dog bowls higher up, we'd already done some simple tasks. Meredith was able to move some of the smaller items of furniture around and removed other hazards like stuff on the stairs, and a runner in the hall. There was still much we felt that could help and I said I'd go away and do some research on things to make life easier. There were probably things around that we could all use. Life should be as easy as possible for any of us, whatever our age.

Maybe a countertop dishwasher would save Vi standing at the sink. A stool in the kitchen so that she could perch on it for any times she needed to be stirring things. Meredith even suggested that an air fryer would be more economical as well as easier than using the oven. And Vi had finally agreed with our suggestion of getting a cleaner, once we'd managed to get on top of everything. Slowly, she was coming round to our way of thinking that it wasn't giving in, it was being practical and giving herself a really good quality of life.

'You and your mum are wonderful. Thank you both. Hopefully now you've helped me, I can keep on top of everything some more. It was just such a daunting and huge task to tackle on my own. And I promise not to hoard stuff any more.'

'Yeah, you didn't really need those one hundred and twenty-seven carrier bags and seventy-five plastic margarine tubs, did you?' We all laughed when Meredith brought this up.

'We laugh, but remember I come from a time where things were rationed and we didn't have much. We had to hang on to everything we had just in case it might come in handy.'

'Yeah, but did you really need that many of each, Vi?'

'You just never know, my dear. You just never know.'

She pulled us both to her for a hug. There was nothing to her, she was so slim these days.

'Are you eating, Vi?' I asked.

'I've not had much of an appetite, and to be honest, I didn't want to eat anything that was cooked in that kitchen. I thought I might catch something nasty. But you could eat off the floor now.'

'Well, there's no need for that. The plates are well within reach now.'

Leaning against the kitchen door before we left, I watched Meredith with Vi. In that moment I was sure she would have been absolutely brilliant with my mum, her grandma. I wished with all of my heart that I'd made more effort to spend time with them both. I'd missed out on so much.

I swallowed a lump in my throat. Regret was painful.

Martin arrived at mine later that afternoon. There were a number of things that I would need his help with too.

After he'd watched me make a cup of tea, we sat in the conservatory.

'I wish you'd have let me do that.'

'I know, love. I could see how much you were wincing while you were watching me.'

He smiled back at me.

'I just want to help, Lydia. You don't have to be so independent all the time. Anyhow, you said you'd got some bits and pieces for me from Vi's. What you got?'

'The carriage clock on the mantelpiece has apparently stopped working and because it was a present for Vi and Albert's twenty-fifth wedding anniversary, she was quite upset about it. There's a music box that's stopped playing music and then there's Theodore, that I mentioned to you. Between us, I'm sure we could try to get some of these precious possessions repaired and back to their former glory to put a smile back on Vi's face. You up for a challenge, my friend?'

Martin loved a challenge. I'd learned this about him over the last year or so. I knew he wouldn't be able to say no to me or Vi, but I let him think that the decision was his. Something I'd learned to do with my many husbands over the years.

Eventually, he nodded. 'Yep! I am indeed.'

'You're a very kind man, Martin Penrose.'

'Thank you, ma'am. You're not so bad yourself.'

I smiled, and looked out to sea.

'Aren't we lucky, Martin?'

'How so?'

'Well, we live in a community that looks out for each other. Some people live in huge towns and cities where they don't even know their neighbours, let alone help them. Just giving some of our time to our friends can really make a difference. Be life-changing even.'

'That's very true. If people thought of others more often and gave up just a little bit of their time, then yes, lives can absolutely be improved. Driftwood Bay does seem to be a place where people really care about the community. We are lucky, Lydia, you are right.'

'Maybe it's easier for us because we're older and have more time to spare. Maybe it's because we're happier in our lives, that makes us want to do more for others.'

'Yes, maybe. But look at Gemma. She's running a busy bistro, helping her sister as much as she can, helping Occy to become a young woman and making time for Jude too, and still finds time to volunteer at the homeless shelter.'

'I suppose it's all about priorities, isn't it? It's about having time or finding it. We all have that same number of hours in the day. It's about making time in the hours you have. And you can either do something for yourself or something for someone else. I just wish people thought of others a little more, then the world would be a much better place.'

'Very philosophical, Lydia. And I reckon that we'll have finished the lovely Dottie very soon too. Agree?'

'I do, I can't wait to meet her owner. How about you give her a call and arrange for her to come over on Friday?'

He made the call and the owner's excitement could be heard from my side of the room. She wouldn't have much longer to wait for her slice of joy.

'Any more tea in that pot, Lydia? I think we should celebrate.'

26

'You've got such a huge heart, Meredith. How do I deserve you?'

'Mum, you don't have to say that just because you are bossing me around, you know.'

I laughed. She really had a wonderful sense of humour. It wasn't often that I thought about her father, and I drifted off to another place, wondering what he was like as a person and whether she was like him.

'Hellooooo! Mum! Are you listening?'

'Sorry, darling, what did you say?'

'I said, isn't it funny how all this happened with Vi when you were laid up! It couldn't have happened when you were physically able to do anything.' She laughed again.

'Well, you know I don't like the thought of breaking a nail.'

'Gosh, good job I didn't have that problem when I started doing the lighthouse up. My hands have never worked so hard or been so disgusting. I wish I'd thought about those things now!'

I stood and looked at her, drinking in her natural beauty, with her hair tied up in a topknot, in jeans and a T-shirt, trainers and her arms encased in bright pink rubber gloves. For a woman in her early fifties, she looked amazing, and a lot of the time far younger than her years. Today, she was having one of those good days; her eyes were bright and she was bursting with energy. I hoped that with a little help from the doctor she'd be feeling like this a lot more often. I pondered whether I should remind her to make an appointment. I didn't want to nag or interfere and I know she didn't take it lightly.

'However, I think after everything I – well, Clem and I – did on the lighthouse, tackling Vi's house is a walk in the park.'

A sleepy woof could be heard from the hallway and a little face peered at us from the door.

'Sorry, Gladys. I know I said the magic W word. I'll take you out on the beach later when I take Alice. I know you're still here, don't worry. Ooh, big stretch. Good girl.'

I looked at her and laughed. 'You don't say that to me when I do my stretches.'

'Sorry, darling. I'll remember that for next time.' We grinned at each other. 'Right, what's next?'

Scanning the list, she said that the lounge was next.

'Dianne will be here any minute to pick Vi up and take her to the café so we can get cracking. Then she'll come back and give us a hand.'

Vi was sat looking at the boxes on the table, shaking her head.

'What do I do with all this stuff? I've got full dinner services here that I'll never use again but they're too good to throw away. It's such a dilemma. These are all my memories. What do I do?'

'How about you take photos of everything you don't use any more. When Dennis comes over at the weekend, perhaps he can pop some of the things that you want to keep in the loft and the stuff that you want to donate to someone else; we can maybe put it on the village Facebook group and see if anyone could use it.

You know, I bet Lucy would love some of the crockery for the B&B, or even Gemma for the café. And we can print all the photos off for you and put them in an album and you can look at them anytime. Is that a rubbish idea or a good one? I'm not sure any more.'

'Oh, Lydia, that's a marvellous idea. Imagine if one day I walked into the café and saw my things being used. Or even at the B&B, the thought that someone else could enjoy them too. Now that would make my heart happy.'

'And your heart being happy is exactly what we want more of, Vi,' I said, 'so let's crack on and I'll drop Lucy and Gemma both a text to see if there's anything that they could use.'

'You are wonderful, you know.'

'Oh, and tomorrow afternoon Meredith and I are going to pop into Nancy's bookshop if you fancy coming with us.'

'It's lovely to see you not letting that ankle stop you doing stuff, Lydia.'

'You can't keep a good woman down. I'm back at the doctor's later this week so hopefully he'll tell me that everything is mending well and I'll be sprinting round the harbour in no time. Meredith can get back to her life. I'm already stealing so much of your time from you at the moment. I don't want Clem falling out with me.'

'I doubt that he'll be that bothered,' she muttered, turning away but both Vi and I clocked it. We looked at each other with 'what's-going-on-there-then' expressions on our faces. I would definitely have to do some more digging around. A love like theirs didn't come round that often and I'd hate to see it go sour, when they both clearly adored each other so much. I wondered whether Clem had said anything at all to his dad. Maybe I could try to see if Martin knows anything.

'Actually, while I'm there, maybe I'll make an appointment to see the doctor.'

'About your mood swings?' Vi asked innocently and I couldn't help but smile and turned away to take a sip of my glass of water, so Meredith couldn't see. 'Or have you got a dry fanny?' I splurted the water out of my mouth and started to cough as everything went down the wrong way and threatened to come out of anywhere that had an opening.

'Oh my God, Vi, really?' Meredith was now bright red in the face but for different reasons to me.

'Well, I presume you're on about that menopause shite that everyone is on about these days. Can't turn the telly on without them talking about it. In my day, you kept schtum and if you had a dry fanny you just spat on your hand and gave yourself a wipe down there! I've lost count of the times my Albert told me to stop being such a miserable bitch. We just got on with it. These days, you have companies giving women a room to go and have a lie down if they feel tired. A lie-down I tell you! Bloody ridiculous! Just looking for trouble and inviting people to take the piss if you're asking my opinion.'

'Well, lucky for the world that we didn't ask for it, our darling Vi.'

I was laughing that hard that I had to sit down. Tears were streaming down my face and Meredith, thank goodness, saw the funny side and a laugh erupted from her too. Within seconds, we were both crying and holding our sides.

'Oh, it's good to laugh, Vi.'

'You won't say that when you're my age and you do a little tinkle when you titter! Or a trump. Or worse! Once I...'

'No!! We don't want to know!'

'I was only going to say that sometimes, your teeth fly out. You won't be thinking it's so funny when your teeth end up on your mantelpiece! It's all about concentrating on keeping things inside your body when you get to my age. And you girls these days think menopause is hard.'

That just set us off again. Vi was incorrigible. She knew exactly what she was doing when she said these outrageous things and her eyes were bright and crinkly.

There was a knock at the door and a yoo-hoo from Dianne came echoing up the hallway.

'Thank God you're here, Dianne. You can bring some decorum to the conversation. Take me to the café, these pair are being quite rude and laughing at me.'

'Oh yes, come on then, poppet. I'll be back soon to help you and you can tell me what on earth has been going on here.'

Wiping tears away from our eyes, Meredith and I went back to the list.

27

Dianne, Meredith, and I worked in harmony, the radio playing in the background, and we sang along decluttering where we could and cleaning where we couldn't.

Doing this spring clean of Vi's house today made me realise just how much we took for granted and that old people who wanted to stay living in their own homes, really did need help.

'I couldn't help but open the wardrobe, Lydia, to see if there was any room for any of the stuff that's lying around. She's got blooming tons of clothes, you know. Packed full it is.'

Another thing I adored doing was nosing in people's wardrobes and looking at their clothes. Every item of clothing held a special memory for the owner, an important occasion maybe, or an everyday reminder of a life lived. Especially someone of Vi's years. I bet the clothes she had stashed away could tell a story or two.

When I was a little girl, there was nothing I loved more than going to my grandmother's house and dressing up in her clothes, entertaining the family as I came downstairs dressed as 'Nan'. It would make her howl.

As I ran my fingers over the clothes in Vi's wardrobe, wondering about the memories that were stored there, my hand stopped at a white lace gown sheathed in a transparent garment bag. Curiosity made me reach up and remove it, a desire to study it closer, and as I unzipped the bag, the scent of cologne and nostalgia filled my senses. I shuffled closer and hung the coat hanger over the top of the wardrobe door. As a five-time bride, I'd seen more than a wedding dress or two in my day but I could honestly say that in all my years, I had never seen a garment as beautiful as this one.

'Ah, my wedding gown.'

I turned to find Vi in the doorway.

'I'm so sorry, Vi, you must think me terribly nosy. I didn't mean to snoop.'

'Snoop away, my love. That dress was the finished product of weeks of my mother's hard work. Beautiful, isn't it?'

My fingers caressed the material. I had always been a tactile person and as a child was always told off for touching things that I wasn't meant to but it was my way.

Vi moved across to the dressing table where she lifted a photograph and handed it to me with a smile.

'My wedding day. We'd have been married sixty-five years today you know. And seventy-five years since the day we met at school.'

The hand not holding the photograph rested on my heart.

'Why didn't you tell us? It's such a special day.'

'I don't know really. I suppose it doesn't seem real. And I just celebrated with a cup of tea and a full English breakfast. My Albert would have approved of that I can tell you.'

'You are so beautiful in this photo. Look at you both. And this dress. It's magnificent. Your mother was so gifted.'

'Ah, do you know my lovely mum spent hours and hours sitting up late at night individually hand-sewing every single one of those beads on that bodice. Gorgeous, isn't it? Don't look too closely though, Lydia. It's moth-eaten in a couple of places around the bottom. Heartbroken I was when I saw it. It might even be worse now. It's been a while since I had it out of the wrapper and there's a bit of damage at the back too.'

'May I?'

Vi nodded her approval so I carefully teased the dress from the garment bag and let it unravel, the delicate lace bodice perfectly complementing the luxurious silk skirt which rippled like a gentle waterfall until the folds fell into place. I studied the hem and sure enough there were some holes, where clearly it had been eaten away. As I turned it around to examine the back, I could see that the silk skirt had come away from the bodice. What a shame. It was such a stunning garment and I knew how I felt when a precious item got damaged. I was inconsolable when I first discovered my dance dress was ruined.

I caressed the fabric with my fingers. It was very similar material to that which I had restored Dottie the doll's dress. My heart began to pound and my brain started to whir as I tried to remember how much of the fabric was left in the workshop.

'Have you ever looked at getting it repaired at all?'

'I didn't think anything could be done so I've never bothered. Why? Do you think it could be mended?'

Not wanting to get her hopes up, I tried to keep my excitement in. I had sat beside my mother for so many years, watching as she repaired our clothes and even took in some of her friends' and neighbours' too. I sat as she lovingly created my crimson dance dress. And even though the other girls in my class bought theirs, mine was the most beautiful one, fondly hand-stitched all the way. I was feeling quietly confident that I could make this wearable again. The risk was huge but the result, if it worked, might be worth the gamble.

'I suppose I could take a look at it for you?'

Her hand went to her chest. 'Really?'

'I can't promise anything but I can take a closer look once I get it under decent light. Maybe Martin would take it up to the church for me and I could examine it under a magnifying glass. At least that way we'll know what's involved and whether I can do something with it.'

'Oh, Lydia. You are my fairy godmother. If you could take a closer look that would be amazing. I'd lost all hope of it ever being worn again. Silly really but I always dreamed that it would be passed on throughout the family. There's only really Dennis and his future wife now that would ever use it. There's no one else.'

'I didn't realise Dennis had a girlfriend.'

'He doesn't. Dozy dipstick works all the time and doesn't have time to find himself anyone. Or should I say he hasn't met anyone yet who has made him want to work less than he does. And even if he did, what's to say that they'd ever want to wear a silly old woman's wedding dress? I live in hope that he'll meet someone lovely. It's been such a while since he's had a love life. Well, one that I know of anyway. Bless him. I wish he would find someone. Maybe one day...'

'Who knows what the future holds for any of us?'

I reached to my chest and rested my hand there. What I hadn't shared with anyone was that I was going to the doctor tomorrow. They wanted to discuss the results of my recent tests and had requested an in-person appointment. I'd felt permanently sick since I'd had the call earlier that morning and especially when they asked if I could go tomorrow. Surely if everything was OK, they'd have said. Would the universe be so cruel as to wait for me to be properly reunited and in a wonderful relationship with my daughter before throwing an awful diagnosis at me? Just when things were very nearly perfect.

I had tried to put it to the back of my mind. Worrying about it wouldn't make any difference whatsoever but it was just there all the time. Keeping busy at Vi's was the best thing for me right now.

'Are you OK, Lydia?'

Vi's question brought me back to the present.

'Yes, sorry. Drifted off there for a mo. I'll see what I can do.'

'Thank you, treasure. What would we do without you?'

I sincerely hoped that she wouldn't have to find out.

Friday finally rolled around even though it felt like it had been forever. The throaty purr of a car engine alerted us to the fact that we were no longer alone.

'That'll be Dorothy. Come on, you, we've got a little old lady to make happy. God, I hope she likes it.'

'Are you allowed to say "God" when you're here?'

He grinned back at me. 'I've said far worse while I've been in the church, I can tell you. I never gave that a thought.' He pulled me up to a standing position.

I didn't realise how much I'd been anticipating this moment and hoped with all my heart that we'd make someone happy today.

When Dorothy's son walked her into the church, I was

surprised by how much like George Clooney he looked and it was clear that he got his looks from his mother. Dorothy was a striking-looking woman, with smooth silver bobbed hair and wearing a classy royal blue trouser suit with a camisole top and a silk scarf tied loosely around her neck. She must have been an absolute beauty in her youth. She looked a little nervous and walked slowly up the path towards the gate, a little unsteady on her feet, as she held on to her son's arm and looked around. He looked at his mother with such love in his eyes and I knew that these people were something special.

'Do you know, Martin, I was thinking after I came here the other day, it's such a travesty that a church like this is not operating as a church any longer, but how super that you are using it for such a wonderful purpose.' She enunciated her words precisely. 'And who do we have here then?'

I stepped forward. 'Hello, I'm Lydia and I've been helping Martin bring your doll back to life. I do so hope that you think we've done you justice.'

'Well, it's lovely to meet you, Lydia. You know that I'm Dorothy and this is my son Graham.'

Graham smiled and it struck me again just how handsome he was. 'Mum hasn't stopped talking about the doll for days. I know you won't be able to get her working again but just a good clean-up will make Mum so happy.'

'I think we've done better than that.'

Martin offered Dorothy his arm.

'Not far to go now, just over here.' He took her from Graham and led her over to a bench with a chair by the side of it and invited her to take a seat. The doll was on the table but covered by a ruby red velvet blanket. 'Now are you ready?'

She put her hand to her throat and took a deep breath and then nodded.

'Ta-dah!'

Dorothy held her hands to her mouth and stifled a cry. 'Oh, my golly gosh.'

'Is that a good golly gosh?'

Dorothy stood and approached the table. Her hands were unsteady as she reached out and put her hand up to the doll's face and gently stroked her cheek.

'Oh, my darling, Dottie. You are beautiful again.'

My heart soared when I realised that the doll clearly had the same name. It was no wonder they had a deep connection.

She turned to Martin and tried to say something but couldn't seem to find the words.

Graham spoke instead. 'Did you know that Dottie is seventy-five years old?'

It was my turn to gasp. The doll was older than me. That made me realise just how precious she was.

'Oh my! Martin, you never told me that.'

'I didn't think you needed that kind of pressure, and to be honest, I wanted to let you find out yourself.'

I turned to Dorothy, who seemed to have calmed down a bit more now. 'She must be very important to you, Dorothy.'

Dorothy seemed to have calmed down enough to tell me her story.

'Dottie was a birthday gift to me on my tenth birthday. She was my parents' last hope for me.'

I tilted my head, my eyebrows furrowed.

'When I was nine years old, I had an accident. I was trampled on by a horse. Horses were part of our family life as we lived on a farm. But I became afraid of them, and we'd taken on a feisty old stallion who wasn't at all happy at being cooped up. I went in to clean his stable one day with my mother and something spooked him. We never knew what it was, but he went berserk, rearing up and kicking out. He kicked me and then trampled on me. My mother was beside herself trying to rescue me and got knocked unconscious in the process. My father was out of the country for work and it wasn't until one of the farmhands came looking for us that we were found. He called for help and we were both taken to hospital.'

She was wringing her shaking hands; the incident clearly still affected her all these years later.

'After hours of surgery – a nerve had been severed in my spine – I was told that I'd never walk again. That I'd be confined to a wheelchair. We were all distraught obviously. After weeks of being stuck in hospital alone, I became more and more depressed and refused to get out of bed for weeks on end. I just didn't want to live. All my friends were running round playing at school and I'd be stuck in a wheelchair for the rest of my life. I did go to school a few times but it was clear that I would never fit in again. I remember saying that I may as well be dead.

'After months of my parents trying and failing to encourage me to get out of bed, we had a change of doctor and he suggested something contentious. My dad called him a quack but my mama would have tried anything to get me to come back to life. For my next birthday Mama and Papa bought me Dottie. She was a walking doll and they hoped that she might help me.'

A tear escaped my eye and I tried to wipe it away inconspicuously. This tragedy hadn't happened to me, yet I was the one getting upset.

'Put simply, Dottie rescued me. She rescued me then and I wanted to rescue her back, so what you've done to bring her back to life is truly wonderful. She was my friend when I didn't have anyone else and just gave up. She brought me back to life.'

'Wait, Dorothy. The best is yet to come.'

She looked at Martin, confusion showing on her face.

'Would you like to see her walk?' he asked.

Dorothy clutched her chest and gasped, eyes wide.

'She can walk? Can she? Can she really?' Her whole body began to shake.

'Watch.'

Martin placed Dottie at the edge of the workbench and pressed a button on her back. She slowly came to life and walked across the bench.

'Oh, my darling girl. You can walk again.' Dorothy's breath caught as she started to sob.

There were tears all round. Dorothy was clearly overwhelmed that Dottie had been restored fully. She lifted the doll to her chest and held her to her heart. We were all in bits. Martin got a hanky out of his back pocket and gave his nose a good old blow. The noise broke the silence and we all laughed.

'You've brought back some many wonderful memories to me. How can I ever thank you for what you two have done? What a wonderful team you make. Tell me what you did.'

I went to put the kettle on while Martin explained how he'd had to take Dottie apart to get to the walking mechanism, clean it all up, do some soldering of parts, and then put her back together again. He described how I'd lovingly cleaned her body with a flannel and carefully washed her hair and got her back to the beautiful face that she would have been all those years ago, before dressing her in her new outfit, edged with bits of the original lace dress.

'You clever girl.' Dorothy flung herself at me and clung on tightly. 'You two honestly don't know what this means to me. Thank you from the bottom of my heart. I will never forget what you've both done.'

'My grandma bought Dottie for Mum to try to see if they could use her to teach her to walk again. And that's exactly what she did. She helped her to recover both physically and mentally. Mum wanted to pass her on to my daughters now they're old enough to appreciate her but when we fetched her out of the loft recently, we discovered that she'd seized up. Dottie that is. Not Mum. Don't worry, we don't keep Mum up in the loft.' He winked at me, clearly someone with a great sense of humour. 'She was devastated so I did some asking around and was recommended this fella here.' He pointed at Martin. 'You're amazing you know. You have truly worked wonders and we're so very grateful to you. Money doesn't seem to be enough to pay you. How can we ever thank you properly?'

'It's our pleasure. Lydia played a huge part too. And I'm sure she feels the same and that just seeing Dorothy's face is payment enough.'

Graham handed an envelope to Martin and he put it on the bench. He then reached across and gave Martin a hearty hug before coming round to me and giving me a more delicate embrace.

'Thank you both so very much. This really does mean the absolute world to us. Thank you again.' He held his hands to his heart. What a lovely, sincere family these people were from.

As we stood at the church gate, waving them off, for the first time in a long time, I felt a real sense of achievement. Emotional satisfaction, right deep down inside my heart. Maybe after all these years of searching, I'd finally found my purpose.

'I'm buzzing. I just know how happy we made her. That doll and her legacy will live on in that family and passed down for generations to come. I hope they'll always know the story of Dottie and what an important part she played in their family history. And how just one small thing can change something so huge. If Dorothy's mother hadn't listened to the doctor and given the doll a try, it would have been a whole different story.'

'It sure would. So, was this a one-off then, Lydia? Have you had enough of helping me? Or do you fancy sticking around for more?'

'Try and stop me! What's next?'

28

Meredith collected me on her way to the doctor's and as we chatted in the waiting room, I felt a little guilty that she thought I was there about my ankle when it was about something completely different. Meredith's name was called first by the receptionist and when she came out she was smiling.

'You look brighter, darling. That looks hopeful.'

'Yes, absolutely. I told him I'd done all my research and explained about my symptoms. He didn't think I was mad, Mum. I'm so pleased.'

'That's wonderful, Mere. So, what's the next steps?'

'The nurses are going to take some blood and checks first, but all being well I can try HRT.'

'Let's hope that they get results back quickly then and you can get started. You'll be feeling like yourself in no time.'

'That would be so nice. That's exactly what I need. Thanks for giving me a kick up the backside to get here. I really do appreciate it.' She leant across and kissed my cheek as the receptionist called my name.

* * *

'Come on in, let's take a look at that ankle first, shall we?'

The doctor frowned as he looked at the bruising and I nearly shot out of the chair when he touched it.

'Have you been resting like I advised?'

'Well... kind of. A bit I suppose, but I'm busy and I've had things to do.'

'Mrs Robinson, do you remember me telling you that you needed to look after a badly sprained ankle more than you do a broken foot?'

'I do. But I...'

'I'm sorry but there has to be no but. I'm afraid that you've put yourself even further back.'

'What? Surely not. I can't have done. I have a dance competition soon.'

'You will not be fit to even walk if you don't rest it like you've been told, Mrs Robinson. It is now imperative that you do as I say. Unless it's absolutely necessary, you are to keep off this ankle and there is absolutely no way that you are going to be able to compete in a dance competition.'

I dropped my head into my hands. Seriously. Could this day get any worse?

Well, yes, apparently it could!

'Now regarding the other reason you came to see me. I'm sorry it's not better news, Mrs Robinson but we can confirm that we'd like to do a small operation to get the lump removed and then when we've sent it off for further analysis, we'll know a little bit more.'

I realised that he was still speaking, but I hadn't heard a word he'd said.

'Sorry, can you repeat that please?'

'Yes, are you OK, Mrs Robinson? Would you like me to get your daughter for you?'

'No!'

'Sometimes it's better to have someone with you. They hear things that sometimes you miss.'

I shook my head, feeling dazed as I placed the leaflet he'd handed me inside my jacket pocket. Had he really just told me that I had a lump that needed to be removed and investigated further? Had I heard right?

'No. It's important to me that she knows nothing of this. I presume I can rely on your confidentiality in this?'

'Of course. And I'm sorry. I know it's a lot to take in. The removal will show whether that's enough or whether further treatment is required.'

'No, it's fine. I'll be... I'm OK. Thank you, Doctor.'

As I walked from his room, I wondered how that poor young man felt, having to dish out such a mix of news throughout his day. One sentence from him could completely flip someone's life from happy to God knows what. Horror, pain, fear. I wasn't quite sure of the feeling I had right now. Numb maybe.

'You OK, Mum? You're as white as a sheet.'

'Yes, love, thanks. My ankle is just hurting a bit after being prodded and poked. I'll be fine.'

I had to swallow down a lump in my throat. Would I be fine though?

29

Going through the motions was bloody tough. I postponed our afternoon outing to the bookshop to the following day, citing discomfort as the reason why. But it wasn't the pain in my foot that was the issue. It was the pain in my heart. Keeping up the pretence of being fine was one of the hardest things I'd had to do but as I closed my front door, watching Meredith walk back to her car, I threw my crutches across the room, slid to the floor and wept. I wept for the years I'd selfishly put myself ahead of my daughter and for the years of joy that I thought we had left together and that I may never see. For the dancer that I might never be. For all the things that I thought I would have time to do and now may not. My body shuddered, shock finally settling in and I gulped in air, feeling like I couldn't breathe, trying to make sense of the situation.

I wasn't sure how long I'd been there for when there was a knock at the door. I ignored it. There wasn't a person in the world I wanted to see, or one that I wanted to see me. However, the universe clearly had a different plan, because I may have closed the door, but I hadn't thought to lock it. The handle moved and suddenly the door was bashing into my thigh.

'Dear God, Lydia. Did you fall? Let me help you? You don't look like you've fallen.'

I heard a whimper of pain and when Dianne bent to my level, and pulled me to her, the tears that I thought had finally stopped flowing came flooding back and I realised that the wailing sound was coming from me. All I could feel was a heaviness in my heart. An overwhelming sadness sapping my energy. Dianne's kindness and the soothing sensation of her rocking my body against hers released something within me and suddenly the weight of holding everything in burst free and I blurted everything out. She listened carefully while we both sat on the kitchen floor, sympathising in all of the right places. Whilst I'd previously thought her quite loud and brash, I realised that she was kind and warm. She was also just what I needed right then.

I wiped my particularly snotty nose on the arm of my blouse, released myself from her hold, and started to haul myself up.

'I think we need a cup of tea.'

'Sod a cup of tea, mate,' she answered. 'This calls for something much stronger.'

I gave a derisive laugh.

'Sadly, I'm not allowed alcohol. The doctor at the hospital warned me off it.'

'Bugger that. Doctor Dianne says that a small one won't hurt. Right, just need to pop next door? Back in a jiffy. Bear with!'

Whilst I felt emotionally spent, not having to keep all of this to myself any longer felt better. She'd left the door slightly ajar and the next thing I knew, a cold nose pressed up against my cheek and a loud sniff alerted me to the fact that I once again had company.

'Hello, Hobson, darling. Oh, thank you, I think.' I laughed

out loud as he turned around and pressed his backside up against me, eventually plonking himself on my lap.

'Make yourself at home, why don't you, Hobson? It's a good job I like you because you have no manners and certainly no concept of personal space. Urgh!' He gave me a big slobbery wet kiss.

Dianne appeared, waving a bottle of brandy at me.

'Glasses?'

'Top right, next to the fridge.'

'Ah, perfect.' She took down two large balloon glasses and handed one with a very hefty measure of brandy down to me, and stood over me.

I sipped at the warm brown liquid and it burnt my throat on the way down.

'Are you getting up, or am I coming down there?' Dianne raised her eyebrows at me. She didn't look like she actually had any intention of coming down to me.

As I lifted myself from the floor, using the cupboard to haul myself up, my phone rang. I was going to let it go to the answerphone but recognised the number.

'Hello?'

'Mrs Robinson, it's Doctor Antony.'

I felt a sense of panic sweep over me, wondering why he was calling.

He continued. 'There's been an appointment become vacant for ten o'clock tomorrow morning for a pre-assessment at the hospital. And a date for a lumpectomy next week. I wondered whether you might like it?'

'Oh.'

It seemed like the only word I was capable of at the moment.

'Well, when I say like it, you know what I mean. I have asked them to hold it for you until I confirm it with them. I always think that speed is of the essence in a situation like this.'

Panic made my heart beat faster as I imagined the desperate scenario before me.

'Are you saying that it's that urgent that I need to have this appointment?'

'I'm not. I'm saying that there's an appointment that's become available because someone has a bad cold and isn't fit enough to have the operation right now, so it's yours if you want it. Could save you several weeks of waiting for another to come through.'

I could tell that Dianne was trying to decipher what was going on from this side of the conversation. She was pulling 'what?' faces at me so I mouthed to her what the doctor was saying.

'Take it,' she replied, aloud this time. 'Get it over and done with one way or another. I'll come with you.'

'Are you sure?'

'Never been surer!'

I took a deep breath and returned my focus to the phone. 'Yes please,' I told the doctor. 'I'll take it.'

'I think that's wise, Mrs Robinson.'

'Can you do me a favour, Doctor?'

'Of course.'

'Can you call me Lydia please? You make me feel ancient!'

A little deep throaty laugh came back. 'OK, Lydia. I'll get the hospital to send the details over to you by text if that's OK. Hope it goes well and I'll be in touch.'

As I ended the call, I couldn't remember whether I'd even said goodbye. It was all starting to get a bit real right now.

30

'How are you feeling now?' Dianne asked.

'Guilty?'

'For what?'

'For keeping it from everyone.'

'How about thinking about it like this? You're not keeping it from anyone. You don't really have anything to tell them right now. You're protecting them from being worried about something that you don't know the outcome of yourself. That's all.'

'Yep, that works.'

'Come on, let's get that foot up on that footstool. If you're still planning to have Martin and Meredith here tonight to practise their dancing, despite my protests, I think you might need a cuppa and power nap to get you through.'

As she walked past, I grabbed her hand and stopped her in her tracks.

'Thank you, Dianne.'

'Ah, it's no bother. We all have secrets, Lydia.'

She drifted back off into the kitchen and I could hear her pottering around. I closed my eyes, wondering what she was hiding. Had I missed something obvious? Was this to do with Martin?

* * *

Dianne stayed for a while and it was lovely to have the company as a distraction. Thank God I'd shared with her what was happening. She really had come up trumps. When she first arrived in Driftwood Bay, I really didn't know what to expect and I must admit that I did judge her a little. This was a reminder to me not to do that again. Instead of being bold and brash, she'd surprised me by being warm and wonderful. Kind and compassionate. She was fast becoming a wonderful friend and I was truly grateful.

Having Martin and Meredith with me later that evening was pure delight. It was a beautiful evening out, so we used the garden as the dance floor. Meredith seemed happier since her visit to the doctor. Ironic really, as while her world was getting better, mine was completely in jeopardy, with this operation hanging over my head.

When the doctor gave me my news, it felt like I'd never laugh again, but it's amazing what good company and friends and family do to lift your spirits. I did laugh that evening. Lots. It was balm for the soul and my heart felt happy. Sitting watching my daughter dancing in the evening air, with the soft undulating waves in the background was only second best to being able to do it myself. If the prognosis was bad, then at least the last couple of years had been special for me and I had my peace.

Sadly, the next morning, my spirits were not the same. Bad dreams had meant that my sleep was fitful. I woke up tired, grumpy and miserable. It hit me now that I was unable to dance in the competition, the one thing that had brought me more joy

in the last few weeks than for most of my life. I needed a procedure to remove a lump which they were unaware of whether it
was life-threatening or not. I felt like I'd been kicked in the teeth
and that life was treating me really unfairly right then. Without
giving it too much more thought, I picked up my dance shoes,
my scarlet dress and my journal and hobbled with them under
my arm and dumped them in the skip on Celia's drive before
knocking to let Dianne know I was ready to go to the hospital. I
wouldn't be needing any of them again. In fact, since they'd
arrived I'd had nothing but bad luck. Hopefully they would be
buried under other junk of theirs that would be thrown away
and I could forget all about them. Maybe history didn't heal the
future. You couldn't rewrite the past no matter how hard you
tried.

'Oh, you're early.' Dianne answered her door, pulling a
cardigan around her shoulders. 'Give me two minutes and I'll be
with you. You OK, love? All ready?'

'Ready as I'll ever be.'

We pretty much drove to the hospital in silence. I stared out
of the window for most of the journey, and Dianne seemed to
know that's what I needed and didn't try to push conversation.
She rubbed my arm reassuringly and smiled as the nurse called
me through.

'You don't have to stay, Dianne.'

She smiled, sat down and opened her book.

'I know.'

Much as I knew I wasn't great company that morning, I didn't
seem capable of making an effort to be more grateful. As you get
older, you seem to just do what your body tells you to do, rather
than falsify a situation for the sake of others.

I met the team who would be performing the operation next
week, had bruises on my arms from the blood tests they did

while I was there, had a heart and lung function test and filled in many forms. It was actually quite exhausting and that was just the pre-op checks. By the time I'd finished, and I'd hobbled back to the car, my sleepless night had caught up with me, and closing my eyes to rest them resulted in me falling asleep for most of the journey home. Dianne, bless her, had had the foresight to put a spaghetti Bolognese in her slow cooker before we went out, and she insisted that I stay with her for tea before she walked me home.

My house phone was ringing as I walked through my front door. It doesn't ring often these days so I picked it up saying hello, quite nervously wondering if it was going to be someone trying to sell me something. When I heard the familiar voice of my ex-husband, asking me how I was, it really caught me off guard and I couldn't help but crumple again. I'd held it together all day but everything came tumbling out. Poor Peter. He hadn't bargained for that, when he thought he'd give me a call to see how I was getting on. I moaned about the fact that I couldn't visit Meredith because I couldn't get up the stairs of the lighthouse. I whined about the fact that I was just about to be a surrogate grandma to Lucy's baby Taran and help them out more and wouldn't be able to do that for a good while.

It was good to have someone to share all these negative emotions I was having with. It was lovely to chat with him again and I was glad that we'd kept in touch. We'd parted as great friends, but we were not in love with each other and he knew that I needed something else to fulfil me in my life and he wanted someone to adore and pander to him. After four other husbands and heading towards my seventieth birthday, I didn't have the energy which is why he sent me off to a retreat to find myself while we set about separating our lives. It absolutely was the right thing to do at the time but hearing the familiarity in his voice, his gentle sympathetic tones, and the fact that I was feeling incredibly sorry for myself, made me miss him more than ever and question whether our decision was the right one.

In these later years of our lives, maybe companionship was enough after all. Perhaps I shouldn't have still expected the bells and whistles of young love; the pounding heartbeat and pure unadulterated lust that made your legs tremble when someone who filled you with desire only had to look at you and you couldn't wait be in their arms, lips locked together in harmony.

However, just chatting to him did make me feel slightly more uplifted. He could always tell when I was feeling low and also knew how to make me laugh and I did put the phone down that evening feeling slightly better in myself. Pouring my heart out to someone who knew me as well as I knew myself was different to talking to Dianne. There was still so much about me that I held back from her, I'd not long met her so wasn't going to share my life story with her. Yet Peter knew everything about me that there was to know, so I held nothing back. I slept better that night, and after bearing my soul, I felt a little lighter. Maybe a problem shared was a problem halved after all.

31

'I'm coming,' I yelled from the conservatory. These bloody crutches of mine meant that it took me ages to get to the door. Most of the time, I left it unlocked so people could walk straight in, but this was clearly someone I didn't know. When the knock came again, I yelled even louder in an exasperated voice that left the offending door knocker in no doubt that they had infuriated me. I couldn't go any quicker if I tried.

When I flung the door open, I couldn't have been more surprised.

'Oh! My! God! What the hell are you doing here?'

'Is that any way to greet your favourite ex-husband?' Outstretched arms greeted me and I fell into their familiarity, breathing him in.

'Well, if one of my favourite ex-husbands had informed me two days ago when we last spoke that they were likely to turn up on my doorstep, I might have been more affable. I also might not have been in my dressing gown with no make-up on and bed hair. Seriously though, Peter. Why are you here?'

'Speaking to you on the phone the other night made me

realise something. I've missed you, girl. You were really low and I wanted to come and cheer you up and two, so I thought I'd surprise you. Now are you going to invite me in or not? I'd love a cup of English breakfast tea.'

As I pulled the door to, I glanced across at Dianne's house and noticed that she was just heading down to the field to feed the animals. She would have seen the scene unfolding on my doorstep, and goodness knows what she'd make of it. The last thing I wanted was to have gossip about me all around the village. I gave a little wave to show her that I had nothing to hide so hopefully it wouldn't be a big deal.

It certainly was a surprise to have Peter here. I hadn't seen him for well over a year, and in that time, his hair had got a little whiter than it was before, and he looked like he had more wrinkles. Glancing down, I noticed that he had quite a large suitcase with him and much as I wanted to know if he was planning to go off elsewhere, I was a little afraid to ask. It was strange to have him in my house. Almost like my previous world was infiltrating my present one and I wasn't totally sure how I felt about that.

Sitting and passing the time of day with Peter wasn't unpleasant but something felt a bit off. Maybe that was just how it would be when we hadn't been in each other's company for such a long time. I excused myself.

'I'm just going to take a shower. I was about to go in when you arrived.'

'OK, honey. When you come out, we can decide how we can spend the day. Maybe you can show me around this funny little village of yours.'

On behalf of Driftwood Bay, I felt a little offended and I frowned, however clearly not as discreetly as I originally thought.

'Maybe funny was the wrong word, cute. Yes, cute is more

fitting.'

If I removed myself from the situation temporarily, I'd hopefully have some time to think and ground myself again. My chakras were all over the place. I was feeling particularly discombobulated and quite grumpy at the assumption that I would drop everything at his request. I had arranged to go to the church today to look at Vi's wedding dress and see if there was anything I could do to restore it. It would have been lovely to catch up with Martin too as I hadn't seen him for a couple of days. I was hoping to chat to him about the Meredith and Clem situation which was really playing on my mind. Would I now have to change my plans?

Raised male voices from the kitchen surprised me and as quickly as I could with a dodgy ankle, I threw some clothes on and opened the bathroom door. Peter and Martin were glaring at each other from opposite sides of the kitchen table.

'What's all the noise?'

'This fella just walked into your house. I walked out of the hallway and practically bumped into him. I thought you were being robbed.'

I smiled at my guest despite feeling quite light-headed. 'Peter, this is Martin, who I can honestly say, would never steal a thing from me. He's more than likely to bring things with him. He's Meredith's father-in-law and he is a wonderful friend to me.'

'I bet he is...'

'Don't be childish, dear. Martin is also my dance partner. Well, he was till I went and did this.' I indicated to my foot.

'And might still be too if you'd rest it like people are telling you to.' He grinned back at me.

'But you can't just go walking into other people's houses. It's not right.'

'Well, firstly, as my friend, Martin would know that he could knock and come in. Even before I had a bad ankle. And secondly, it's kind of what we do around here. Doors don't really get locked. We're a community.'

'A bit strange if you ask me.'

'I didn't realise that Lydia had asked you.'

'OK, both of you, enough now. Martin, I'm sorry but my plans have very unexpectedly changed for today and I won't be able to come to the church with you.'

Peter looked very smug as he glowered at Martin. They were worse than a pair of teenagers.

'I'll get out of your hair then and will see you later at the beach.' I hadn't got the heart to say I didn't know whether I'd be able to make it tonight but I'd sort that out later. He strode across the kitchen and out of the door.

'Peter. Please do not be rude to my friends. You can't just come whisking into my life and expect everything to change because you decided to fly thousands of miles on a whim.'

He did have the good grace to look a little sheepish, but came to my side and held my arm, guiding me into the conservatory.

'Come and sit down, my love. Can I get you anything?'

'No thank you, I'm perfectly capable of managing.'

'With a little help from your friends, obviously.'

'Yes, that's what friends do.'

'I think I'm a bit cranky. Tiredness has just swept over me. It must be the long flight.' He raised the back of his hand to his forehead, never been one to hold back on a dramatic gesture. He moved towards my bedroom. 'I might just go and have a lie down.'

I pointed to the corridor which led to the spare rooms. 'There's a room that's all made up. You can go in there.'

'Not in your room?'

'No, Peter. Not in my room.'

'But the other room isn't as nice as yours.'

'And you'd know that how?'

'Oh, err, yes. Well… I went for a little wander earlier when you were in the shower. I didn't think you'd mind. And I thought it might be nice if we shared a room.'

'Oh, so you're planning to stay here then, are you? Without even asking whether that would be OK? Rather presumptuous don't you think?'

'Oh, sweets. I'm your husband. Surely we still get to share the same room. It'll be nice to be together again.'

I tutted.

'Ex-husband.' Maybe we were both a little tetchy; a break would do us good. 'Go and lie down, Peter, and we'll talk when you wake.'

As it happened, I could have gone to the church and I wished I had done, as Peter slept for four hours. When he eventually woke, I knew I was going to have to be brave and set some ground rules for this temporary living arrangement we appeared to have found ourselves in.

'Thank you for allowing me to sleep. So, what shall we do today?'

'Not sure. I had plans which have already had to change. I do have a life here, you know. You turning up out of the blue has already meant that my day has changed.'

'So tell me your plans, honey. Don't mind me. I'll just tag along.'

I raised my eyebrows.

'If that's OK with you, of course. I'm not here to cause trouble, Lydia. I wanted to be here to support you and help. I knew how down you were when we spoke and I thought that, as your friend, I could be here for you. And as your husband, that's what I promised.'

As I'd already pointed it out a couple of times this morning, I didn't feel that it was necessary right now to remind him of the significant two-lettered word 'ex' which came before husband and totally changed the context.

'So, what are we doing then?'

'Well, today I was going to Martin's workshop to do some work on a dress that needs restoring and then early evening we have a dance class and then there's a group of us meeting up at the bistro for supper before quiz night at the pub.'

'Oh, that's a shame. I was hoping that you and I might go out for dinner alone.'

'Peter, I haven't been sitting around for the last two years pining for you. I have a life here. I hope you realise that.'

'Well, I could see that when that man walked in.'

'Oh, stop being ridiculous. That man has been a very good friend to me.'

He scoffed and then held his hands up.

'Sorry. Well, hopefully, I can just slip seamlessly into your routine. Is your car insured for any driver? Maybe I can be your chauffeur for the day. OK if I go and freshen up before we go out? Shall I put my case in your bedroom?'

I nodded in response and then pointed to the corridor that led to the bedrooms. 'You can put your case in the spare room.'

'If you say so. It is wonderful to see you, you know, Lydia.'

He came towards me, wrapped his arms around me and gently kissed my cheek. It had been a while since I'd been held affectionately in this way and the familiarity of his hug took my breath away. Yes, I'd had hugs from friends and from Meredith, but it's a different type of hug from someone who truly cares about you. It made me realise just how much I missed human touch. And also, how despite loving my new life, I really had missed him.

32

By the time Peter woke up the following morning, I had gone through a multitude of emotions, from pleasure in someone sweeping in to take over my life and look after me both mentally and physically, pandering to my every need, to feeling a little suffocated. Then from seething to sheer disappointment. The whole situation reminded me of our marriage and how unhappy I had been for such a long time. Our relationship had started with Peter sweeping me off my feet, whisking me away to glamorous locations, taking me to lavish parties and completely adoring me. Then over time it changed. I remembered the occasions that I had waited around for him to come home for tea, to be told, when he arrived late, that he'd already eaten, or when he changed plans at the last minute that I was looking forward to. I hadn't realised until my time at the retreat that it was a control thing and it wasn't until I was away from him that I was able to process this; able to think about how his behaviour affected not only our marriage but also my self-confidence, which had diminished so much towards the end that I hardly recognised myself.

'Gosh, I hadn't realised how tired I was. Not the young fella I thought I was.'

'Well, I hope you are feeling better for sleeping for so long. I'll make some coffee and then could you drop me off at Vi's when you are dressed.'

'Oh, I thought we'd be spending the day together.'

'You'll have to fend for yourself for a few hours today. I promised Vi I'd go round this morning.'

Not only did I want to help her more in the house, I thought a chat with her would do me the world of good.

He rolled his eyes before he looked away, which made me even more determined to go.

'We can talk when I'm back. If Dennis is there perhaps he'll give me a lift back, but if not...'

'OK, darling.' He came over to me and gave me another lingering hug. 'You know, Lydia, I think we were meant to be together for the rest of our lives. Yes, we had a blip along the way, but companionship in our later years is all that matters surely. I'd love to muddle along with you for the rest of my life. I hope you feel the same. It makes so much sense.'

Did it?

The previous evening had been somewhat of a disaster. Martin and Meredith came to pick me up on the golf cart to take me down to the cove and Peter insisted on coming along inside it, yet complained all the way there about how bumpy it was. I tried to remind him that if it wasn't for that golf cart, I wouldn't even have been able to get to the cove. During Martin and Meredith's rehearsal, he undermined all my dancing instructions, and generally put a dampener on the whole experience. It had been a few days since I'd been along to watch them, though they were definitely improving.

When we got to the bistro, he and Martin disagreed about

literally everything, from the food to the wine and all in between; I felt like a referee. Or maybe a nursery schoolteacher would be a better comparison. They were certainly behaving like kids, squabbling and both quite territorial over me which I found completely bizarre. The quiz wasn't much better, them bickering over the answers, and I noticed furtive glances passing between Clem and Meredith when they thought I wasn't looking. The atmosphere was just off. And then, to top it off, Peter announced to the table that I was the love of his life and that he had come to rescue me. It left me completely bewildered.

When we arrived home around 10.30, he completely changed personality and was the loving, caring Peter that I'd first met. Before we went to bed he asked if he could have a word.

'Lydia, I adore you. I have missed you more in the last couple of years than I ever thought I would. I think we should get remarried and start all over again. I really do think it's the best idea all round.'

Flabbergasted by his words, I couldn't speak and he kissed me gently on the cheek and said that he would give me some time to think about it, before he took himself off to bed.

Astonished at the unexpected proposal, I hardly slept a wink all night, reliving our lives, the good times and the bad and still not quite knowing whether it was the best idea he'd ever had, or the most ridiculous one I'd ever heard in my life. Do I go back to someone because of their familiarity, because I was feeling low, or should I battle on with my new life? My mind was in turmoil.

It was a tonic to see Vi the next day. Dennis was still there, having decided to extend his stay for a few more days. He made us a drink before saying he was off to the bookshop.

'Again, Dennis? You were only there yesterday.'

'Yeah, I've discovered a love of reading again.'

'Funny that!'

She winked at me.

'Don't suppose it has anything to do with a pretty bookshop owner at all, does it?'

'Well, Nancy did say that she'd got some boxes to shift today and I said if I was passing, I'd give her a hand.'

'Oh, so you're just going to be passing then. What a coincidence. Why don't you just admit to everyone, including her, that you fancy the pants off her? Save an awful lot of time if you are upfront right from the start. Just get on with it, lad.'

'You're a meddling old woman. Whatever happened to romance?' He laughed and kissed the top of her head. 'Good job I love you, Nan.'

'Not as much as I love you.'

'If you really want to know why I'm going it's because I'm helping her with some business advice.'

'Oh, is that what you call it these days?'

'I'm pretending I didn't hear that. Lydia, call me when you want a lift home.'

'Thanks, love. That's really kind of you.'

He beamed at me and I noticed how much more relaxed he was looking now than when he arrived. Maybe Nancy was putting that smile on his face.

As the door slammed, she turned to me.

'What's up with your face then? You look like you've lost a shilling and found a penny.'

A loud and deflated sigh escaped my body.

'Come on, spit it out. I'm old and could die at any moment, you know. I haven't got time to waste these days.'

'Oh, Vi, don't say that.' I hated to think of her not being in my life as I classed her as a great friend. She would be a loss to the whole village.

'Don't worry, I'm not planning to go anywhere for a long time. I just like to be dramatic.'

Even Vi's witty repertoire wasn't able to raise a smile from me today. I had so much swirling around my head.

'I need some words of wisdom from my wise old friend.'

'Tell your Aunty Vi all about it, me darlin'.'

It all came pouring out. My worry over waiting for my results. The thought that I might die. Worrying about Meredith and what would happen to her if I wasn't around. My thoughts around Peter and how in love with him I'd once been and whether it would be better to spend my remaining years with someone who loved me, so that I wasn't lonely. She absorbed it all and closed her eyes. I waited. And waited.

'Vi?'

She opened one beady eye and glanced at me.

'I'm thinking. Don't worry, I haven't pegged it yet.'

After a minute or two, in which I did wonder if she'd fallen asleep, she suddenly bolted upright in her chair.

'I understand loneliness more than anyone, you know. When my Albert died, I didn't want to be in this world without him but then I realised that we have a duty to those who die to live our best lives because they can't. Loneliness is horrendous. People think if you're lonely that you just need to keep busy and be surrounded by people. But that doesn't fix it. Loneliness is an empty feeling deep down inside the very core of you that no amount of company can fix. People popping by and saying that you should just give them a call when you're feeling alone... it's all very kind, but it doesn't stop you from feeling that way. Having another person in your life gives you a very particular comfort, and no one else replicate that. Someone who cares about you as much as they do their selves.'

Funnily enough, as she said this, it was Martin's face that flashed into my mind and not Peter's. That was interesting.

'Much as you have history with Peter and loved him once and probably still do, it doesn't mean that he's right for you now. You can't make a decision based on nostalgia, Lydia.'

33

Those words about not making a decision based on nostalgia were the ones that were whirring around in my mind as Dennis dropped me back up to Bay View Cottage. Peter was sat in the conservatory looking out at the sea. I didn't think he'd heard me come in.

'Beautiful, isn't it?'

He turned at the sound of my voice and smiled.

'It really is.'

I knew that it was better to get everything out in to the open as soon as I could. I'd bottled up my thoughts for a while now and it wasn't helping either of us. It was only fair of me to let him know my decision sooner than later.

'We need to talk, Peter.'

'We do. I have something I want to say first if I may.'

Nodding, I took a seat on the sofa opposite observing my ex-husband. He looked nervous sat on the edge of the chair, creating space between his shirt collar and his neck with his index finger. He gave a dramatic sigh and his voice was thick with emotion.

'Darling, Lydia. Being here with you has reminded me of how much I love you. How much I want to take care of you. I know I wasn't a perfect husband, and that we've had our ups and downs but what marriage doesn't have that? If you would give me another chance, I will be the man that you want me to be.'

I bit my lip. He was putting doubts in my mind again. My mind was becoming confused again yet minutes ago I knew exactly what I wanted to say. He was making me wonder about that safe option again. Peter continued, taking my silence as an invitation to go on.

'Remember how happy we once were? We could be that happy again. More in fact. They say you never know the value of what you've lost, until you don't have it any more, and it's so true. I feel your loss as an ache in my heart. The loss of a limb. When we spoke on the phone the other evening, I knew that I had to get on a plane and come to tell you how I was feeling. To give this a shot. Please allow me... us to give our marriage another try.' He moved to my feet, knelt and grabbed my hand. 'Please?'

I hovered. This had completely derailed me. Him being here at all had completely derailed me. One minute I thought us getting back together was preposterous and the next it seemed a sensible thing for me to do. I'd been on my own for a while now but maybe I was just feeling insecure and incapable because of my injury. Would he even consider a move to Drift-wood Bay? Would he fit in here, with my friends. With my daughter. She was now a huge part of my life which I would never again give up. So many questions. It was making my head hurt.

His big brown puppy-dog eyes locked onto mine. 'What do you reckon?'

There was so much going through my mind. My silence gave him the opportunity to keep talking.

'We can pack up all your stuff and be back in the States by the end of the week.'

Woah! Did I just hear that right?

'What did you say?'

'We can pack everything up and be back within the week.'

'What about Driftwood Bay?'

'What about Driftwood Bay? It's very quaint, but it's not real life, is it? It's like everyone is permanently on holiday.'

'Isn't that the whole point though?'

'Not for me, thank you.'

My heart sank. I'd come to love Driftwood Bay and the fact that it felt like I was on a permanent holiday was one of the many things that I adored about it.

'What about Meredith?'

'Well, now you've repaired your relationship and apologised for being a shit mum, you've done what you need to do. If you want to see her, she can always come and visit. We'll only be a plane ride away.'

I obviously knew that I'd not been the best mum to Meredith in the past and that's why I was here doing all I could to make it up to her. Nobody was ever going to take me away from her again. Only death would ever part us and even if my prognosis was bad, I'd go down fighting my last breath to be here with her as long as I possibly could.

'Peter, please get up.'

I couldn't bear to see him pleading with me. My mind was made up and nothing was going to change it. I knew I was doing the right thing.

He returned to his chair. I looked out at the bay beyond. To the village that had captured my heart. But to be honest, anywhere Meredith was would capture my heart. To be able to look out and see the lighthouse from my window was both comforting and life-affirming. That she was right there in front of me all the time. Maybe when I eventually do die, this would be what it's like in heaven. Being able to watch over your loved ones still.

'I'm sorry, Peter, but I'm staying here.'

As soon as the words had left my mouth, I felt like a weight had been lifted from my shoulders. Funny how just saying a sentence out loud could be so life-changing yet life-affirming. They were just words. But words were so very powerful.

Crestfallen, he seemed to realise that he'd lost his battle to win me over as he nodded.

'I knew it was a long shot but I hoped I could persuade you. She clearly means more to you than I do.'

'It's not a competition. However, she is my everything.'

'And Martin? What is he?'

'Like I said, he is my friend. A very good one at that. He is honest and kind. A good man. I wish you'd given him more of a chance. You'd like him.'

'You've changed so much, Lydia.'

'I know. I'm excited about life. I have so much life left in me. So many things I want to do. But they're things I want to do for me. I'm no longer living my life for someone else, making their dreams come true instead of my own. I think after all these years I've finally found me.'

'You seemed so unhappy when we spoke.'

'I was unhappy. But only temporarily. I had a dance competition to practise for and I'd bloody twisted my ankle and was told I couldn't compete in it. How do you expect me to feel? Elated? I'm happier here in Driftwood Bay than I've ever been in my life. I get to spend time with my daughter. My beautiful, bright, clever, talented daughter. I'm trying to make up for the years I was away from her and want to be the mother that I've never been.'

'It looks like you're achieving that. The relationship you have is wonderful. I can see that from the short time that I've been here.'

I smiled. I felt it but it was always good to hear that someone else recognised it too. It meant the absolute world to me.

'Can we still be friends?'

'I'd like that. I hope we'll always be friends. We have history together. We just don't have a future.'

'I wish you nothing but love and happiness, Lydia. I really do.'

'Thank you. I hope you find your happiness too. I've been looking all my life for someone to make me happy. I just didn't realise that it was inside me all the time and that I just needed to find it. It was me all along.'

34

Peter had insisted before he flew back to the States that he should take me to the hospital for my appointment. I felt bad that Dianne had already offered, but she was very magnanimous and said that she was happy for him to take me.

The procedure didn't take long at all, and they were keen to get me home as quickly as possible once they knew that I hadn't reacted to the anaesthesia and before long we were home. I felt a little tender for a couple of days and he was a big help around the place, although I would have absolutely managed without him and was a little fed up of him fussing around me.

'The taxi is here, love. Are you sure you don't want to change your mind?'

I smiled. It was a huge relief to me once I'd told him that we wouldn't be getting back together, and as I waved him off to the airport, I knew that I couldn't wait to get my house back to myself. That night I slept better than I had for weeks.

* * *

Dianne was on her way out and dropped me at Martin's workshop the following day. I was determined that I would keep busy to keep my mind off getting the results and Martin's face lit up as I walked through the big old oak doors, which were propped open. It was a beautiful spring day and the blue skies and sunshine made my heart happy. I hoped that it was the start of things to come.

'He's gone.' I wanted to be upfront.

'Everything OK, Lydia?' he enquired politely.

'More than OK. Thank you for bearing with me.'

'Well, in that case, let's have a cuppa and get on with some repairs, shall we?'

He winked and headed out to the kitchen. That little skippy feeling was back in my heart. I knew that I felt something for Martin but I couldn't put a name to it. Maybe it didn't need one. It was just something that felt right. Being with him felt right. He didn't ask any more questions about Peter and I didn't offer anything more. There was nothing to be said. We were back to our familiar relationship and worked companionably side by side, one of us occasionally glancing across at the other and smiling. All felt well with the world.

* * *

Exactly one week later, I was sitting in bed reading, when the letter box rattled loudly. I hesitated before swinging my legs round off the bed and hobbling into the kitchen. My sleep had been restless with so much on my mind as well as the thundery weather we'd had. It had been stiflingly hot for days and particularly sticky and humid. We'd all said we could do with a good thunderstorm to clear the air. It certainly felt a bit fresher this morning, but the rain hadn't totally gone away.

As I sorted through the day's post, the envelope with the hospital stamp on it was the one that stopped me in my tracks.

I made myself a coffee and carried that and the envelope through to the conservatory where I propped it up against the window while I thought about how something so small could hold my fate. I ripped open the sealed part and unfolded the piece of paper. Before I read it, I looked out at the bay, with the sun battling with the grey rain clouds, threatening to overpower them, and the spots of rain that were already splattering against the windowpane, showing me who was winning. Even though I wasn't religious, I made up a small prayer begging whoever was in control of our fates to be kind to me.

I didn't realise that I was crying until a wet tear plopped on the paper.

We would like to confirm that the results from the recent excisional breast biopsy show that the tissue that was removed showed zero cancer cells and therefore, no further treatment is required. We do, however, recommend that a mammogram is undertaken in one year's time and will ensure that you are on our system to receive an appointment.

The relief I felt at that moment was intense. It felt like my heart literally fell through my body and I heard a deep guttural groan from deep within. I couldn't however, help wonder how I would be feeling should the results have not been as positive. And how many other women were waking up, around the world, opening a letter such as this but getting a completely different result. I looked up as the sun broke through the clouds and smiled as a stunning full and vibrant rainbow arced over the bay and whispered, 'Thank you.'

I jumped up, not easy when you've got a dodgy foot, a sense

of energy suddenly filling my body. I scooted to the door and managed to get round to Dianne's, waving my letter at her as she flung open her front door.

'By heck, you're a sight this morning, lady. What's that you've got there?'

'Oh, Dianne... You'll never guess...'

The ringing sound of the phone that she was holding was getting louder and louder.

'Hang on, let me just see who that is and get rid of them. Hello?' She turned as white as a sheet as she slumped down on the bench seat in the hallway, and as I listened intently to the one-sided conversation, I was trying to decipher what on earth was going on. Looking at me with wide eyes, Dianne's expression kept going from one of deep frowning, to blowing out air through her pursed lips in bewilderment. 'OK, I'll tell her and yes, we'll be over as soon as possible.'

'Whatever is the matter?'

'That was Martin. He couldn't get hold of you so he called me. It's the community centre. It's on fire.'

As we headed to Dianne's back window, me hobbling behind her, sure enough we could see billowing smoke and the occasional orange flame against the blue sky. The sound of sirens cut through the silence of the morning and the acrid smell of smoke filled the air. The community centre was next to the church and I was worried to death it might spread to the workshop and that all Martin's hard work would be ruined.

'Oh no! What on earth has happened?'

'Kids apparently. They use the grounds at night from time to time and last night's campfire wasn't put out properly and was still smouldering this morning. A gust of wind set it off, according to Martin.'

'There's only a week to go to the dance competition. Maybe if there's not too much damage Clem will be able to repair it. Surely there'll be enough time. Clem is marvellous; he can fix anything.'

'That's what I was thinking but Clem is already there. The roof was the first thing to go. And when I say go, Martin said the whole roof has gone. I'm sorry, Lydia, but they've said that there's no way that the dance competition can be held there. It will probably have to be cancelled.'

My hand flew to my chest. What was it with this blessed dance competition? There had been more obstacles in my way than I could have ever imagined. It was doomed.

35

An emergency committee meeting was called later that afternoon in Gemma's bistro. Clem burst through the door just as Jude Adams, a local fire officer as well as Gemma's partner, was relaying the extent of the damage at the centre and interrupted him.

'Sorry to butt in, Jude, but please don't worry, folks. It can still go ahead. We have a new venue.' He garbled between excited breaths.

'What the blithering hell are you wittering about, lad. Spit it out and put us all out of our misery.' Vi was never one to mince her words.

'You know I've been working over at Driftwood Manor? Well, the owner has a huge ballroom and said that if we can get it done in time, then she's happy for us to use it. I've spent the last couple of hours calling in favours from a number of mates who are tradesmen and Meredith and a couple of other people, and if we start tomorrow, we reckon we can sort it. It'll be a job and a half and it'll be all hands on deck like our own *DIY SOS* but it's doable. We can still have the dance competition.'

A cheer went around the room.

'Who is the owner, Clem?' Vi asked.

'Now that I'm not allowed to tell you, I'm afraid. But you will find out soon. At the competition in fact as they'd like to come along and are having quite a lot to do with the evening's plans along with our lovely Occy here who has been an absolute star. However, don't be asking her either, as we've all been sworn to secrecy. It will be a nice surprise though, we promise you that.'

'Well, as long as they've got lots of disco balls then that's fine by me,' Vi muttered.

My own fate was to be decided on the day of the competition as miraculously my eight weeks suggested recovery time were up on that exact day which had now come around incredibly quickly in one way, but it felt like I've been off this blooming ankle for ever.

I'd invited Martin around for a bite to eat and when he arrived, told him my plan for the evening. He was nervous about me trying to test my ankle before the doctor had approved me to, but I was adamant that it would be fine.

'But what if you bugger it up even more, Lydia. That will annoy you more than anything.'

'I won't, Martin. I'm just going to take it easy and I promise that I'll rest up straight away. I'm not taking no for an answer, so you can either help me or I'll do it another way. I will always find a way.'

'Honestly, you women never cease to amaze me.'

'Well, you'd have thought by your time of life that you'd have learnt by now we are always right.'

He smiled. 'And you'd have thought by now that you'd realise we just let you think you are. Come on, Hopalong. Let's get it over and done with.'

Without much room in my house, we could only manage a few steps but we still fitted together beautifully and danced carefully and that was all I needed to know that I could, in my own mind, go ahead. It would bloody hurt afterwards, but physically I could do it. Whether Doctor Antony agreed was to be decided when I saw him on the day of the competition. On my little roller coaster of life at that moment, I was at the top and I couldn't stop grinning. The competition was back on and as long as I got the all clear from the doc, I would be taking part. Joy was back in my heart.

* * *

Competition day soon came around. The bay had been a hive of activity for the week, with comings and goings and more vans and trucks than we'd ever seen before heading up to Driftwood Manor.

When I arrived at the surgery Dr Antony asked me lots of questions about both the recent procedure and then he poked and prodded my ankle.

'Please, Lydia, respect my position as your doctor and don't tell me what you think I want to hear. This is your wellness we're talking about. You've managed to get over one huge health hurdle recently, and you have your whole life ahead of you. So, let's not put any more in your way.'

'OK, so it does hurt a tiny bit when I've done too much, but I've done everything you said I should and I've rested it as much as I can. I haven't even practised any dances. Martin and Meredith have done it all without me. I've not been near the manor house either to help with the decorations. I was banned.'

He smirked. 'Your friends are clearly smart. And obviously want you to be well enough.'

His cold hands gently cupped my warm skin as he manipulated my ankle.

'So come on, Doc. What's the verdict?'

He ummed and ahhed, frowned a bit and then his face broke out into a huge smile.

'I say Lydiarella can go to the ball!' He grinned.

'I can?' My heart skipped a beat.

'Go and have fun. But that does not mean dance all night, Lydia. At your—' he coughed '—time of life, you can do irreparable damage to an injury like this, so I do recommend that you go and do your dance for the competition and then sit most of the evening out. Maybe one or two other gentle dances and absolutely no more than that. And rest up again tomorrow. You'll thank me for it one day, I promise.'

'I promise.' I could feel my beam reaching from ear to ear.

'There's a huge difference between dancing at a party and competing in a competition. I just hope they are gentle dances. Please tell me you're not doing a jive or something too energetic. I'll be up at Driftwood Manor tonight myself. My mother and father are taking part, so I might even take you for a very short gentle spin myself.'

I reached the door, and as my fingers touched the handle, on a whim I turned back, crossed the room, and to his surprise, grabbed him and squeezed him tight. Then I rushed out, while dialling Meredith's number on my phone ignoring Dr Antony's cries of, 'Do be careful, Lydia, for goodness' sake.'

I yelled down the phone. 'Oh God, Meredith! I can dance. I'm so happy but now I have to find something sparkly to wear.'

I hadn't wanted to jinx anything by buying something new beforehand just in case. I would have been so disappointed.

Where the hell was I going to find a competition-worthy dress from at this short notice? I always knew I'd go along, and had plenty of things to wear, but that was very different to competing.

I grinned, happier than I had felt for weeks. My heart felt happy at the thought of being able to take part in the competition.

Luckily, Meredith said that she had a number of dresses that would be suitable. What a fabulous daughter I had, who, at the drop of a hat, could produce something for this occasion. None quite as beautiful as the one I had stupidly thrown away, and was regretting very much, but there was one in particular that she said was very pretty and would do the job perfectly.

Martin was over the moon to hear I was fit and able to dance. I suggested we met up an hour beforehand but he said that he'd bumped into Dr Antony in the mini-mart and he'd told him that under no circumstances was he allowed to agree to any practice dances before the main event.

Driftwood Manor owner's identity was under wraps to most of the village, but Meredith had told me and sworn me to secrecy. The excitement at meeting her was getting me in a right old tizzy.

Martin had offered to pick me up at 6 p.m. and Dianne, on hearing my news when she had also bumped into Martin and Dr Antony, had offered to come round and curl my hair and do my make-up.

'So, what are we doing?' she asked.

'Knock ten years off me but at the same time make me look subtle and natural.'

Dianne laughed and looked at her watch. 'We haven't got that long!'

I swatted her arm. 'Ooh, you cheeky mare!'

'But that's one of the many things that you love about me though, Lydia.'

'Very true.'

'So how are you feeling?'

'Excited. Petrified. Sick with nerves.' I'd been trying to keep all these emotions under wraps, but now that Dianne had asked me about them, they came pouring out. 'Worried I'll mess up. Worried my ankle won't hold out. Worried I'll show myself up and look a complete and utter fool. Shall I keep going? You did ask.'

'You'll be grand, kid. Just grand.'

Silence just enhanced my trepidation and I couldn't think of anything to say while Dianne spruced me up and eventually we heard a car door slam outside.

'Yoo-hoo!'

'Hi, Martin, come in, we're just finishing off.' I pulled my kimono around me a little tighter. I looked up at him. 'Are you not getting changed into your dance suit?'

'No, not yet. Meredith asked me to give you this.' He hung the garment bag on the door frame. 'I'll just leave it here and put these here.' He placed a box on the kitchen table. 'Can't stop. I'll see you there if that's OK.' He bent to kiss my cheek. 'I'm glad you can dance tonight, Lydia. It wouldn't be right without you.' The door slammed behind him.

Dianne's raised eyebrows told a story.

'Don't start, madam. It's nothing. We're just friends.'

'Has someone told him that? He looks at you like a lost puppy.'

'Don't be ridiculous.' I brushed away her comment but wondered if he really did look at me that way. My tummy started to churn.

Dianne drew in a big breath. 'Mark my words, Lydia. He is a very good man who admires you very much. Trust me. I know.'

She looked a little sad and her eyes lingered on me.

I wondered how she seemed to know so much about Martin and how he felt. Was she jealous of the time that he and I had been spending together? Did she have feelings for him? It was really the first time that I'd considered this. What sort of friend had I been to her?

'You're all done. That OK for you?'

What reflected back at me from the mirror was a sight to behold. I bounced the curls that fell onto my shoulder in the palm of my hand.

'Thank you. I love it.'

'Right, I'm going to go back next door and if you'll be OK, I'll go and get ready myself. Clem is coming to pick us up at 6 p.m. so I'd better get on.'

'Thanks, Dianne. You're a real pal, you know. If Celia can't be next door, I'm glad you are there instead.'

'Me too, kid. Me too. See you in a bit.'

I carried the garment bag through to my room and hung it over the door, faffing around with spraying deodorant and Chanel No. 5 in my bra, pants and hold-up stockings before reaching for the zip to release the dress.

A loud gasp escaped me and I held my chest while my heart did a little skip as I realised what hung before me. How on earth? What the hell?

36

Meredith's phone was ringing out. Martin's phone went to answerphone. Why wasn't anyone answering? Where was everyone?

As I slid my beautiful crimson dress from its protective cover, the years fell away and I was eighteen all over again. About to dance in a competition. Fired up and raring to go. Although in those days, I had the shoes to go with it. The box that Martin had also brought around in popped into my mind. Surely not.

But it was so. In the shoebox, somehow, were my stunning red sparkly shoes. I ran my fingers over the satin upper, the original jewels back to their original shiny glory. I turned them over to stroke the suede soles, searching for where one had broken but it was nowhere to be seen. Like magic, they were back to their original state. I honestly couldn't get my head around it. Was I dreaming?

I slid my stockinged feet in and they were the absolute perfect fit. I slipped the dress over my head. The silk bodice clung to me like a second skin across the bust area and then fell away into the loose folds of the nearly full-length flowing skirt. I felt like a princess. There was a bit of me wondering whether something magical had happened, but the realist in me knew that magic wasn't real. That someone very special had done this. For me.

A car horn beeped and then there was a knock at the door. Clem.

A loud wolf whistle greeted me as I walked into the kitchen.

'Wit woo, Lydia. Has your fairy godmother been waving her wand? If I wasn't madly in love with your daughter, I'd be whisking you away.'

I spun round in a little twirl.

'Stunning. A friend of mine once said that if you want to know what the woman you love is going to end up like, take a look at her mother. And you look amazing. I'm a lucky man.'

'Thank you, darling boy, you little charmer you. But how the hell am I standing in my dress and shoes from fifty years ago?'

'Ah. I'm sure Dad and Mere will explain when they see you. I'm just glad they fit. God, can you imagine what would have happened if they didn't? It doesn't bear thinking about. So, is Cinderella ready to go to the ball?'

There was another knock at the door.

'Only me!' Dianne trilled as she let herself in.

'Oh, Dianne. If only your sister was here too, I'd have the perfect joke.' He grinned at his own wit but Dianne screwed up her face, totally unaware of the context.

'Come on, you two. Let's get you to the dance. There's a competition to be won!'

* * *

Clem's car pulled up outside the front entrance to Driftwood Manor and Mere and Martin stepped out.

'Mum, you look...' She scanned my outfit from head to toe. 'Absolutely stunning. God, I'm glad it fits.'

'Like a glove but how on earth? Last time I saw this dress I chucked it in the skip. Along with the shoes.'

'Yes and a journal. But Dianne saw you do it and she pulled them back out.'

'Oh. So, you found the journal then?'

'Yep, and I promised myself that I wouldn't read it.'

'Thank God!'

'Ah, don't thank him yet, because then I did.'

Shame washed over me and I put my head in my hands but she took them and hers and pulled mine away.

'You have nothing to be ashamed about, Mum. It's me who should be apologising to you. I should never have read it but I couldn't seem to stop myself. But it's all worked out OK, hasn't it? Our life together now; it's really good, isn't it?'

I looked deeply into my daughter's eyes. My beautiful, kind, forgiving daughter. Even after reading my innermost thoughts, she still had the generosity of a saint and a heart as big as an ocean.

'It's OK, Mum. It's OK.' She pulled me to her carefully, so as to not crush the dress.

Martin stepped forward. 'So, you approve of what Mere and I did then?'

'You both did this? For me?'

'We did. I fixed the shoes. Meredith fixed the dress.'

'But how? And when? How on earth have you had the time?'

'We'll tell you all about it later. How's the foot? Can you manage in those shoes? You could always go barefoot until the competition starts.'

'Yeah, all good.' I didn't have the heart to tell them it was already aching. He must have somehow put a lower heel on them because I'm sure they used to be higher.

'Right, let's go and see what order the contestants are dancing in then. Shall we?' Martin crooked his arm for me to take and grinned. 'You look amazing, Ginger.'

'You're looking rather dapper yourself, Fred.'

He was wearing a pair of black trousers with a satin stripe down the leg, and a matching open-necked, black satin shirt, with a red cummerbund and shiny patent leather shoes.

'And, Meredith, you look fabulous too.'

I noticed a look pass between the two of them, one I couldn't decipher.

Meredith was wearing a stunning turquoise gown, covered in tiny diamantés. She looked like the sea, glittering away as the lights made it sparkle.

'Well, I couldn't have some of these contestants out-sparkle me now, could I? As the interior designer of the hall, I thought I should make the effort and a night like this is all about the glitz and the glamour, right?'

I gasped as she opened the double doors into main ballroom. Huge ornate chandeliers hung from the high, white-painted wood-panelled ceilings and between them shiny disco balls dangled at intermittent intervals. Lavish ivory drapes hung at the floor-to-ceiling windows matching to fabric on the chairs placed around a black and white chequered dance floor.

'Wowsers. How does someone have a room like this in their house?' I tried to take it all in, but it was quite overwhelming. It was like nothing I'd seen before. A small stage sat at the very rear of the room, with three small ornate thrones. I looked at Meredith and raised my eyebrows.

'For the judges.'

'You did all this?'

'Well, I had a little help.'

A tall, blonde woman approached us and I gasped, honoured to be in her presence. I recognised her straight away from a period drama I'd recently seen, as well as many other shows before that. She held a beautifully manicured hand out to me.

'Now you must be Meredith's mother. You are so alike.' My daughter and I smiled at each other. 'Oh look, your eyes both crinkled up in exactly the same way. I love that. Welcome to Driftwood Manor. I do hope you like what we've done so far. For God's sake though, Lydia, don't go anywhere but the hallway, here and the lavs. Don't tell anyone else but the rest of the house is a total shithole!'

We all laughed. She was so nice.

* * *

'Come on then, cherub, let's see the schedule.'

There were six couples in total. We were on fifth, after Geoff from the pub and Dylis from the supermarket. I didn't want to be gloaty, but I didn't think either of those two would be particularly gifted in the dancing department. But we were followed by Nancy's mother and her brother, who apparently were ballroom champions in their younger years. Now they were what I considered to be competition, and being the last couple on, they would be the ones that people might remember the most. The first two couples were people I'd met before, but didn't know well, so had no idea of what their standard of dancing would be. I hoped that by the time we came on, people would had forgotten about them. And the third couple were Dr Antony's parents and he'd already told me that they weren't as good as they thought they were. Gosh, this evening really was bringing out the competitive side in me.

Clem and Martin wandered out to find the gents' as Meredith returned. I nodded in Clem's direction.

'How's things with lover boy?'

'Not sure really.'

Sadness tinged her eyes. I know how much they each thought of each other and it worried me that even though I was in her life now, abandoning her as a child was still damaging her relationships.

She'd done so much for me recently. Her generosity of spirit really was a very special quality that not many human beings had. I really hoped that they would sort things out. I had to do something to help them.

But not right now, because as the lights dimmed, a drum rolled and a spotlight shone on a centre spot on the small stage, gasps came from all around the room when a familiar voice boomed out.

37

Jason Martin, who was a host on a daytime TV quiz show, appeared with a microphone in his hand.

'Ladies and gentlemen, welcome to Driftwood Manor. Some of you might be surprised to see me here this evening, but when Samantha told me what she was up to, I asked if I could come along and be a compere. Samantha and I have been friends since we met as children and our families used to come to Driftwood Bay on our holidays. We thought it would be a nice little gift to the community who have made Samantha so very welcome. So, I do hope you don't mind me muscling in on your evening and being your host.'

Cheers rose all round and everyone gave him a huge grin. I was surprised to see he looked a little nervous prior to his little speech. Funny how you don't imagine people who are famous being apprehensive at events, but I suppose they must have some sort of nerves to fuel them. He announced the contestants and began to introduce the three judges.

'Please put your hands together for the chair of the charity, who are responsible for this evening's competition, Richard Walker.'

Mr Walker was I would have said around fifty years old, incredibly good-looking in a very obvious tall, dark and handsome way in a black velvet dinner suit, with a pink sequinned bow tie and a sexy smile that had already got a few of the womenfolk of the village in a little bit of tizzy.

'Our second judge tonight is the Mayor of Truro. Thank you so much for joining us, Mayor Angela Bateman. You are looking gorgeous this evening. Love how the gold dress matches your ceremonial chains!'

The mayor was much younger than I expected her to be and much more glamorous too.

'And finally, our very own Samantha Murphy who has very kindly and generously given up her glorious house for the evening.' Samantha sashayed into the room in a tight-fitting iridescent mermaid gown and gave a little wave before she took her seat. 'You are looking hot, hot, hot tonight! Thank God they killed her off in that drama so that she could return to this wonderful part of the world and host this fabulous event. So without further ado, I will ask you to take your seats, wish our contestants the very best of luck and let the dancing begin.'

My own nerves were now beginning to kick in. Would I remember the steps? It had been so long since I'd danced them. I'd been teaching Martin his steps as well as teaching Meredith hers, so I knew both roles well. Why was I doubting myself now?

The lights dimmed and a collective gasp from the audience made my heart start to pound. Deep breathing soothed me only a little as from our seats beside the dance floor, I watched the first couple walk out. The only sound breaking the silence was the tip-tap sound of their shoes on the dance floor. It felt like everyone in the room was holding their breath until the music started and they danced their hearts out to an incredible samba. They were followed by couples two and three with a square tango and a lindy hop. Roars of approval from the audience after each performance showed just how much they were enjoying the display even after one half of the second couple fell over and very quickly righted himself.

When Dylis and Geoff's names were called, my stomach started to do summersaults, knowing that we were up next. Geoff imitated a very masterful matador and Dylis's impression of a bull created a fabulous mix of comedy and drama rolled into one. Proper showmanship.

'Ladies and gentlemen, the next couple to dance this evening are Lydia Robinson and Martin Penrose.'

Martin squeezed my hand. My legs suddenly felt like jelly and I couldn't stop trembling.

'You OK?' he asked.

This was it. No turning back now. I should have danced over fifty years ago but things had not turned out how I expected them to. Tonight all the pent-up emotions of a young woman called Lydia were merging with those of the much older and should-be wiser Lydia of today. It was all quite overwhelming and suddenly Meredith and Martin were by my side as I breathed in, held for the count of four and exhaled loudly. My eyes landed on the familiar face of Miguel our dance teacher. He gave me a double thumbs up and mouthed 'You've got this.' I wanted to smile back at him, but it must have appeared as more of a grimace. I was feeling quite nervous and my tummy felt quite jittery. Three deep breaths seemed to ground me a little.

Martin smiled and mouthed, 'You've got this.'

I stared deeply into his eyes and thought about how much I'd enjoyed getting to know him more over the time we'd spent together. He really was the nicest man I thought I'd ever met and

I knew that I wouldn't want to be having this experience with anyone else. I couldn't drag my eyes away. He was the first to break our locked gaze.

As I waited for him to take my hand and walk to the centre of the dance floor, so that we could start our waltz in the hold position, he grinned, bent to kiss my cheek and wished me luck.

And then he walked away.

38

'Martin!' I shout-whispered to his retreating back. 'Martin. We're on now. Get back here. Now!'

I turned to Meredith who had appeared beside me at the edge of the dance floor. I was so confused.

'What's going on, Mere? Where has he gone?'

She reached her hand out to me, palm upwards, an unspoken invitation to take her hand.

'Dance with me, Mum?' she asked.

'What?' I didn't realise how loud my question had been. 'We can't dance together. We can't both do the women's steps. It won't work.'

'I've been learning Martin's steps. Miguel has been teaching me. I want to dance with my mum.'

'But women can't dance together. Women don't do that.'

'They do, Mum. Didn't you watch the last couple of *Strictly* series? Same sex couples dance together all the time now. Let's set a trend. Who says that mothers and daughters can't dance together? Who sets the rules?'

I shrugged my shoulders at her, still in disbelief. I was totally discombobulated, never been so surprised I didn't think in my life.

'We do. That's who. If you taught me anything in my life, it's that I can do anything that I set my mind and my heart to. That if I want something badly enough, I can go out and get it. You taught me that, Mum. You. And you continue to teach me every single day. So what if we didn't have the life we thought we should have had. I've had a bloody good life and the life I have now, with you and Clem at the centre, is amazing.' She looked across at Clem and his love bubbled over in his beaming smile, his face was full of love and adoration for this woman who stood before me.

'But I let you down, Meredith! I'm so sorry.'

'Mum, I read your journal.'

'Ah yes, I forgot about that.'

My daughter knew all my innermost thoughts and feelings from all those years ago. I had never really been one for voicing my emotions, but she knew everything.

'Mum, I keep telling you. I forgive you for the past. You have to forgive yourself at some point. Only then will you be able to move past everything. Your journal has made me realise, and I know you've told me before, but reading it in black and white really made it sink in. All along, I thought that you didn't love me and that's why you left. What I didn't really get until now is that you left me because you loved me.'

A wet slow tear trickled down my cheek. Meredith reached up and wiped it away with her thumb.

'And I mean. Look at me. I'm bloody fabulous, so it clearly didn't do me any harm.'

'You are fabulous. And I don't deserve you.'

'It's all OK, Mum. I love you. It's going to be OK.'

My recent prognosis sprung back to mind and I realised how

lucky I was to have the results that I did. If things had been different, I might be now living on borrowed time.

'I love you too, Meredith. So very much.'

'What's more beautiful than the love between a mother and daughter?'

This was probably the maddest and most spontaneous thing I'd ever been asked to do in all my seventy-one years.

That hand reached out to me again.

'Come on, Mum. Are you going to dance with me? Say yes. We've got this!'

I threw my head back and laughed. I nodded.

As I looked up, a piece of paper had been handed over to the host, by one of the organisers and he read it and grinned. After a brief discussion, a moment later the announcement was made.

'Ladies and gentlemen, there has been a change of plan, which we know you are going to love. Please welcome onto the dance floor mother and daughter pairing, Lydia and Meredith Robinson.'

I looked over to where Martin and Clem stood whooping and hollering, and as the thunderous applause when we reached the dance floor eventually died down and silence fell, Meredith and I faced each other. She placed her hand just below my shoulder blade and we joined hands and held them high in the air and stood proudly. Together we danced the most beautiful and graceful waltz that I could possibly imagine. Our bodies in perfect symmetry, mirroring each other's moves; not a single step out of place. The unwavering, unconditional love between a mother and a daughter so deep and wholesome and shining through above everything in the whole wide world.

When our dance finished and we held hands and took a bow, I looked across at my daughter and she flung herself into my arms. Our dance may have finished but our bond would never break. Could never be broken. As the spotlights moved to light up the audience, I gazed around the room and every single person was on their feet clapping. There were a few people dabbing at their eyes with tissues. I couldn't believe that we'd made such an impression.

My heart felt like it could burst. I had honestly never been so happy. There was me all my life, looking for the perfect man to complete me, when all along I just needed the love of my life which had been right there all along.

My daughter.

Her acceptance and her love. They were everything to me. And all I needed.

And that's how our mother and daughter dance set our little world of Driftwood Bay on fire.

39

Nancy's mum and her brother never stood a chance, even though they gave a faultless performance. When Jason announced that Meredith and I had won, I was honestly shocked to the core. As he handed over the shiny glitter-ball trophy and Meredith waved it in the air, the music kicked in and we got to dance a few steps of our waltz again before the floor opened up to everyone.

The first people to join us were Vi and Dianne.

'I don't think I'm one of those, you know...' Vi mouthed the word 'lesbian' at me, over pronouncing the words. 'But hey, never say never. At my age, beggars can't afford to be choosers. And you'd never have guessed that Dianne was one of them, would you? She just told me. Dark horse that one.' She winked at me as she flounced off and twirled Dianne around the dance floor.

Well, that was a turn up for the books. So that was Dianne's secret.

Martin and Clem appeared at our respective sides.

'May I?' Martin asked and took a dramatic bow.

I laughed and looked over at Meredith, who was totally

focused on Clem.

I heard him say, 'You were spectacular tonight, Mere. You will never know how much you mean to me.'

The relief that flooded through my body was quite unbelievable. I knew the one final thing I could do to help them.

'I'll dance with you, but only if you promise to help me tomorrow with something, Martin.'

'You know I'd do anything for you, Lydia. You are... well, you know...'

I tilted my head, wondering what he was alluding to. His eyes bore into mine and then down to my lips. His head bent towards mine and I realised that he was going to kiss me. What I realised, in that moment, was how much I wanted him to. I closed my eyes.

'Umphh! Sorry!'

I was physically shoved away from Martin as Vi and Dianne bumped into us as they whisked on by.

The moment had been lost.

'You're my best friend,' he finished. 'That's what you are. Now are you going to finally dance with me or what?'

I smiled to hide my disappointment. 'Can I just do something first, please?'

His frown showed his utter confusion as he questioned what I was going to do next.

I reached down and undid the buckle on my shoes. I did consider using one foot to push off the other shoe and then kick them both away, like I would have done if I was eighteen, but these were vintage Lydia Robinson. They'd lasted fifty years and maybe I'd find someone else to pass them on to in time and they might last another fifty. But they were shoes that held a story. Every item that people possess holds a story one way or another; some happy, some sad, some poignant, some insignificant and some even untold, but there's always a story. And my own had come full circle.

I placed them carefully to one side and we danced barefoot until I spied Miguel heading our way. I smiled as he caught my eye. At that precise moment Vi and Dianne careered into him and he fell to the floor. He screamed as his mop of curly black hair gave way to a short ginger head of hair. Martin and I both gasped, before going to his aid.

He held up his hands. 'Don't say a thing.' And there was that strong Brummie accent that Martin had sensed previously.

'Miguel, what the hell?'

'It's Callum. Not Miguel. Callum from Cannock. Not Miguel from Madrid. I thought it was more exotic. Would get me more business. I'm sorry I lied.'

'Callum from Cannock, eh?' I laughed. 'Fancy taking me for a spin?'

Callum whisked me around a circuit of the dance floor and chatted all the way. He was hilarious and now he'd unmasked himself, his broad Midlands accent was so apparent.

'You didn't have to lie to us, Callum. Why did you feel the need?'

'I never felt like I was enough, I guess.'

'You, my dear, are way more than enough and don't you dare ever forget that. Do you really think we care where you are from? You are the most remarkable dancer I've ever seen and it's my pleasure to dance with you.'

He grinned.

What a funny old world.

* * *

Meredith appeared, flinging her arm across my shoulders.

'Happy?' she asked me.

'Happier than I've ever been, darling.' I kissed her cheek. 'You?'

'Yes. I really do think I am.' I saw her glance at Clem again. 'We just need to find you your happy-ever-after now.'

I looked around me and realised that I'd already found it. Tonight had made me feel like I was a huge part of Driftwood Bay. I hadn't felt like I'd belonged anywhere for a long time, but this was now my home and I never wanted to leave.

Clem drove us all back to Bay View Cottage and we opened a bottle of champagne that was on the top shelf of my fridge. Something one of my husbands had taught me, I can't quite remember which, was that you should always have a bottle of something special chilling. You never knew when you might need to celebrate.

Martin hovered as Clem and Meredith walked to the car. We stood looking up at the stars above, neither of us quite knowing what to say after that moment earlier when I thought he was going to kiss me. He shuffled from one foot to the other but still neither of us spoke. Suddenly, he leant towards me, kissed my cheek and blew out air.

'Thank you for one of the best nights of my life, Lydia. You are very, very special.'

As suddenly as he kissed me, he walked away.

As I walked barefoot to my front door, my heart felt fuller than it had ever felt before in my life. I thought back to the conversation that Martin and I had had on the beach about finding the joy and happiness in life.

I knew that I had finally found mine and I was truly blessed. I knew now that I didn't need a man in my life, but needing and wanting were two very different thing. It might be nice to take things slow and see where it took us.

40

I'd asked Meredith to pop round to see me. We needed to talk about the journal.

Communication was everything. It was the reason why couples split up, why people argue, why families drift apart, why governments fail, why wars start. My lovely mum always used to say that if only people would just sit down and talk, there wasn't much that couldn't be solved with a nice cup of tea and a chat. I didn't think she was wrong.

Meredith looked worried when she arrived. I held her in my arms and didn't want to let her go but I released her before she could accuse me of being a weirdo. That was something she had done in her youth. I remember once coming back from America, and clinging on to her for dear life, never wanting to let go, and she'd laughed at me.

I handed her a drink and we took a seat in the conservatory.

'I just want to apologise for everything, Meredith. I know we've talked before but there are things I'd like to say.'

'I've read the journal, Mum. Every word. Three times in fact. So I know what happened. Everything.'

'I'm sorry you didn't have a proper family, Meredith. It was hardly conventional, was it? At the time I hated that you didn't know your father. That you were the product of something so sordid and wrong.'

'Mum, you didn't ask to be taken advantage of. It must have been awful for you. You only did what you could. It's all OK. My life was good. Nana and I had a wonderful life. She was my best friend.'

'That's what hurts. I was jealous of my own mother. What sort of a person does that make me?'

'Mum, that's life. It's human nature. And I think it's probably envy rather than jealousy. Jealousy is when you feel threatened by something yet envy is a painful feeling of wanting something that someone else has. I'm envious of Lucy and James. That they have a baby and I'm too old to ever have children. Even Gemma who couldn't have children has an adopted stepdaughter. And I'm envious of her too because of that. And I'm even envious of baby Taran, that poor little soul who knows nothing about life. I crave the attention he gets from Clem. More than anything, I'm envious of the time that you spend with Lucy and Taran and that you're wonderful with her. And it breaks my heart that we never got that chance. For you to be a grandma and me to be a mother. But it doesn't mean that I don't love them too. It means that I'm human.'

I moved to sit beside her, taking the cup from her hand and placing it on the table beside me. I took both of her hands in mine.

'All of that makes me so sad, Mere. You're missing out on things.'

'But that's the thing I've realised now and to be honest it's taken me a while. You can feel sad for the things you haven't had or got, or you can get stuck into life and live it the best way you know how, being grateful for the things you do have. You can live with regrets but make sure they're the regrets for the things you've tried to do, or that have really happened, not the ones that live in your head. You coming to live in Driftwood Bay is one of the best things that's ever happened to me. I hope you know that this is not where our story ends. This is where it begins.'

'How did my daughter get to be so lovely and so bloody wise?'

'Maybe it's in my genes.'

I smiled through my tears.

'How about we both stop beating ourselves up so much. Let's talk about it whenever we feel something is in the way, truthfully, and help each other. Understand. Communicate.'

'Yes. That sounds like a great idea. I do love you, Mum.'

'I love you too, darling. And that's why I want you to go to my little bay at lunchtime. At 1 p.m. to be precise. I have a surprise for you.'

She looked into my eyes, questioning my words.

'I'm not telling you any more than that so don't ask. All I will say is that I would do anything for you and for your happiness. Promise me you'll trust me and that you'll be there?'

She nodded. 'OK. I do and I will.'

* * *

I was glancing at my watch every five seconds and looking out the window which wasn't helping my nerves at all. I hoped Martin had done everything that I'd asked of him. The relief I felt when I saw him appear at the end of my drive was overwhelming.

'Come in. Did you follow my instructions to the letter?'

'As if I'd dare not to!' He grinned.

'So you set up the music player with their favourite song on repeat?'

'Yep, Ed Sheeran's "Perfect" will be playing about three hundred times back-to-back as we speak.'

'And you left the bottle of champagne?'

'Of course. Left it as instructed in the cool box surrounded by lots of ice packs and then the two wine glasses on the rock that you described.'

'Wonderful. Oh, and you gave Clem my letter?'

'You think I would have left something off the list? More than my life's worth.'

I smiled back at his cheeky question.

'God, I hope they're talking. I hope they don't mind me interfering.'

'It's all been done with the most genuine intentions, my lovely. Now make me a cuppa and stop worrying. I'm sure we'll hear from them soon.'

* * *

A knock at the door made me jump out of my skin.

'Anyone in?' came a familiar voice.

'We're out the back, Dianne. There's tea in the pot if you want to grab a cup on your way through.'

'Oh, fabulous. Will do.'

Dianne appeared and busied herself pouring tea and milk. I could see however that her hands were shaking.

'Are you OK, love?'

'I wanted to apologise to you, Lydia.'

'Whatever for?'

'For not telling you truth about who I really am. I didn't want you to treat me any differently if you knew the truth about me.'

'Why on earth would you think that?' My eyes widened.

'Well people do, you know.' Her voice had a tinge of years of disappointment.

'People are daft,' Martin replied.

We all stared out at the sea pondering life.

'I only really have one n, you know.'

'Uh?' Martin's face was a picture; screwed up, not having a clue what she was talking about. I smiled, cottoning on straight away.

'I'm really only Diane with one n, not two,' she continued. 'I thought I'd be more interesting if I had two.'

'Seriously?' he asked, quite abruptly.

Dianne's neck and face were turning red. 'I'm a silly old fool, aren't I?'

'Yes, you are,' he replied.

She hung her head and I knew that the words that I said next would stay with her forever, so I needed to make them count.

'Dianne. Whether you have two ns or one, it doesn't make a scrap of difference. I think you are one of the nicest, kindest, most interesting people that I know. You moving into Celia's house while she's away is one of the best things that has ever happened to me.'

She clutched at her chest. 'Really?'

'Really! And I honestly don't care if you are one of those, you know... lesbians.' I mimicked the way that Vi had said it last night and she laughed.

'I couldn't care less whether you are gay, straight, bi or pan sexual. You're still Dianne to me and I hope you'll be my friend for the rest of my life.'

'Oh, look at you being all diverse.' We laughed. 'You mean that though? You really don't care?'

'I really do mean it and I really don't care. I'm sure you're the same, aren't you, Martin?'

'Ah well, Dianne and I have had a few chats recently and I had an inkling when she told me about a painful break-up she'd had over in Australia and that she'd come to the UK to start afresh. But I don't care either. I hope you know that, Dianne. Whether you have one n or two, you're still our friend.'

'That's good because you're going to be stuck with me. Celia is staying away for longer. She's met a man.'

'Oh wow! That's exciting. Did she meet that handsome yacht-owning millionaire that she was imagining?'

'Sadly not, but she did say that she'd met an old hippy with a beard and a dinghy.'

We all laughed.

'Well, if my sister can do it, maybe there's hope for us all. Just goes to show that it's never too late to find love.'

Martin and I locked eyes, unspoken words between us heavy in the air before he whispered his next words.

'Also, you're never too old, eh?' His question was directly to me.

It seemed like an age before either of us looked away. When we did, we all continued to stare at the view beyond.

Dianne's words jolted me back into the room.

'Thank you both.'

'What for?' I asked.

'For being wonderful friends.'

'That's what friends are for, Dianne.'

She blinked back tears and grabbed my arm in an unusual gesture of affection. She reached out to Martin.

'Come on, Martin. It's group hug time.'

She pulled us both in tight. She was an absolute gem and I thanked my lucky stars to have her in my life.

'Christ! I never realised that when I said I wanted some excitement in my life, that I'd end up in a thruple.' Martin scratched his head in astonishment.

Dianne smacked him on the arm while we fell about laughing.

'You should be so lucky! You're lovely, Martin, but you're really not my type. Neither of you are to be honest.'

'Charming. Don't hold back, will you?' he replied with fake offence.

'I'll take another friends hug though if there's one going.' She held her arms out to us again and I was the first to step into them.

'Always my friend. Always.'

'But keep your wandering hands off my bottom this time please, Lydia. I've already told you, you're really not my type.' We all laughed out loud before she pulled us both back into her. Laughter with friends is one of the best medicines ever.

41

When Meredith and Clem appeared at the end of my drive,
while I was filling the kettle again, they were both laughing and
my heart skipped a beat.

'Everything OK?'

'More than OK. Thank you, Mum.'

'Yes, thank you for everything, Lydia,' Clem added.

'What have I missed?' Dianne, nosy as ever, stuck her head
around the kitchen door.

Clem looked at Meredith and she nodded back at him. There
were never many secrets in Driftwood Bay.

'We'd got our wires seriously crossed. Meredith thought that
me spending time with baby Taran was because I was getting
broody and it couldn't have been further than the truth. He's a
little belter, but at my age, it's bloody exhausting to spend time
with a baby. I'm always glad to give him back to be honest but I
just wanted to give my mate James a break. He's shattered so I
was just trying to help out.'

He reached out for Meredith's hand, who gave a dramatic
sigh before speaking.

'And I thought that he was going off me when he wasn't. Not sure how we got it so wrong to be honest.'

Dianne shook her head at them and tutted.

'What a pair you are. Do you know what Celia would say if she were here right now?'

We all looked at her with bated breath.

'You need your heads banging together. That's what our dad used to say to us when we were kids.'

'Yes, they definitely needed their heads banging together for sure.' Martin laughed.

'So, are you OK now? Sorted everything out?' I hoped that by meddling a little I had helped their situation rather than made it worse. The initial signs of them holding hands tightly and grinning at each other were looking overwhelmingly positive.

'Very much. In fact...' Clem looked to Meredith for her approval and she nodded.

'I've asked Meredith to marry me.'

A squeal escaped Dianne's mouth and an excitable gasp from mine. When I planned for them to spend some quality time together on the beach, I had no idea that this might be the outcome. Clem popping the question was more than I could ever have wished for.

Meredith's face lit up into the biggest grin I'd ever seen from her. I was delighted for her. For them both. They were made for each other.

'And you said... Come on, stop keeping us in suspenders.' We all laughed at Dianne's misquote.

'Yes. I said yes.'

'Oh, thank God. I was scared that you'd both hate me for meddling. I just know how much you love each other and know how right you are for each other too. Love like that doesn't come around many times. I know that Driftwood Bay has given my daughter a second chance at life and I'm so glad that she gets her second chance with you, Clem.'

'Not just with me though, Lydia. She gets her second chance with you too. I know how important that is to you both.'

'Congratulations to you both. I'm so happy for you. I really am.' As I pulled them both to me, tears streamed down my cheeks. All was well with the world and the future was looking brighter than ever.

'We're going to head off if you don't mind.' Clem had a twinkle in his eye and Meredith was positively glowing.

'I'm going to head off too. Celia is FaceTiming me in ten minutes. So much to tell her. Normally all I have to say is how many poos the goats have had that day, and how many eggs I've picked out of the coop. She's going to have a field day with all the gossip today. Laters, darlings, and congrats again to you all.'

'Just you and me then kid.' Martin smiled. 'Shall we have that other cuppa?'

42

As we sat chatting, I realised something special. That I could sit and talk to Martin for hours. He was so honest, interesting and animated, especially when talking about the passion he'd found for restoring things when people thought that they were beyond revitalising. Giving them a new lease of life.

'Restoring these items that belong to people, has taught me everything I need to know about life. People, places, relationships, friends – they're the things that create memories. It's the memories that are the important things in life, that bring us joy, not material things. It's the feelings and the emotions that these things stir within us. If Miranda dying taught me something it's that life is for living. Life is to be treasured because it's not promised to anyone and could be wiped out in a heartbeat. And it's to be lived while we have the chance. Within that living is love, and to love someone is not a thing to protect ourselves from but to throw ourselves into. I want to start living again, Lydia. And there's no one I'd rather do that with than you.'

What he was saying made a lot of sense, but as always I felt cautious. Both rational and irrational thoughts were racing through my mind. I'd spent my whole life worrying about what people thought of me. Maybe it was time to set myself free and live my life for me instead. Surely we all deserved this. There were just a couple of questions that I needed answers to first though.

'Do you not feel a little disloyal to Miranda? How do you think Clem will feel?'

'I think he'd be delighted to see his old dad living his best life. Loving after death isn't being disloyal. The love I had for Miranda is like no other. She was literally the love of my life. But maybe it was more the love of our lifetime together. This is now the life I have left and...' He coughed. 'The feelings that I have for you is love. I know that now, but it's a different love. It's more about companionship and friendship and realising that we have a duty to those who have gone before us to live life to the full. I don't even know if I'm making sense. Someone wise once said to me that there are gardeners and flowers in life. Gardeners are the ones that do the looking after and I miss that. I want to be a gardener again. And I reckon it's probably time for you to be a flower. Let someone look after you and let you bloom. I'd like to be that someone. Your gardener.'

Blimey. That hit home. I always felt like I'd always been the gardener in my relationships and yes, it would be bloody lovely to have someone look after me for once. I would love to be his flower.

I turned to him. 'Do you think we're too old to change, Martin?'

'I think that we're never too old for anything. I do think that we have a chance here and I'd really like us to take it. We could be so good together. We already make a formidable business partnership. I haven't enjoyed myself as much as I do when I'm with you. When I wake up in the morning, I look forward to seeing you. Spending time with you is my favourite time of the day. I love doing things for you, even if it's just making you a cup of tea. Just being with someone again is giving me a new lease of life. I love just pottering away in our own little worlds in the same workspace. Sometimes I look over at you and the concentration on your face takes my breath away. It's so clear that you are loving what you do. And I think we could find a lot of other things that we could love to do. We could travel. See more of the world. We could stay here. It doesn't matter where though. What matters is that we do it together.'

I understood exactly what he meant. To live is to love. A life without love is like a flower without petals, a tree without leaves. And I'd missed being loved. I'd missed loving someone else. Yes, I had found myself and I liked the me I was now. That could surely only be a good thing. This would be a different me going into another relationship. A me that didn't need someone else to validate me, but a me who was already happy. So anything else that added to that, surely, was just a bonus?

'You know I'm not great at relationships, don't you? I've had five husbands.'

'Pah! Only five? Elizabeth Taylor had seven, you know. Or was it eight?'

I threw my head back and laughed. Since I'd known him, he'd made me laugh. Every single day.

'So how about it, kiddo? Fancy doing something fun with me for the rest of your life?' He moved from his chair across the room to a standing point before me and held both of his hands out, laying himself before me, vulnerable yet courageous, bearing all that he was, waiting for my answer.

My heart was beating fast. I was apprehensive. But it also felt right. My guru at the retreat once said to me that fear is only a four-letter word – a teeny word, but which holds so much power.

He told me to never let something so tiny have so much power and that it should never hold me back.

I took a deep breath and, in that moment, it hit me that we must be brave to move forward. So what if we fail? Me failing at my previous marriages brought me to the place I was today. If not for them, I wouldn't have been in this gorgeous house, surrounded by this magnificent beauty, part of an amazing community, with my wonderful daughter, surrounded by my fabulous friends. This incredible man who was part of my present could be the answer to a fulfilling and fabulous future. Life is for living. I knew that I wanted to live mine to the full. With him.

When I stood and nodded, he wrapped me in his arms and pressed a kiss to my temple, pulling me tight to his chest.

A warm familiar feeling flooded my whole body, and as I lifted my head to his, and he lowered his and gently kissed my lips, my heart soared. This might not be the bells and whistles of young love. But it was something else. Something quite wonderful. In that moment, I felt safe. I felt loved. I felt complete. And I was excited to see what the rest of my life could hold. With this lovely, kind, gentle, remarkable man. I was grateful for another chance at life. And I reckoned that, together, we were a force to be reckoned with.

'Here's to our future and whatever it may hold.'

'Here's to a joyful life together.'

'And memories too, Martin. Here's to making memories.'

ACKNOWLEDGEMENTS

As always to my sister Lisa. It's been a tough old time lately but I hope you know how much I love and appreciate you. By each other's side, we can get through anything. You're the best sister I ever had! LOL! Or would want. My best friend too. Love you loads. x

To the many amazing friends, who inspire me to write about special friendships. I am so very lucky to have people like you in my life; particularly to Bev, Steph, Lisa B, Emma and Becky. Thank you for being you. x

To my writing tribes. Firstly, Sue Watson, Emma Robinson and Susie Lynes; for making me laugh more than ever and allowing me to cry when I need to. Thank you for your understanding, your love and your support. Secondly to Laura Bambrey; for being one of the kindest and most thoughtful people I know. Though a long way in distance, you are never further than a message away. Thank you for everything along with your motivation, encouragement and writing sprints and for making me get off my arse and write. x

To the whole team at Boldwood Books but particularly my editor Emily Yau. This was a tough old book. Thank you for helping me to shape it. I promise the next one should be easier (famous last words). And big love to Susan too for confusing you with my timeline. And to everyone else at Boldwood. Your passion for books and your authors and all of the hard work that you do is so much appreciated. There is so much that goes on behind the scenes which never gets recognised publicly. To my cover designer Clare Stacey for creating the Driftwood Bay world so perfectly. You are all wonderful. Thank you for everything you do to bring my books into the hands of readers. x

To the book community – the authors, the readers, the influencers – one of the most supportive I've ever known. You keep me going every single day with your messages, reviews, GIFs, social media posts. Thank you for everything. You'll never know how much of a difference that you make to authors. x

And last and absolutely not least to my son Ollie. I'm honoured to be your mom. You make me laugh every single day and are growing up to be such a lovely young man with a huge personality that we love. Your papa would have been so proud of you and I wish beyond words that my mom had got to meet you. She would have loved you so much.

Thank you, Ollie, for not minding too much for yelling at you when you are doing keepy-uppy next to me when I'm writing because 'I'M TRYING TO BE CREATIVE!' Thank you for being proud of me and my books and not being too mortified when we drive down the high street and see my books in the bookshop window. I love you, son; you are my world. x

ABOUT THE AUTHOR

Kim Nash is the author of uplifting, romantic fiction and an energetic blogger alongside her day job as Digital Publicity Director at Bookouture.

Sign up to Kim Nash's mailing list for news, competitions and updates on future books.

Visit Kim's website: https://www.kimthebookworm.co.uk/

Follow Kim on social media here:

facebook.com/KimTheBookWorm
x.com/KimTheBookworm
instagram.com/kim_the_bookworm
bookbub.com/authors/kim-nash

ALSO BY KIM NASH

The Cornish Cove Series

Hopeful Hearts at the Cornish Cove

Finding Family at the Cornish Cove

Making Memories at the Cornish Cove

LOVE NOTES

LOVE IN EVERY CHAPTER

WHERE ALL YOUR ROMANCE
DREAMS COME TRUE!

THE HOME OF BESTSELLING
ROMANCE AND WOMEN'S
FICTION

 WARNING:
MAY CONTAIN SPICE

SIGN UP TO OUR
NEWSLETTER

https://bit.ly/Lovenotesnews

Boldwood

Boldwood Books is an award-winning fiction publishing company seeking out the best stories from around the world.

Find out more at www.boldwoodbooks.com

Join our reader community for brilliant books, competitions and offers!

Follow us
@BoldwoodBooks
@TheBoldBookClub

Sign up to our weekly deals newsletter

https://bit.ly/BoldwoodBNewsletter

Printed in Great Britain
by Amazon

41818362R00155